BARRY E WC

T0314787

MOLOCK'S *Wänd*

A Daughter's Revenge
Wields a Deadly Weapon

BARRY E WOODHAM

MOLOCK'S WAND

MEREO

Cirencester

Published by Mereo

Mereo is an imprint of Memoirs Publishing

25 Market Place, Cirencester, Gloucestershire GL7 2NX
Tel: 01285 640485, Email: info@mereobooks.com
www.memoirspublishing.com, www.mereobooks.com

Molock's Wand

ISBN: 978-1861510037

Book jacket design Ray Lipscombe
Printed in England

ABOUT THE AUTHOR

Barry Woodham was born in 1943 and has lived in Swindon, Wiltshire in England all of his life. He is married with three sons all in their forties and lives happily in retirement with his wife Janet! (48 good years & more to come!)

He spent his working life as a design engineer/draughtsman and worked on the nuclear fusion project for thirteen years. Finding himself with nothing to read one lunch-time, he began to write the saga of the Gnathe and the Genesis Project. The thought occurred to him that any life form evolved to live in this world would not be able to cope with the micro-organisms of another eco-system on an alien planet. After many of his colleagues began to read the chapters as quickly as he could finish them he continued on and finished the first book.

The alien Gnathe are instinctive genetic engineers and alter living creatures to be their tools by the use of their brooding pouches controlled by the third sex. This first book is set millions of years after the sun has entered its red giant stage and is set on a vastly altered Jupiter. Humanity and intelligent Pan-chimpanzees are recreated by four Guardians made of nano-technology sent towards the stars from the dying Earth, to bring back mankind. One ship is stuck in the Kuiper Belt until it begins to fall towards the new sun and the crew are activated.

He was able to take early retirement through a legacy and continued to write the next book following on from Genesis 2, called The Genesis Debt. These have both been self-published on Amazon some years ago.

Recently he decided to put all 15 years-worth of writing in the hands of a new publisher and spend some of his son's inheritance!

While writing Weapon he decided to link all the books together as 'The Genesis Project' and write all the books into a series. He is now written a forth; - 'The Genesis Search' set hundreds of thousands of years after the events that occurred in Weapon. This part of the saga concerns the deliberate collision of the Andromeda Galaxy with ours in the distant future. What kind of entity could cause this to happen and why? This book attempts to settle those questions and concerns building a hunter/killer group from the ones who defeated the 'Goss' in Book Three by going back in time to remove their DNA and clone them, restoring their stored minds into young healthy bodies. At the same time whole solar systems are being rebuilt and moved by wormhole technology to the other side of our galaxy to be launched as a globular cluster towards the Greater Magellanic Clouds and safety.

Whilst writing this forth book the idea came to be, that the group of mixed human and aliens would find themselves having to deal with the abandoned machine intelligence of Von-Neumann probes left behind by the events produced by the 'Harvester' and this would be worth considering as the fifth Book;– Genesis 3, A New Beginning. He then considered what would happen after this universe runs down and how to build a new one to take its place!

The Elf War followed and by so many asking if he could go back to the Elf World, he did and Molock's Wand was the result.

I hope that you will enjoy reading these books as much as all the others and as much as I have enjoyed writing them!

Barry.E.Woodham.
Science Fiction Author.
barry.e.woodham@btinternet.com
The Genesis Project.

Book 1 - Genesis 2

Book 2 - The Genesis Debt

Book 3 – Genesis Weapon

Book 4 - The Genesis Search.

Book 5 - Genesis 3 ; - A New Beginning

The Elf-war & Molock's Wand.

Tales of the Ferryman can be read on his blog;-
http://sci-fiauthor.blogspot.co.uk

MOLOCK'S WAND

CHAPTER ONE

Over the centuries I had grown used to the voices in my mind. I am now the High King of the Elven Kingdom that straddles two worlds. My name is Peterkin, and I taught my people to kill Dark Elves, known as the Dokka'lfar. If I had not they would have destroyed everything that we stood for. My people were pacifists and abhorred violence of all kinds. This reluctance to defend themselves had almost destroyed them.

A chance mutation many thousands of years ago had produced the first wingless, Dark Elf, called Molock. When he became mature his mental powers outstripped those of his parents and he murdered his father and raped his mother to produce others of his kind. He then 'pressed' the minds of as many female elves he could capture to be his private breeding stock. My ancestors were appalled at his behaviour, but did nothing, hampered by the 'unwritten law' that elves did not do violence to other elves. It was unthinkable to them and they did not stop him and his perversions. We lived long lives and controlled our rate of increase and had never outstripped the land's capacity to feed us. We numbered but a few hundred thousand and had stayed that way for eons.

My people exiled themselves from the Dokka'lfar and moved as far away from them as they could, in the end,

1

looking for another solution. Finally it was too late to do anything at all as they bred by the millions and turned Alfheimr our home world into a wilderness stripped of anything edible. That was when they turned on our kind, the elder race and practised cannibalism against us, the Ljo'sa'lfar. They fanatically lusted after the flesh of my people and began to prey upon us.

I took the mantle of the High King and forged my gentle people into a fighting force. I was born with the ability to kill others of my kind, as all of the High King's bloodline could. This was my heritage hidden from the sight of others of my kind. It was a heavy burden for me to carry and it cost the lives of every Dark Elf and the hell-spawn of their indiscriminate breeding. I had no choice and with the aid of human friends and their weapons we finally prevailed. I had other allies that stood fast with us.

When Auberon had taken the last of my kind in the Spellbinder to Earth, they had settled amongst the Neanderthal peoples of northern Europe. His father the High King Freyr, had lain down his life to save his people. He kept the hordes of Dokka'lfar away from the reality-shifting ship until it was full, by expending his mental energy using the Star of Light. When he weakened, they ate him alive. I know, because I have his mind in mine, just as I have all the High Kings minds imprisoned inside my skull. Auberon took his place and ruled on Earth until the increased working of iron forced my people to relocate again to this world we named Haven. The Dokka'lfar found the link to Earth and plundered a vast number of humans as a food source and slaves, taking them with them. Eventually they made a bridge to this world and the great siege began after their craft went insane here, by Abaddon, keeping the bridge open.

We lived on a mountain in the centre of a vast crater teeming with dinosaurs, which had only one exit, through the great gorge. This we filled with a poisoned brier that grew far faster than it could be removed. This only entrance was patrolled by the dwarves. The Dokka'lfar spent centuries trying to get in without success.

On this world the dinosaurs had not completely died out and the raptors had evolved intelligence. They had mastered fire and used tools. They too became allies in the struggle against the Dark Elves. They in turn found them an acceptable food source. One of the Ljo'sa'lfar genetic experts developed a virus that would sterilise the Dokka'lfar and kill most of them. We spread it into the army that was trying to get in. My people drove hungry T Rex's that had their tiny minds 'pressed' to eat only the Dark Elves and look upon all else as 'not food,' through the open gate into our home world of Aifheimr. With them fled the infected Dokka'lfar, spreading the virus wherever they hid. I infected the rest of the world taking the virus in the Spellbinder and dropped off more meat-eating dinosaurs to mop up any survivors. The virus was fast acting and spread as fast as the wind could blow the spores.

When I eventually returned to Molock's castle to see if he had survived I found that this had enabled the humans imprisoned on that world, to revolt and overthrow him. They had soon found that by wearing iron collars it stopped him from dominating their minds. They had exacted a terrible revenge upon him by removing his legs and feasting on them in front of the cage in which they had imprisoned him. He had developed a healing salve that would allow his kind to eat the humans piece by piece, or allow them to grow back a limb after removal, but first he turned them into cocaine addicts to season the flesh. They had applied this to his stumps so that he did not die, leaving his fate to me.

I killed him with an AK-47, left him inside the cage and destroyed the abomination of his castle using explosives. My human friends, Sam Pitts and John Smith had set them well and all the walls had fallen inwards, leaving just a mountain of rubble where the atrocity had stood. I made sure that no-one would ever go near it again. Or so I thought!

As the years went by, my colony of humans increased and spread out over the empty lands of Aifheimr and developed farming to a great trading system. None of them wanted to return to Earth and I used the resources of my engineering business to buy equipment, seed and stock. Certain people were selected and offered a one way ticket to this empty world so we had doctors, teachers and all manner of skilled artisans living here. Life was getting more and more dangerous in the human world and things were building up to a crisis.

Finally a full scale war broke out and I would no longer use the Spellbinder to travel to the Earth anymore. I managed to bring all of the workers who had managed Acme Engineering back to Aifheimr safely before the bombs began to drop. Reluctantly I was adamant that there would not be any more trips back to their home-world in the future. A great number of my people elected to return to the old homelands and live with the humans there. I decided to stay here on Haven and continue to live at the castle that my ancestors had built.

The other thing that I did was to impound every Earth weapon that had been given to elf, dwarf, human, goblin and gnome. These firearms were covered in grease and stored in the basements of the castle along with any other ordinance. My human friends had taken some time to adjust to my edict as they were so used to being able to carry arms. I made the point that there was no need to be able to kill at a distance farther than a bow could reach. We had no enemies now and anyone foolish enough to wander through Prime's territory deserved what happened to them.

The last of the meat-eaters had been eradicated from

Alfheimr, once all of the Dokka'lfar had perished. A vast restocking took place all over the planet of not just domestic animals, but also wild creatures from Earth and Haven. Many of the dinosaurs had adjusted to eating the plants that had been transferred from Earth thousands of years ago by the Ljo'sa'lfar. These vegetarians packed on the meat at a steady rate and made good eating as did the eggs so they were transferred to the Elven world.

As the years went by everything stabilised nicely and the effort in recolonizing the two worlds took up the majority of my time. My son Elthred grew up in a world in which many different sentient creatures flourished. He carried the High King's genes and was born to rule our people and after two centuries had passed by I allowed him to be in charge of Aifheimr and to mastermind the rebuilding of the elf home-world. Humans, goblins, and gnomes all lived together amicably without any problems. The humans were quite happy to have escaped the violent world of their birth and settle on the Elven world. The dwarves decided to stay on Haven and made sure that there would be no competition between the Neanderthal stock and Homo-sapiens. Both off-shoots of humanity got on very well, but both wanted to keep racial purity given what had happened in the past.

Slowly over the years the memory of the Dokka'lfar and their excesses began to fade.

Eloen was a Halfling. Molock had been her father, but a human woman had been her mother. Out of all the many women he had 'favoured' with his attention only this one had become pregnant. She had been born over three centuries before, long before Molock's death and had kept to the fringes of the Dokka'lfar society. She had watched her mother die of old age while she stayed young. Eloen had all the mental powers of her father and many of his vices. She was strong and clever; dominating any of Molock's other children with ease as she rose in power, building her own small empire, separated from the mainland of what would have been Europe on Earth. Here on an island she ruled supreme, making sure that the mindless Dokka'lfar did not breed themselves into starvation, while she picked through the ones that were sentient and controlled them with a light mental leash. Life was good until a strange sickness began to rage throughout her people, except the humans that she bred for food and sport. Suddenly a new menace began to prowl through the lands; reptilian meat-eaters that targeted only the Dark Elves and would not kill the humans. They were unstoppable, as all of them wore iron collars around their necks making them uncontrollable by mental pressure. It did not take long before the humans realised this and they all wore iron around their necks as well.

A systematic slaughter of her people took place as dinosaurs and humans worked together ferreting out those who had fallen sick and making easy access to them for the meat-eaters. It had not taken them long to tear down the walls of her stronghold and let the beasts inside. There were many of the large killers that stood four times the height of an elf, but the deadliest ones proved to be the ones the same size, as they could wriggle into small spaces and drag the terrified Dark Elves into the light. There they would be torn to pieces and eaten. Even in the middle of a feeding frenzy the dinosaurs ignored the humans that fought amongst them. It was obvious to Eloen that they had been 'pressed' to do so. It had to be the Ljo'sa'lfar that had found the will to fight back after thousands of years of pacifism.

She reasoned that it could be the only explanation for the sudden collapse of the Dark Elves power. Her reaction to the sickness that had spread through her people was slight and it had to be the human part of her that was resistant to it that had saved her life. Eloen dressed herself for battle in hardened leather and bronze, carrying little more than her knives of obsidian. Across her back she carried her bow and arrows with a length of rope. As the outer walls came tumbling inwards, she had made her way to the far side of her stronghold and let herself out of a window, leaving the disease stricken Dokka'lfar to slow down the assault by man and beast. At the foot of the tower she shook the rope loose and made her way towards the trees. By now the stronghold was well alight and flames were pouring out of the window that she had just vacated. Once the humans had found that she was nowhere to be found they would search her stronghold and then the countryside around it. She realised that she did not have a great deal of time before this happened.

She made her way down the roadway that had been flattened through the surrounding woods at a steady run. As she topped a rise Eloen stopped short and stared at the sight that unfolded in front of her. A beast that seemed to be all head and teeth was crunching up one of her kind. It tilted its head and the remains slid down the throat into its stomach. It heard her as she trod on dry twig, making an audible snap and stood erect on its huge hindquarters with its tail counterbalancing the weight of its front end. The beast sniffed the air and shuffled towards her, casting its head from side to side.

Eloen stood very still and assessed the situation, watching the animal as it swung its head towards her. She could plainly see a metallic collar around its neck and realised that it must be iron, as she could not get into its mind. Droplets of saliva mixed with Dark Elf blood hung from the hinge of its jaws. The teeth were longer than her obsidian daggers and the ridiculously tiny front arms were still bigger than hers, carrying claws that were long and sharp. As it advanced towards her she caught the stench of its breath and she wet herself with fear.

The beast snorted and shook its head, stopping short of where she stood. It leaned uncertainly forwards and sniffed Eloen's face and slowly down to her feet. It sneezed over her and stood back, uncertain in its actions. The Halfling suddenly realised that she did not smell like the other Dokka'lfar and an idea presented itself. She edged forwards until she was once more in front of the confused beast and as it swung its head to one side, she side-stepped it and quickly ran up the base of its tail and up onto its shoulders. Eloen grabbed hold of the metal collar covered in greased leather and drew her head close to the animal's tiny brain. Before it could react to the unaccustomed weight on its shoulders Eloen had dominated it and 'pressed' it into her service.

To the tiny mind of the T Rex the weight on her shoulders had always been there. It was to be ignored. It was her young that needed to be protected at all costs. She would hunt for it and carry it wherever it needed to go. Eloen was satisfied now that she had the means of escape from the immediate surroundings. Now was the time to cover as much distance as she could. She turned the beast towards the road and urged it onwards. The beast could run! It charged off in a loping run that soon ate up the miles and took them far away from her old home. It did not take long before they came upon a homestead where a Dokka'lfar 'family' had settled with a few human slaves.

The area looked well managed so the dominant Dark Elf must have had a reasonable intelligence to make decisions that produced food. There were so many Dokka'lfar spread over the lands of Aifheimr that they had turned it into a devastated hell. Here it seemed that the mindless had been kept at bay and in turn had provided a stringy meal to those who ruled.

Eloen liked her lips in anticipation as her new 'mother' turned her head to follow the scent trail. She swung her head from side to side, hunting for live food and walked through a makeshift fence up to the walls of the farm. The T Rex tore off the roof and buried her head inside bringing out a live Dokka'lfar in her jaws. She turned her head round and offered the screaming child to Eloen crunching down and swallowing the front half. The Halfling quickly stripped the flesh from the legs and buttocks and chewed enthusiastically on the fresh, warm and bloody meat. She tossed the remains down to her protector which swallowed what was left after a quick crunch. The T Rex again plunged her head into the remains of the roof and once again picked off another child, swallowing this tiny morsel whole.

The Halfling gave the beast a command to stay and slipped off the neck of the beast onto the ground. She gave the door a shove and entered the remains of the farm. Inside was water drawn from the well in a bucket and she drank to quench her thirst. She put some of it aside and washed herself, cleaning the blood and dinosaur spittle from her body and leather armour. It was getting dark and she needed to sleep so she found the bedroom that lacked its roof and settled down to sleep. There would be no rain tonight so she would remain dry. She had survived being killed by the human slaves at her stronghold and had added a new 'friend' to her arsenal. In the morning she would try and find out what had happened to turn her life upside down. Now she would sleep content.

It was just before dawn that something awoke her by intruding into her senses. She sprang from her bed and naked, rushed outside and found her protector looking up at the sky. Eloen leapt to her side and wound her arm around the iron collar pressing her forehead to the body heat of the metal. There in the sky was a bubble that distorted the clouds behind it and it was filled with Ljo'sa'lfar! She could feel their minds with hers for just one moment and then the contact went fuzzy. Gnomes! It had to be gnomes that were aiding the Light Elves. Old folklore had been handed down about the old races that once had lived on Aifheimr before the Dokka'lfar had driven them out.

Eloen returned to the inside of the farmhouse and dressed herself. She then searched through the bottom of the building until she found the tools tucked away inside a wooden box. There were bronze cutters and spades in abundance, but little that would suit the purpose that she had in mind. What she needed was something that housed a diamond edge as bronze would never cut through iron unless the iron was soft. She had spent enough time holding onto the beast's collar to know that it had been hammered shut and was quite hard. At last she found a glass cutter wrapped in a soft leather pouch. Eloen held it aloft and watched the sunlight catch the facets in the diamond. It had been worked to present a sharp edge and she checked it by rubbing a finger down its edge. A small bead of blood trickled down her palm.

She went outside where the 'pressed' T Rex sat in the morning sun waiting for her. Eloen climbed the beast until she was once more perched upon the massive neck and began to rotate the collar around the creature's neck until she came to the join. The metal was thinner here as it had been hammered together. The Halfling began to scribe the diamond's edge back and forth to bite into the metal. She sent her mind into the metal and destabilised the molecular substance, softening it. She had never met a Dark Elf that had this power of hers and all of them reacted badly to iron. Whilst iron shielded telepathic contact it did not affect her telekinetic ability. Since the sickness had left her she had noticed that in some ways it had extended her mental powers once she had thrown off the infection.

The sweat began to roll down her forehead and cheeks as she toiled on. The muscles on her arms and shoulders bulged out as she began to pull the collar away from the beast, bending it along the deeply scribed line. She then began to press it down so that the metal bent inwards. As she worked the collar up and down, she was aware of a heat building up at the fault line where her unique gift had softened the metal. The T Rex began to get uneasy and it took all of her mental powers to keep it still because of the iron collar's inhibiting, mental shielding abilities. At last after a time when the sun had climbed to the mid-day position the collar came free. Eloen slid down the beast's back with her prize.

Now the tiny brain of the T Rex was completely under her power and she could do the next stage of her plan. She sent her off to find whatever food was in the area as she could smell carrion on the mid-day air. There were many dead Dokka'lfar scattered over the countryside so the strong constitution of the T Rex would not be fussy. She needed to get to work on the collar as soon as she could. Eloen soon located a hammer and a hard marble stone that would do for an anvil. She got a fire going in the dead hearth of the kitchen and pushed the end of the collar into the flames and waited for it to get red hot. Once it had started to glow she pulled it out with a leather holder and began to hammer it flatter. Over and over again she carried out this action until she had enough to bend around her neck. She had watched the humans work metal for their elfish masters, making all manner of things out of bronze. Working iron took more effort, but the shielding effect would make her invisible to the Ljo'sa'lfar as long as she wore the collar. The problem would be controlling the T Rex from time to time, so she had to make sure that the collar would come off easily, but not so easy that it came off at the wrong time. To prevent that she fashioned a leather loop on each end with a lace holding the open ends together.

Satisfied with this she looked at the length of collar that was left and had a thought. She pushed the iron into the fire and began the whole process again until she had a number of metal strips that she could fold around her arms. Unlike the other Dokka'lfar she was neither black, nor flame red and was the same brownish colour as her mother. She had the same cat's eyes and pointed ears of an elf and could have passed as one of the Ljo'sa'lfar were it not for the hatred in her heart and the lack of wings. Without a close inspection she could also pass as a human woman.

It was evening and she was hungry, so she began to systematically search through the kitchen of the homestead and found jars of potted meat and vegetables. Not trusting the age and toxic properties of the contents raw, she put them inside a bronze pot and heated them up on the kitchen fire. There was a crashing sound from outside as her adopted mother began to look for her young by pushing her head through the doorway. She caught the smell of fire as the wind changed direction and snorted with fear. Eloen's mind reached out to the T Rex and soothed its fears. She went outside and stretched out her hands to the saliva dripping mouth of teeth and was rewarded by the stench of long dead Dokka'lfar in the creature's breath. Eloen retched and turned aside gasping. She climbed the back of the beast and gripped the neck with her legs as she passed a rope beneath the massive neck and knotted it firmly. Now at least she had something to hold onto while they travelled together. She eased the T Rex away from the farm and pointed her away from her stronghold's borders towards the east and the sea. The dinosaur was well equipped to travel and hunt at night so it would not hurt to keep it travelling at a steady pace. Once the renegade humans had found no trace of her they would begin a search looking beyond the stone walls of her old home.

Eloen would make sure that she was an unfeasibly long distance away from all efforts to find her. She swore one thing in her heart and that she would be avenged against those who had ripped her life apart, no matter how long it took. She had ransacked the farmstead and gathered up anything of use that she could carry. This was proving awkward to carry while she balanced herself on the T Rex's shoulders so she instructed the beast to stop. Now that Eloen had put a few more miles between that last meal of carrion, the beast's breath had reached a more reasonable level. Eloen wrapped the coil of rope around the beast's chest, looping it around the tiny arms to keep it in place and got her to lean forwards so that she could pass the rope over her back. Fortunately the moon was full and enabled Eloen to see quite clearly with her eyes fully dilated what she needed to be able to do. Now she could tie the straps of the bag of tools and supplies securely to the makeshift harness.

Whilst the country was in chaos she intended to put as much mileage behind her as she could. She could see that the Dokka'lfar had been hit hard by whatever the Ljo'sa'lfar had released and it had been a stroke of perverted genius to release these programmed, giant meat-eaters into the countryside to finish the job, wearing iron collars. Fortunately iron was not a poison to Eloen due to her human side and she would use that knowledge to her advantage.

MOLOCK'S WAND

CHAPTER TWO

Eloen awoke cradled between the T Rex's huge hind feet and stretched her arms to the rising sun. What she needed most of all was information. What had happened to her world and what or who was responsible? She had dominated this area around her stronghold ever since she had wrested control from the resident master. Others had done her bidding and had lived because of their attention to her will. Now she had nothing! The puny humans could never have taken control without help from someone. Eloen cast her mind back to the distortion that she had seen passing over her and the fleeting connexion with elvish minds and the fuzziness that cut off her contact. It had to be the Ljo'sa'lfar who had fled from this world thousands of years ago and Eloen knew practically nothing about them. She knew of her father's curse that while one Light Elf lived he would not rest until that heart was stilled, but that was all.

A raw hatred filled her soul as she began to ready herself for another day's travelling with her 'pressed' defender. She determined there and then that somehow she would find her father's castle and the truth behind his people's destruction. All she remembered of the time that she had spent growing up adjacent to it, was that it lay to the east, beyond the sea that separated this large island from the mainland. Her mother had escaped her father's notice by emptying her mind and just walking steadily away. Molock had plenty of diversions to keep him happy and cocaine-addicted fresh human meat was one of them. Her mother, Isabel, was one of many female humans that he kept for his own use and would not be missed. He never knew that her mother was pregnant and had he been aware, he would not have been interested.

Eloen had all of her father's mental powers and they were very much stronger than most of the Dokka'lfar, plus she had developed the ability to reach out with her mind to touch things. She commanded the T Rex to lower her head and climbed aboard the thick muscular neck, checking that she had everything that she had scavenged from the farm house. The beast's mind was buzzing with the fact that she was hungry and her excellent sense of smell picked up the scent of carrion wafting on the breeze. Fortunately the wind was blowing from the east and that was where Eloen wanted to go so she encouraged the dinosaur to steadily trot in that direction. After several miles had gone by the T Rex slowed and waved its head back and forth until it began to head off towards a rise in the scrubby undergrowth. When they breasted the small hill, below them was another farmstead and smoke was coming from the chimney. Outside and in the yard was a pile of dead elves that were beginning to ripen in the hot noonday sun. This was what the T Rex had smelt on the morning breeze.

As the beast shuffled forwards into the yard she could see the door slam shut, that faced out onto the pile of dead. Eloen smiled to herself as the humour of the situation presented itself. The size of her companion was enough to instil fear into anything made of flesh and blood. Also the fact that the rows of teeth were longer than most knives would make sure that the fear of meeting that mouth at close quarters would be all you could think about. She sent her mind inside the farm and felt the presence of a few Dokka'lfar, lying terrified upon the floor pushing benches against the front door. The Halfling slid off the dinosaur's shoulders and left her to feed on the mound of dead.

Eloen gripped the low level minds inside with brutal pressure, "Open the door. Now!"

Unable to resist the summons, the Dark Elves inside began to pull the benches away from the door until the door could open. The fact that forty feet of hungry dinosaur was dominating the yard outside eating the dead elves made no difference. With one glance Eloen could see that the only survivors of the virus were the nearly mindless Dokka'lfar that bred indiscriminately and that served the overseers that were one generation down from Molock. They were of no use to her so she sent them towards the T Rex's feast and watched as her protector left the stinking carrion for fresher prey. Inside the farmhouse it was all too evident that the surviving elves had stripped the food cupboards bare, so she re-entered the yard and stopped the T-Rex from eating any more of them. She looked at what she had to use as food and selected a young female that did not look too stringy. Eloen cut her throat and drank the arterial gush that spouted from the dying elf. It would do for the moment, but she needed to consider the immediate future. She butchered the Dark elf into manageable strips and carried the meat into the kitchen. There she lit a fire and smoked the meat to preserve it. After this she wrapped the strips of meat in soft leather bags that probably had once been the backs of dead Dokka'lfar sewn together.

Once again she washed herself and scrubbed herself down in the kitchen with water that had been drawn from the well.

She searched the kitchen for water containers and found some leather ones with laced up ends. Some were foul and mouldy, but several fresh looking ones were all that she required and these she filled. Eloen looked outside at the setting sun and decided that this place would do as well as anywhere to sleep. She checked on her protector and found the T-Rex fast asleep draped over the pile of carrion with belly distended.

Eloen smiled and said to the sleeping beast, "I'll bet that's it's been a long time since that fat belly was full! Sleep well!"

Leaving the dinosaur to its rest, she re-entered the building and found where the dominant Dokka'lfar slept. It was a very large bed, quite capable for a group to sleep in. She shook the blankets to get rid of most of the infesting creatures that had taken up residence and wrapped them around herself and slept.

When she awoke the sun was streaming through the windows and she felt the warmth on her skin. Eloen dressed and made her way outside where she searched the immediate area for her protector. The heap of carrion had been eaten in the early morning and had practically vanished. The Halfling cast out with her mind's power and found the beast had rooted out a hole on the edge of the trees and was busily laying a clutch of eggs. As Eloen got closer to the T Rex she swung her head round and hissed at the Halfling in defensive fury. She retreated from the maddened onslaught and warily probed the mother's mind. She realised that she was now to be driven off to make room for the hatchlings that would emerge from the clutch of new eggs. Try as she might she could not override the mothering instinct that filled the beast's small mind.

Eloen eased herself out of sight of the obsessed dinosaur and it calmed down, spreading dung and earth over the eggs to cover them. The last thing that she needed was an uncooperative T Rex. She would have to part the beast from her eggs and rub it out of her mind. Eloen probed the new mother's mind and began to blank out the recent memories. She planted a false memory of the beast discovering the clutch of eggs and labelled them as food and reinforced the 'family ties' that she had installed in the T Rex's mind when they had first met. Now she approached the huge mouthful of teeth with confidence and bent the beast to her will and she got her to dig out the eggs that she had laid during the night. There were three that had been carefully nudged into a triangle shape all about the size of Eloen's head. These would make a pleasant change instead of elfin flesh. The T Rex's stomach was still very full of Dokka'lfar, so she was not bothered when Eloen packed the eggs into a bag and hung it on the side of the harness attached around the shoulders. She was back in the frame of mind that the Halfling was her own young and would now protect her again.

Once again she turned the T Rex towards the rising sun and put some miles between her old stronghold and themselves. As the days went by she was guided by the dinosaur's keen sense of smell as she could scent carrion miles away. Very often where there was carrion, live Dokka'lfar could also be found trying to eke out existence from the barren and exhausted lands. These elves could always be 'persuaded' to feed Eloen and her beast.

The one creature she needed to find was a human who knew what had happened on this world. She needed to be able to control her informant and leave them with no memory of the interview. All she was sure of was that the Light Elves had somehow struck back and destroyed her world. She was still young for an elf and could allow time to pass until she got her answers. Whatever controlled her aging process seemed to be elfin in nature. She had none of the human frailties and had never picked up any of the many human diseases that afflicted her slaves. By this time she was sure that the humans that had stormed her broken stronghold had ransacked and taken whatever she had amassed over the centuries. What they had not thought about was that she would run from all that she had built over the long years. They expected to find her diseased racked and weakened body waiting to die. Eloen had made sure that she left no trace behind her of where she had gone.

She had now been on the run for over a month and had made her way from Dokka'lfar stronghold to isolated farmsteads all of which she had found practically empty of live elves. There was less and less for her large protector and beast of burden to feed upon as even the carrion had been reduced to bones by the crows. Eloen had managed to trap the odd rabbit now and then and had dug some edible roots from various gardens. Without the constant state of famine where anything edible had been gathered from the land, things were beginning to grow and flourish, but meat was getting scarce. Already the T Rex was getting more and more difficult to control as it became hungrier every day. The bones were beginning to show through the skinny frame. Each rib stood out and the powerful legs began to fail. By now in its natural state the T Rex would have eaten her young to survive and was very conscious that sat upon her skinny shoulders was a morsel of food.

Eloen drove the beast ever onwards towards the sea and that evening she stopped the dinosaur by another deserted farmstead and dismounted. As she loosened the rope harness the great head swung round towards her and the mouth opened wide to snap onto her head. The Halfling ducked underneath the slavering jaws and nimbly stepped to the side. She sent her mind into the beast's brain and made her blind and also deadened her incredible sense of smell. As the beast staggered round seeking the meat she needed, Eloen loosed an arrow deep into the beast's open mouth and into its throat. She followed it with another that slammed into an artery at the back of the T Rex's cavernous mouth. It began to drown in its own blood and in its weakened state the dinosaur soon fell onto her side, the tiny arms scratching uselessly at the soil it bled to death upon. Eloen built a good fire and began to butcher the huge animal. To reach any usable meat it would require her to get inside the beast and cut out its heart. The liver she would ignore as she was not sure as to what extent a carnivorous creature's organs would carry poisonous toxins. She was cutting deep into the chest and under the rib cage to get at it when her mind picked up approaching thoughts. It was a group of humans who had seen her fire. Eloen hacked through the arteries and blood vessels and dragged the heart out of the bloody hole, spearing it onto a long sharpened stake. She dragged her makeshift harness into the fire to destroy it and waited for her visitors to arrive while she roasted the dinosaur's heart in the flames.

While she waited for the new arrivals she altered her appearance by masking her pointed ears by combing her jet black hair over them. The next thing that she did was to carefully place her iron neck collar over the hair to keep it all in place. This effectively shut off the telepathic chatter that she would have picked up from the group of humans and would also show them that she felt vulnerable to any surviving ruling Dokka'lfar. As it was evening her pupils would be fully dilated and not showing the elfin cat's eyes that would have immediately shown her up as different. She now looked human enough that the newcomers would not think about it. Once they were asleep they would never notice it again.

A voice shouted out, "Hello. We mean you no harm. We saw the fire and would like to warm ourselves. We also have a little food to share."

Eloen stood and answered, "Welcome. I have more than a little food to spare. I am on my own and have been so for the last month or more. Come to the fire. There are no Dokka'lfar here. All of them are long dead and the farm is empty."

One by one the group walked out of the increasing darkness and stared at the dead T Rex in disbelief.

Their leader came further into the firelight and asked, "How in hell did you manage to kill that?"

"It was weak and two well-placed arrows into the back of its open mouth were sufficient," Eloen replied. "I would guess that most of the thing is just skin and bones, so I cut out its heart and I am roasting that. Feel free to cut it into strips and cook your own. There is plenty there to share round."

With that the Halfling lifted the heart out of the embers and sliced off a large strip for herself and handed it over. The hungry group soon cut the heart into strips and hung them over the red-hot embers to part cook. Their leader reached into his bag and threw over some hard unleavened bread to Eloen.

"Where did you get this?" she asked.

"We found some wheat growing wild and ground it up ourselves between a couple of flat stones, added some water and oil we 'found' and baked it. Mind your teeth! It's a bit gritty, but it helps to fill the belly," he replied. "I see you are wearing an iron collar! I doubt that you will need that anymore. I'm sure by now all the Dokka'lfar are dead. Any that might be still alive are easy to kill, as it seems that only the very primitive types seemed to have survived. Very few of the overseers have we seen and those we quickly killed as they had no power over us as long as we wore the collars that the Ljo'sa'lfar gave us before they travelled on."

Eloen sat upright and stared at the human chewing on the T Rex's stringy heart and said, "What are Ljo'sa'lfar and where did these monsters come from?"

"Where have you been this last month or so? Have you been isolated all this time?"

Eloen replied, "When the sickness came to my master I fled into the fields and just kept going. I found this iron collar on a chewed up girl. She seemed to have been attacked and then spat out and ignored. I recognised the collar as iron. It has always been a death sentence to possess iron in any shape or form because of what it does to the dark ones' mind control so I thanked my luck and put it on. Since then I have assumed that they could not feel my mind and have kept on running."

"Wear it if it gives you a feeling of security," the leader said, "but I can assure you that the majority of the Dokka'lfar are dead. Now I for one am tired and intend to sleep soundly inside that abandoned farmstead. My name is John and these people follow me of their own free will. This is Sam. He was with me when our master fell sick and helped me kill him when he collapsed. The two women are Jane and Saffia and the two children are Jimmy and Susan. We don't know where they came from except they were hiding in the cellar at the last farmstead we searched."

"I am called Eloen," she replied and shook hands with John and the others and gave the children a reassuring cuddle.

She wiped her hands on a swathe of grass to clean the grease and blood from off them. The next thing she did was to unstring her bow and place it carefully in the quiver with her arrows. She tied a leather throng around her bag to keep her knives safe and what possessions she had gathered on her travels, lifted it onto her shoulder and also made her way inside the farmhouse.

"I will sleep downstairs and leave the beds to you," she declared and dropped her bag and quiver onto the floor by a soft looking rug.

"Thanks," John replied, "we will see you in the morning

and then you can decide whether you want to join up with us. We are making for the sea where there should be others of our kind. There will be safety in numbers and we can all pool our labour. Also I think that there may well be a thriving community there that we could join. We have met others who are doing the same thing."

"That sounds good to me," Eloen answered, "I will make my decision right here and now. I'm coming with you if you will have me?"

"I'm tired and my belly is full," complained Saffia, "and all I want is to sleep! Come to bed all of you, or I shall fall asleep on these stairs!"

Eloen waited for the noises above her to cease and went to work.

She sent her mind into the sleeping thoughts of the leader, John, altering his perception of her so that her eyes and ears would look the same as the rest of the humans. This she did to all of the sleeping slaves to be. Next she went deeper into their memories to extract the knowledge of what had happened to her world. Much of it was speculation because of the events that all of them had taken part in. There was one fact that stood out and that was that Sam had seen a distortion in the air come down onto the ground and a group of the fearsome beasts had come leaping out of nowhere. They had immediately begun to hunt down the Dokka'lfar ignoring all of the humans. A mixture of strange and different creatures also poured out of the hole in reality spreading a mist that was being squirted into the air. A human approached Sam carrying an armful of iron collars.

He had said, "Put these on and the Dokka'lfar cannot get into your minds. They will sicken and many of them will die. When this is over, make your way to the sea, by the big river. There will be help there for all those who come. We must go now as we have so much to do. The beasts will not harm you. They have been 'pressed' into eating only one food and that is your old masters."

After that brief interchange he stepped back into the hole and disappeared. Eloen had recognised some of the odd creatures that had joined with the human. There were goblins and gnomes working side by side with another type of human that she did could not identify. They were not very tall, but very muscular and very hairy. They carried something made of metal that spat fire and killed the Dark Elves at some distance. She was amazed to see the gnomes using the metal sticks to kill her kind while the goblins squirted the mist into the air. Something very fundamental had to have happened to do this. Gnomes and goblins were without courage or aggression and were just a sub-species of elf. What had changed them?

She played back all of Sam's memories and then she just got a quick flash of something in the air. Eloen played back that brief sighting in the sky and saw a winged elf, just before the human turned his head. Ljo'sa'lfar! A Light Elf! The ultimate pacifists had somehow changed into killers! It could only be them who could have had the knowledge to travel to their home world and wrest it away from the domination of the Dokka'lfar! There was much that she did not know about her history, let alone the history of her father's struggle to destroy the people that he had sprung from. What she needed was to capture one of the Ljo'sa'lfar and pump him or her dry of information. Again she replayed Sam's memories of what the human had said to him. She had been right to travel towards the sea and away from the ruins of her stronghold. Whatever 'help' there was at the river mouth it had to involve the Light Elves and that was where she needed to be.

Exhausted, Eloen wrapped herself in the warm rug and

slept contentedly and was woken up by the children as they opened the door to go outside and relive themselves. Her mouth watered as she contemplated the fresh young meat that was parading past her reach. Noises from the kitchen made her take stock of her situation and she lightly touched the minds of the two women, encouraging them to cook something for breakfast. The two men she directed to cutting into the carcass of the T Rex to find what meat there was to be had on the bony frame. It did not take much to organise humans to do her pleasure. She made her way into the kitchen and washed off the remaining grease and blood from her body and dressed herself in clean clothes.

John and Sam were cutting into the back legs and tail, separating strips of flesh from the sinews of the beast. Already the heat of the sun was encouraging the flies to cloud around the dead animal. The guts were already starting to swell with gas and a ripe aroma began to circulate, so she allowed the two men to finish what they were doing and take the flesh into the kitchen to smoke and cure. It would keep them from starvation on the long walk ahead and they could forage as they continued towards the sea. Eloen turned towards the well and let the bucket down into the cool depths, slowly as to be certain not to stir up the sediment that collected at the bottom. She wound the rope about the pulley and pulled the full bucket over the wall and set it down. She called the children over and bid them to slake their thirst before she did herself. This had not gone un-noticed by her new companions and gave them even more incentive to trust the raven haired woman that had teamed up with them. They all washed in the 'old water' that was stored in the kitchen and brought cups out to the well filled bucket and drank their fill.

While they were drinking Sam looked sharply at Eloen and asked, "That suit of combat leather fits you well, so I would like to know where you got it from?"

Eloen laughed and replied, "A dead Dokka'lfar gave it to me and she was just my size. Mind you I had to cut her throat first!"

As the sun had risen, her eyes had narrowed to slits and not one of the humans noticed. Now she carried her metal collar loosely linked around her waist and tied into her belt. A leather thong looped about her neck still holding her long hair over her pointed ears. Eloen gave them a mental prod to get things going and watched with satisfaction as her new slaves filled the water-skins and bags of dried meat and carried them towards the east. As they crested the rise at the back of the farm, she could see in the distance a silver ribbon snaking across the lands on its way to the sea. Eloen was quite confident that soon she would have the answers that she craved.

It might take a week or so of walking, but the human had said to Sam, "Walk towards where the river meets the sea. There you will find help."

There would be slimmer pickings the closer that they got to the river mouth as the isolated farmsteads would have been ransacked by other groups. Eloen was not too fussed as she had walking with them two sources of food that could soon be converted into strips of meat and small joints. The humans would never remember what had happened to the children, she would make sure of that.

MOLOCK'S WAND

CHAPTER THREE

At last the skies had blackened enough and a welcome rain began to fall. The dusty band of travellers had made it to the banks of the river a day or so before the rains hit. Others had joined the band and Eloen had ensured that all of them saw her as a human and also they were all protective towards her. The two children from her small group had soon found others to bond with. Fortunately for them the food had not run out and the others that had added to their numbers had food to spare, having come upon food dumps on their travels. It was a very relaxed atmosphere amongst the men and women as all of them told the same story that the cursed Dokka'lfar were practically all dead. Those that had survived had been so weakened by the disease that had spread throughout the lands that their once invincible mental powers were no match for an iron band around the neck and a knife thrust into their black hearts.

Eloen kept her small band of extremely protective humans close to her and dropped her hair into a fringe, hiding her cat's eyes from the occasional stare when they met newcomers. Her ears she also kept hidden underneath her black hair by using a leather thong and fortunately she did not have the antennae on her forehead as the other elves did.

The iron collar she kept around her neck, wrapping beads around it so that it became decorative. By chance, she found that it was when the collar made metal to metal contact; this was when her telepathy cut off. Hidden amongst the increasing band of humans making their way towards the mouth of the river, she experimented on the limits that the ring of iron around her neck possessed. A leather loop pulled tight would bring the naked ends of the collar together and her mind became silent from the thoughts of others. If she left it open to a width of her thumb, she could sense the human minds around her within twice her touching distance. If she left it a fist open she could sense those within a stone's throw. With the collar off altogether her range of sensitivity was about a mile.

When she slept, she made certain that the collar was firmly lashed together so that she did not broadcast her dreams to any of the humans around her. Also the last thing she needed was that the Ljo'sa'lfar might pick up a stray thought and realise that a Dokka'lfar still lived and was in their midst. So she slept each night with John and Sam each side of her with Saffia and Jane by their sides. The children had moved into a crèche with what other small ones had been discovered or were part of a rare family. By now the men and women were quite relaxed and as the days went by and no live Dokka'lfar were to be seen an atmosphere of unsuppressed joy began to infuse the expanding groups. It was obvious that at last after thousands of years, they were free!

The group of people had now reached several hundred as they walked unhurried towards the sea and the river mouth. Now buildings could be seen that had been erected close to where one of the dominant Dokka'lfar had once held sway. The castle had been torn apart and the stones used to build all kinds of useful trades, such as bakeries, butchers, dormitories, blacksmith's and even a water-mill had been built. Stock pens were full of animals that the one-time slaves had never seen before. Sheep, cattle, pigs and birds of all kinds were penned and being looked after by other human beings with help by other strange folk. This was the first time that the humans of Aifheimr had ever seen goblins, gnomes and their close cousins called dwarves or Neanderthals. It was overwhelming!

From out of the sky came the Ljo'sa'lfar with wings spread wide spiralling down. Eloen pulled the laces tight on her collar so that not a single thought could escape. In the silence she very carefully loosened her collar a finger's width so that she could eavesdrop on the human's thoughts beside her and catch the telepathic message from the destroyers of the Dokka'lfar.

"Welcome," sang the thoughts of the Ljo'sa'lfar as the group of refugees stared at the iridescent wings covered in tiny feathers that the new marvels tucked away on their backs. "There is much that you have to know and we apologise for inserting it directly into your minds, but there is no other way. We know of the terrible existence you have endured upon this, our once home-world and the way that you have suffered at the hands and minds of the Dark Elves that used you so cruelly. This time is over and will never return. All the Dokka'lfar are dead and this world is ours once more. We will re-stock the animals and provide seeds and trees. We will teach you how to farm this land and how to make it fruitful. There will be trades for you to learn so that you will become self-sufficient. The age of tyranny is finished. We will not abandon you. We are aware of our responsibilities regarding the new order. All we ask in return that you help to turn this devastated world back to the land of plenty that it can be. This is taking place all over this world as we speak. It is the dawning of a new age. It will be a time without violence and once again no hand will be raised against another's."

Eloen soaked up all of the rest of the telepathic broadcast and drew the leather thongs together to cut off the voices in her head. She had some of the puzzle, but not all of it. That would come later when she took out one of the Light Elves and burned out all of the details that had not been given to the vast group of newcomers.

The weeks turned into months and still Eloen bided her time, living on the fringes of the new society. The four humans that were bonded to her made sure that she wanted for nothing and toiled willingly on whatever projects were being in need of their services. The community prospered and the old ways soon became forgotten by the humans who had once lived only to serve the Dokka'lfar. Family life became a certainty instead of a rarity and children were born knowing their parents and growing up with them. Both of her females had got pregnant several times, but Eloen had terminated the tiny life sparks before they grew to any size in the womb. She also found that in some way she benefitted from the tiny life forces that she snuffed out. Eloen always felt more alive after each tiny death, so she experimented by wandering through the community and occasionally taking an infant's soul for her own.

She made sure that she took only those who were slightly sickly as too many healthy one would have aroused suspicion. Human doctors had been transported to this world with cabinets of drugs to treat the sick and the occasional injured. With them from time to time would be Ljo'sa'lfar doing what they could with their mental powers to aid the medicine available. Eloen tried many times to eavesdrop into these equally as powerful minds without success. The moment that she exerted any pressure the Light Elf would become aware of her, so that when they were nearby, she kept the iron collar tightly shut.

Eloen began to think of an easier target and considered something else. Amongst the crowds that were busy building a town at the river's mouth were many goblins who by nature were inclined to be solitary by inclination. They enjoyed each other's company, but also did not mind spending a lot of time on their own. She had 'overheard' some stray thoughts of this particular goblin when he was relaxing with a group of his own kind. He had been there when the vessel known as the Spellbinder had entered this realm and was talking about it. The language he spoke was different to anything that Eloen had heard so she could not understand it, but she had picked up a wisp of thought about coming here and the destruction of a vast castle.

Eloen looked at the goblin's greenish, round face and thought about that last picture in his mind. It was impossible for her to tell if this creature was young or old! His eyes were large and very dark with long eyelashes. The ears were similar to the elves, but were pointed at top and bottom. Large tufts of hair sprouted from each ear. His hands were long and spindly as were his arms and legs. He had pointed teeth and a pointed nose with a bald head. He came up to her shoulder, so overpowering him would not be difficult. All she needed to do was to follow him on his many journeys into the countryside. He was setting up animal management courses and was teaching human beings how to keep pigs and chickens. Scattered around the town that they called New London were now a number of smallholdings that had been built by human beings brought through by the Ljo'sa'lfar with building experience. This skill they had passed on to the people that had been slaves and worse to the Dokka'lfar. Now the art of farming was being passed on and the goblins were very good at it.

The goblin was mounted on a pony and had packed it for

a long stay with a sleeping bag and provisions to last for several weeks. Eloen had soon mastered the ability of riding a horse as had many of the humans who had been born on this world. This animal had been part of human development for thousands of years. It had not evolved on Aifheimr and the elves had taken them from Earth to Haven. Now once more the horse was in demand and had been brought to this world also. Shire horses were now pulling ploughs and turning the soil far deeper than had been done by human beings pulling them. The land was being changed from its period of desolation to a more fruitful usage. Now that millions of the Dokka'lfar had disappeared, already the land was beginning to recover and brown was being transformed into green.

Eloen rode up to the goblin who slackened the pace to allow her to draw by his side.

"Good day, human, my name is Jolene," he said, "are you going far?"

"About as far as that clump of trees," she replied and pointed to a stand of oak that was nearby. "Shall we rest there for a while and sit in the shade. I have plenty of provisions that I can share with you. I am mapping out the territory and marking the different types of wood for logging usage for the town."

"I can rest for a while," the goblin replied. "I have plenty of time on my hands and I am not expected. This is a roving visit, just to make sure all is well at the homesteads and I am there if help is needed."

Eloen gave a savage smile at the news and urged her horse into the shade. She unclipped the iron collar and widened the gap ready to seize the goblin's mind as she swung her leg over the horse.

The goblin dismounted his pony and threw the reins over a branch and reached into his provisions looking for a water bottle. That was when Eloen hit him with the full force of her mind. Jolene was taken by surprise, but fought back as best he could. The first thing that Eloen did was to make him blind and deaf and looped an iron amulet around his neck. Now he was isolated from all of his own kind. The only voice he could hear was Eloen's. She cleared his sight for a few moments to allow him to see her slitted eyes and pointed ears and make him panic."

"What are you?" his mind screamed.

"I appear to be the last of the Dokka'lfar. I am a Halfling. My mother was a human, but my father was the great Molock himself. Now I need to know how he died and who was responsible for his destruction. You were there. I have heard you speak of it to the others. Now you will tell me!"

Eloen dug deep into Jolene's mind and memories while the goblin screamed in agony as she extracted all she needed. She was there when Sam Pitts and John Smith detonated the explosives and sent the walls inwards. Now she knew where her father's castle was located far across the sea and she knew the history of the wingless elf that had become High King. It was this maimed Ljo'sa'lfar that had rallied his people and led them into the otherwise aberrant behaviour of being able to commit violence against the Dark Elves. She watched as the new High King battled the Dark Lord Abaddon and destroyed the command chair and Staff of Power. Wait! She ran that through again more slowly and watched the Staff of Power vanish from sight in a downfall of rubble as the arch collapsed in front of the Spellbinder. To the goblin's knowledge no-one had ever been back there to retrieve it. Eloen realised that it was still there under the ruins located on Haven. Somehow she needed to hitch a ride on the Spellbinder and travel back to Peterkin's realm. To do this she would need more information about the comings and goings of the ruling Ljo'sa'lfar.

She gave back the sight and hearing to the terrified goblin, after she made sure that his bonds were tight.

"Tell me about the Spellbinder, Jolene. How often does it come to this world and where does it come to once it's here? Does it come to New London very often and when it comes; is there any warning of its intending visit? If you speak freely to me I may grant you your life and just make you forget our little chat," Eloen insisted and drew out a sharp obsidian blade from under her cloak.

The goblins eyes were fixed on the blade as Eloen passed it under his sharp nose and sliced the lobe from Jolene's ear. This concentrated his mind on the questions asked by the Halfling so that Eloen picked them out of the terrified creature's mind with ease.

"Good boy," she said, "and well done! Now do I need to keep you alive or not? Is there anything else that I might need to know?"

Eloen chewed thoughtfully on the goblin's lobe and spat it out as it tasted bitter.

"Not!" She said to her captive and drew the obsidian blade across the goblin's skinny throat and watched the arterial fountain spray the tree he was tied to.

The Halfling stood up, walked around the tree and took what provisions would be useful to her from Jolene's pack. She considered killing the pony and cutting steaks from it, but decided that she would set it loose without saddle or bridle. As for the goblin; it might be more sensible to hide the remains. When he did not appear anywhere and began to be missed, no-one would connect her act of murder to his disappearance. It would just seem to have been an accident that had befallen the green-skinned creature. She looked up into the trees and could already see a number of crows gathering, drawn by the scent of spilled blood. Eloen tidied up the corpse by removing every trace of him being tied up and then gutted him so that the scavengers could get at the body quite easily. After a few days of rotting in the undergrowth and being pecked apart, no-one who found him would have any clue that he had had his throat cut.

She mounted her horse and made her way back to the buildings of New London satisfied with the mine of information she had gathered. She had plenty of time and was in no hurry. As the days passed, she saw no-one and was quite sure that by now all traces of her murder of the goblin by her hand had been erased. The information that she had wrenched from Jolene's mind needed to be catalogued into her memory. One of the attributes of her Elven heritage was that she forgot nothing. She could re-run every detail from the goblin's memories at her leisure. She was most interested in the creature's knowledge of the High King and his struggle to gain power. Jolene had lived at the Ljo'sa'lfar's castle long before Peterkin had been born and knew every corridor, nook and cranny. This elf was different to the others under his rule. He was not a pacifist and had altered the frame of mind of his people, to at last rise up against the Dokka'lfar and was ruthless enough to destroy them all.

"All but for one, that is," she thought to herself as she rode slowly along. "All but for one!"

She had plenty of time to prepare and plan ahead as the next visit by the High King and his amazing ship, the Spellbinder would take place next year. She needed to think things through during that time. By then her small group of human beings would need to increase and add several gnomes to the tally. With gnomes 'pressed' into service and part of her band of close knitted companions the chances of a Ljo'sa'lfar picking up her thoughts would be very slim. The goblin had hinted that the ship itself was sentient and would know what she was, if she were not very careful.

There was traffic on the road into the new town as horses pulled carts piled high with tools and provisions were making their way back out into the countryside. A settling program was under way as groups of humans accompanied by a few goblins and gnomes made their way to where the Dokka'lfar homesteads had been located along the banks of the river. It would not take long to re-fashion the poorly built dwellings into more sturdy buildings with proper tools. Eloen smiled to herself as she rode steadily against the flow of refugees, waving to the new families that walked by the sides of the waggons. It would be a good thing for these people to prosper as she would need plenty of them to look after her once she had her father's Staff of Power in her hands.

She rode into the outskirts of New London and was amazed at the changes in a few days as mud gave way to paved areas.

Eloen looked around and thought, "My, these humans could work hard when they were toiling for themselves!"

When she approached the house that they had taken over, she dismounted and led her horse round to the stable at the side. She had been seen by Saffia and Jane who came running out to meet her. They stabled her horse and removed the saddle and bridle, making sure that there was fresh water and feed for the mare.

"We were worried about you, Eloen as you were gone several extra days. John was all for mounting a search for you," Saffia worriedly said and gave the Halfling a welcoming hug.

"Yes," Jane then asked, where have you been, to be gone such a long time? What could have kept you out in the wild countryside for so long?"

Eloen soon tired of all the unwelcome questions and laid a light touch upon their minds turning off their anxieties.

"I am hungry," she replied and walked away leaving the two women stood staring into space for a few moments.

"Prepare me a meal. Make sure that it is something hot and tasty. When John and Sam return from their work, you will tell them that all is well with me and not to worry themselves. Now into the kitchen with you and cook me something."

That evening the two men came back to the house that Eloen had 'liberated' from the family that were living there before they had walked into New London. The Halfling loosened the collar that she kept around her throat and ran their combined memories through her mind. They were employed to build a water mill so that the wheat that was being sown this spring would be able to be turned into flour in late summer. Some of the parts would have to be made elsewhere and brought here by the Ljo'sa'lfar reality-shifting ship, Spellbinder. The large mill wheels could not be fashioned here and many of the parts would have to come from Earth where there was a vast manufacturing base that could be utilised.

During these times the Spellbinder was in constant use, as Peterkin's engineering works and buying and selling enterprise was in full flow. Ivan Koshensky was still the senior buyer at the firm and handled all of the odd and strange orders that were closely related to the recolonizing of the elves home world. Many of the parts were made in separate parts of the country so that firms were scattered about. As Peterkin was the only elf that could motivate the sentient ship he rationed his time between being the only pilot and running the enterprises on three worlds. Ivan made sure that the parts were ferried out to the desert and unloaded far from prying eyes. Peterkin's scientific staff working with John Smith experimented with shielding the influences of iron upon the elves and found that sheets of lead deadened the effect on their mental capacities or a copper net with an AC current pulsing through it.

There were times that the expanding capacity of the

Spellbinder was put to the test when they were exporting millstones. There were groups of humans, elves, goblins and gnomes scattered all over the world of Alfheimr wherever conditions were fair. Without the billions of starving Dokka'lfar eating every green living thing the ruined world began to blossom. Fruit trees were planted and seeds scattered from the open hold of the spellbinder took root. What animals had sought shelter high above on mountain ranges, started to return to the lower levels and bred without any predators to harry them. The Great Plains began to fill up with grazing animals from groups that were released from the wilds of Earth into the wild of the elves home world. Once they were established, predators would be released to offer a check and balance.

Peterkin also transported many types of dinosaurs from Haven that had adapted to the changing environment onto these swampy areas. They would supply plenty of meat to the settlers once they were established. The dwarves soon brought over their riding steeds and showed their new cousins how to care for them and manage the creatures. They then returned to Haven and resumed their own cultures, not wanting to mix too much with the people from Earth.

Years had passed by and the new towns and villages of Aifheimr had prospered and many of the more adventurous Ljo'sa'lfar began to rediscover the old home world. I had prudently made contact with the Amish elders and had transported them to see what we were doing on our old home world. Once they had got over the shock of coming to terms with what we were and the history that had got us to this point, they decided that this world would be the very place for them to settle. In one night the Spellbinder 'swallowed' every farm and barn and transported them to the same area that they occupied on Earth. It hit the inhabitants of Earth with a shock. There were a few that did not want to come and they could not remember how their neighbours had disappeared or why they were still there!

I remember being sorry that not all of them would come as the situation on Earth was becoming more and more dangerous. Time and again I relocated people onto the old elfin home world and made sure that they were well provided for. Communities sprung up and thrived. Alfheimr blossomed as it had never had chance to in thousands of years. The only form of transport over long distances was the Spellbinder. Apart from that, wherever a horse and cart could go was the limit of travel. At our insistence very little iron was used and what could be made of stainless steel and bronze was utilised. Everyone had access to radio and all groups could keep in touch with each other. Every human upon this world had elected to come here and turn their backs upon the rest of humanity. There would be a few more trips back and forth in the Spellbinder and I would rest for a hundred years or so and leave the colonies to their own devices. We too needed to increase our numbers and fill out this world of Haven. If we were needed there were ways of using my long reaching 'gifts' from all those people in my head to reach out beyond this world to Alfheimr.

MOLOCK'S WAND

CHAPTER FOUR

Eloen contained her impatience, but was in a foul humour as she waited for the arrival of the Spellbinder and took to prowling around the town. She had established herself on the outskirts of the vibrant society that had sprung up in the rapidly growing New London. She needed to drain the life-force of someone and refresh herself as she was feeling the weight of her years. Unlike the true elves, she would grow older, very slowly, but the taking of someone's soul would stay the process for some considerable time. The death of the goblin had taken a great deal of her aging away and if truth be told she would not need another draining for maybe another fifty years. Nevertheless she needed that extra energy to do what she needed to accomplish when the Spellbinder came. What she really needed was a fuzzy minded gnome. Eloen was sure that she could take on to her mind the shielding effect of the way that gnomes thought. She just needed to be able to ride inside the Spellbinder when it returned to Haven, so she needed to be able to recreate that fuzzy-mindedness for a short while.

Close to the water-mill was where the bakeries were sited and this area was ceded to the gnomes, as they were master bakers of their craft. Eloen made her way down there as she had many times before. Her four humans all worked at the water-mill heaving sacks of corn that had been brought from Earth as the first harvest had yet to be cut and threshed. Nobody asked what the Halfling did, as no-one could really see her clearly so they dismissed her from their thoughts. She had got used to wearing the iron around her neck and the diminishing of her mental powers, but all it took was a loosening of the closing strap and her mind could reach out with an instant contact.

A cloud went across the sun and laid the area around the back of the bakery in deep shadow. There were no windows looking down on the alleyway between the watermill and the bakery. There was also a slight bend to the lane that led down to the river's edge so that anyone in the street outside could not see past the edge of the bakery.

At last she felt that she had timed it right and followed a young, female gnome to the water-tank by the paddle wheel.

"May I help you with the buckets, lady baker?" she asked.

"Why thank you," she answered and handed a bucket to Eloen. "They do get heavy you know. I like to use the fresh water that swirls out from under the wheel. It's full of bubbles and I always say that it makes a better loaf!"

The two of them walked round the back of the bakery to where the river ran off into a culvert. A post had been hammered into the ground to provide a safe hand-hold, but this would not be needed as there were two of them!

The gnome held out her hand for Eloen to hold as she leaned over the mill-race and dipped the bucket. Eloen loosened the collar and looked round to see if anyone was looking. There was no-one in sight so she swung the wooden bucket over the girl's head and smashed it into her skull. She dropped onto the gnome's back and the two of them went into the torrent. She grasped hold of the gnome and seized her mind in hers while the gnome choked, with her lungs full of water. The gnome stopped struggling and the Halfling made her way to the surface, dragging the girl with her. She had her life-force safely flooding through her blood giving her extra energy and the fuzzy little mind imprisoned inside hers, still alive.

She bobbed up and shouted for help and seemed to be doing her best to keep the gnome afloat and her face out of the water. Almost immediately the river bank filled with people ready to help and someone hurled a rope to her while several others jumped in to help. She grabbed the rope with her free hand and held onto the young girl as other hands came to help. Soon both of them were laid on the bank and Eloen made sure that her pointed ears were tucked underneath her hair. One of the humans started to push the gnome's chest up and down with no response and blew into her mouth. Eloen knew quite sure that the gnome would not resuscitate as she had her life and her mind tightly coiled inside her own body. As the life-force coursed through her body she felt better than she had in a hundred years. The many Dokka'lfar she had killed, over the time she had reigned at her stronghold, had never released so much energy. She wondered what the gnomes tasted like, as it seemed a terrible waste of good meat, but of course her people would want to bury her with some ceremony or other. She hurriedly pulled the collar together and locked out any probing minds as the gnomes from the bakery came to see what had happened.

An old gnome, balding and bearded came running up to the group and fell to his knees by the side of the body. He wore a white apron and there were ribbons tied to the ends of the plaits in his long grey beard. His leather boots were polished and studded on the soles and heels. He ran his hands over his wispy hair, before holding the hands of the still warm gnome.

"What has happened to Viveca? What happened here?" asked Hewit the master baker of the gnomes lodge.

"Master Hewit," cried Eloen, "I was helping Viveca to draw water and we both slipped into the mill-race. I tried to pull us both out, but I fear she hit her head on the bucket and swallowed too much water."

The gnomes gathered round and lifted the young girl onto an empty sack. They lifted her up and took her into the bakery away from the crowd. Hewit came to Eloen and looked up into her face that was showing such sorrow that the gnome cried tears of grief at the sight of it.

"She was the youngest of us all at the bakery. My many times granddaughter. You did all that you could, human. All that you could," he cried, standing up and hugged the Halfling in gratitude around her waist. "If you need anything, anything at all, just ask and it will be yours!"

Eloen chuckled inside and thought, "No trouble little gnome, I have what I came for! Now I shall be ready for the imminent visit of the Spellbinder."

A week or so went by and a distortion in the sky began to drop steadily towards the outskirts of New London. There had been prepared a great palisade to fence off a vast area of land with the river fronting one side. The Ljo'sa'lfar had been hunting and collecting suitable dinosaurs to introduce to the vast empty spaces on this world. They had picked on the Iguanodon as the most useful vegetarian to present to the recovering plant life. The creatures had evolved to eat many of the plants on Haven besides the ferns that their ancestors had fed upon. Fully grown they could attain a length of some thirty-three feet and stand upon their hind legs to feed on the tops of trees as well as graze at ground level. They were placid and easy to drive along. Young ones could easily be broken to be able to ride and when they grew to their maximum size they could still be induced to drag heavy loads. Also the younger ones could also be weeded out and processed for meat. The eggs were considered a delicacy to the Ljo'sa'lfar who kept their consumption to a healthy number. After all it took a voyage of the Spellbinder to bring them and until their numbers increased it would be a waste of resources.

The other dinosaurs that they brought with them were the Quetzalcoatlus, a flying pterosaur that was capable of flying for seven to ten days at fifteen thousand feet. The light Elves had bred them for thousands of years and had the wingspan beyond forty feet and they were quite capable of carrying a human being. The elves although winged, used these creatures for long distance flights. During the war against the Dokka'lfar, many humans had learned to fly and control these magnificent beasts. The only drawback to keeping these huge flyers was that their appetite was for ripe flesh and they needed feeding quite often. Fortunately they were also fish eaters and would forage quite happily over the sea or fresh water.

There were many sacks of wheat to be unloaded from the elfin ship and Eloen's people were part of the crew that were given this task. The Halfling had 'pressed' a number of instructions into the minds of her humans. Once the Spellbinder had left, they would have all memory of her erased from their minds. As she had the same number of fingers as a human, that was another thing that she did not need to hide. She had entered the reality-shifting ship along with John, Sam, Saffia and Jane many times, helping to move the heavy sacks of corn into the mill. Each time she entered she allowed the fuzzy mind she carried to obscure her thoughts from the Ljo'sa'lfar and of course the Spellbinder that was linked to Peterkin's mind.

Since she had murdered the young gnome, she had got rid of her iron collar as the Light Elves were very sensitive to raw iron and would have been aware of her in an instant. She even got quite close to the High King, but shut down all thoughts of hate and revenge. There would be time for this once she had her hands on her father's Staff of Power. As no-one was looking for a stowaway or a threat, she was ignored. Eloen also watched the High King's young son Elthred who also was able to command the Spellbinder, with some interest. Here would be the seeds of her revenge that would flourish in the future.

As sacks of flour were loaded back into the Spellbinder, Eloen made sure that there was a hole large enough to hide inside and also made sure that those who loaded them forgot. She had secreted food and water in the hole. Eloen carried her provisions, wrapped in greased paper in a clean flour-sack and when she was sure that no-one could see her, she burrowed into the centre of the sacks and went to sleep. While she slept, her mind shielded by a mantle of foggy thoughts provided by the captive dead gnome, the loading up of the Spellbinder continued. The size of the reality-shifting vessel decreased once all the dinosaurs had been delivered and assumed a much smaller volume. The hold that the Spellbinder had constructed was already loaded with sacks of flour from other colonies scattered around Aifheimr where water-mills had been built. It increased the volume to accept more by pulling out the walls. Fortunately for Eloen, the cave that she had fashioned from the sacks of flour remained uninterrupted. She slept on undisturbed.

Peterkin sent his mind into the entity of the Spellbinder and it shifted reality to the parallel world of Haven and Eloen woke immediately, alerted by the change of state. She listened with her mind to the passing chatter of elves and humans and tided her provisions into her carry-sack leaving nothing behind her to show that she had stowed away. She patiently waited until a gang began to unload the sacks of flour and fudged their minds so that she joined them without any question, carrying a sack over her shoulder. She became just one more labourer working for the Ljo'sa'lfar in a crowd of many.

Eloen ran through the goblin's memories of the Ljo'sa'lfar castle on Haven and pin-pointed where she was. The spellbinder had fused to the walls by the storage-chambers which were located four flights down from the royal chambers and all the other living quarters. Underneath this floor were the kitchens and bakeries that served the elves. Judging by the amount of fuzzy thoughts there must be more than a hundred gnomes working there. The floor under the kitchens was the homes and workshops of the castle goblins, along with the science laboratories that the elves and humans used to pursue knowledge. This was where the virus had been perfected that had wiped out the Dokka'lfar.

Eloen traced the way out of the storage via the less used passageways by remembering Jolene's knowledge of where he had lived for a great deal of time. She could almost feel his presence in her mind while she rummaged through his memories. The Halfling ruthlessly screwed the remnants of his soul into the same place that she kept Viveca's prisoner.

She heaved the sack of flour she was carrying onto the pile and joined the file of humans who were unloading the Spellbinder, walking at the very back. The Halfling separated from the gang and diverted to a side passage, making her way to where the Quetzalcoatlus were penned. To do this she had to make her way upwards through the goblin's quarters and then through the kitchens. She had managed to find a spiral staircase that took her through both areas without any challenge. The smell of fresh baked bread and pies caused her to divert her journey into the chilling room where the bread and meat pies had been left to cool. As there seemed to be no-one about she quickly filled her sack with freshly baked produce.

"What do you think you are doing?"

A gnome no taller than her chest stood looking up at her with hands on hips.

"Excuse me master baker, I am soon to travel on one of the dragons a far distance," she replied and fingered her obsidian blade. "I shall be gone some time, so I will need to take some food with me. Have you anything that I can take for drink?"

She leant forward and let her hair fall from her ears, fixed the gnome with her slit eyes and saw that he would do as she asked. He nodded and walked over to the bench at the side of the cooling room and carried over three bottles of water.

These he helped to stow in her sack, stood back and said, "Good flying weather my lady. Be careful out there while you are high up in the air. Keep your wings dry!"

Eloen nodded to him and climbed the stairs, passing several Ljo'sa'lfar who were walking down, without any challenge. She concentrated the fuzziness that she had taken from the gnome into a shield that masked her thoughts and continued to ascend to the highest part of the castle until she entered a room. There were wardrobes around the walls full of warm clothes to suit flying in the cold air amongst the clouds. Eloen opened several doors until she found a flying suit to fit her size and rapidly pulled on over-boots, gloves, trousers and a top. She wrapped a cloak and hood around herself and secured it with leather straps.

Now all she needed was a strong flying beast to take her where she needed to go. In the pens there was one very large one on its own, tethered to a post. It was irritable and hungry and snapped its beak at her when she approached it. Eloen picked up a bucket of ripe flesh and bones and offered it to the beast. The long head snaked forwards and seized the rotting flesh, tilting its head upwards to allow its meal to slide down its throat. It eyed the Halfling up and down with eyes that were bigger than her fists, looking for another bucket of carrion. Eloen picked up another bucket and held it forwards, slipping her mind into the simple creature as she did so. She grabbed the leather harness that was already in place and climbed onto the Quetzalcoatlus, making her sack of food secure. Eloen slid her feet into the stirrups and wound the reins around her wrists. She allowed the beast to swallow its meal and urged the pterosaur to walk to the parapet's end and catch the morning thermal. The creature had been ridden for many years and was an old hand at the game. She ran through its memories and how the beast had been controlled and flown. The last thing she needed was that she would make it do something difficult and throw her off. She felt the wings extend as he stepped off and swooped down towards the ground far below, gaining speed. There came a time when he tilted his wings somewhat and gained lift soaring into the air high above the castle ramparts.

Inside the memories of the dead goblin was a picture of the great gorge and this she projected into the pterosaur's mind until it overlapped with its own memories. This was where she wanted to go and this was where the creature would take her. Once there she would review the situation and make her decision as what to do next. There was a good day's worth of flying time left and this beast could stay aloft for days. The only problem was, could she? The flap, flap of the wings became her world and she amused herself by digging out the last bits of the gnome girl's mind and discarding it. She no longer needed the fuzzy mind shield anymore as she was well away from Peterkin's home and any probing minds. It was good to be rid of the girl's pathetic ego and think much clearer. The goblin's she decided to keep a while longer as there might be more for her to extract from the dead creatures memories.

There was an odd memory that she teased out and that was

of a spire that looked like a giant mushroom that was deep in the Plains of Scion and it was called the tower of Absolom. This had been used as a prison for the High King's daughter of the time. I ran through the memories that the goblin had of the new High King's struggle to depose the mad king and his victory over my race of beings the Dokka'lfar. He was a clever and resourceful foe and she would have to be very careful when she struck against him. She eased this memory into the dragon's mind and was rewarded by his recognition of the place. The beast banked to the left and began to drop down through the cloud layer. As they flew through the last of the clouds Eloen saw the plains of Scion for the first time. The sheer wealth of life almost overwhelmed her as the primitive thoughts of the hundreds of thousands of dinosaurs that struggled for survival gave off their energy. She recognised the signature of a T Rex as it hunted below her and many more as she cautiously opened her mind to the clamour of life. Aifheimr had been a quiet world with very little life, except in remote places unscathed by the Dokka'lfar's appetites. It was little wonder that the Ljo'sa'lfar wanted to live here instead of their home-world. Numbers of them had returned there and were helping the humans to bring the planet back to a state of beauty and fruitfulness, but they had been here for thousands of years. This had become home to them. Eloen felt a wave of hatred and envy surge through her body as she thought about the state of near starvation that the Dokka'lfar had endured while Abaddon had tried to take this world for them.

She 'pressed' the mind of the pterosaur to keep flying to this landmark while she slept uneasily upon the creature's back. Eloen had securely lashed herself to the beast so there was little chance that she would fall off.

The change in the flapping of his wings alerted her that something had changed and she awoke immediately. She opened her eyes and her mind and was aware of a large cupola beneath the two of them and a flock of smaller pterosaurs mobbing the Quetzalcoatlus as it tried to spiral down to what looked like a farmstead in the lightening sky. Eloen noticed wisps of smoke drifting up from the chimney. She took control of her mount and made it swoop to the side and deliver a vicious peck at the nearest flyer. At the same time she entered the simple minds of the reptiles with a devastating blow that sent then careering out of the sky with panic. Eloen allowed her beast to hang onto the smaller flyer and plunged to the ground on the top of the 'mushroom.' The pterosaur spread his wings and braked in the air, flicked his head forwards and cast the smaller flyer against a rock, where it lay very still. He then dropped onto his feet, folded his wings and waddled over to his meal. Eloen slipped off his back and 'pressed' his mind to stay where he was while she investigated the occupants of the cottage, carrying her sack of provisions.

The door opened and two figures stood holding an oil lamp aloft. In the golden light she could see that the couple were gnomes and by the fogginess of their minds, quite old for a gnome.

"Welcome, flyer. There is a hot drink inside the lodge and a stew over the embers of the fire. Come in and get warm," the male gnome called out to Eloen. "My name is Rassel and my wife is called Lorena. We were not expecting anyone. Where are you bound for?"

Without giving it any thought, Eloen replied, "I'm on my way to speak with the dwarves at the Great Gorge. I would appreciate some hot food and a rest."

She walked up to the two gnomes and looked down upon them as Rassel lifted the lamp higher to get a better look at the newcomer. Lorena opened the door wide and a warm light spilled out. Eloen walked in and sat herself by the fire and smelt the stew that was bubbling over the embers. She removed her cloak and hood, gloves and over-boots setting them down by her side. She did not loosen her jacket as the two gnomes would have noticed the lack of wings. She allowed her hair to fall away from her pointed ears so that the gnomes would see them and not think to question her appearance. Her eyes had reduced to slits in the bright light showing her elfin heritage.

The two gnomes fussed around her and treated her as an honoured guest. They gave her a bowl of stew, a bronze spoon and a hunk of fresh bread and sat down by the fire sipping a hot drink of a sweetened herb that filled the air with a pleasant, pungent smell.

Rassel, turned to the Halfling and said, "Is there any news from the castle? We see very few people now since the Dokka'lfar have been destroyed. Not that I'm worried about that as we no longer have Abaddon at the Great Gorge and his hoards of darkness trying to destroy our world. Were you involved with the struggle at all?"

"Not I," answered Eloen. "I did visit the home world though and saw the devastation that nearly destroyed it. There is much going on there and the humans are settling in. Great areas of farmland are being put to the plough pulled by great horses that have been brought from Earth. Many different crops have been planted and will soon be harvested. Meanwhile the High King travels back and forth carrying seeds to be planted and flour that has been milled on the home world. Everyone is very busy. Now if you don't mind I would like to sleep in a soft bed for a change."

"Of course my lady," Rassel answered and led the way to a private room with a bed that was built for her kind.

He opened the door for her and she entered the room and sat upon the bed.

"Thank you Rassel," she said. "Would you please leave me now and shut the door. I will join you again after I have had a few hours' sleep.

The gnome shut the door and went into the kitchen to help himself to another hot cup of herbal tea.

He sat by his wife and said, "It's nice to have company now and again. It makes a welcome change, but I feel something odd about her!"

Lorena swung round in the chair and fixed her husband with a steely glare.

"Is your eyesight so bad that you did not see her clearly? She is no Ljo'sa'lfar! Fog your mind more than usual and fight not to let her in. Did you not see her hands? Four fingers not five! There was no bulge under her jacket to take the folded wings. Oh yes, she has elfin eyes and ears, but little else. The fact that she wears her hair in a fringe over her forehead did not hide the fact to me that she has no antennae over her eyes! If she can control a large flying dragon, then she has the mental abilities of the elves, but which kind, my love? Come; let us get out of this house while she sleeps. Pack a travelling bag. We must get off this rock and make our way over the plains of Scion and get to the High King or we will die here!"

Rassel nodded and replied, "I believe you, wife. I felt something about her; a certain ruthlessness that leaked out, while she fed on our stew. I'll pack while you rustle up as much food as you think we can carry. It's as well there is a tunnel leading down to the ground or we would be trapped and in her power."

"I'll tell you something else that I felt leak out of her mind. There was a gnomish wisp about her; a young girl. I caught it just for a moment and then it was gone. Hurry my husband! We must get going and soon. I feel our lives depend on it.

Eloen slept soundly until midday.

MOLOCK'S WAND

CHAPTER FIVE

Eloen had dressed to fly, opened the door and walked into the empty kitchen. The fire was out and there were no sign of the two gnomes. She let out a screech of anger as she realised that they had seen through her efforts to be unrecognised. She ran out into the neat and tidy garden and could see no trace of them. Her dragon was still stood where she had left him 'pressed' into staying put until she came for him. He had eaten the smaller pterosaur last night and was still hungry. In this state he was inclined to be awkward and more unnecessarily difficult to control, so she gritted her teeth and swept the skies for any of the flyers. There was a small flock wheeling over the cupola, rising on the thermals and she directed her thoughts towards them 'calling' them closer.

Her mount tilted his elongated head towards the sky and waited, held still by Eloen's mind. As the flock dived down towards them, she blinded them cutting off all sense of sight to their tiny brains. One by one they thudded into the ground by her Quetzalcoatlus who waddled over to them and one by one picked them up, tilted his head and slid them down his neck. This then caused him to evacuate his bowels and Eloen moved away from the stench back into the small lodge to take what food she could find.

Inside the kitchen she found that the food that had been stored inside the cupboards had been either taken or spoiled with salt. Jars that had been full of preserves had been emptied into a bucket of slops. The leftover stew smelt odd and she was sure that things had been added to it just for her. The gnomes had been very thorough in their despoiling efforts and there was enough disquiet left behind to make sure that she would not dare to eat anything that was left behind. She still had some of the food left that she had taken from the castle bakery, so she would have to do with that.

Furious, she stormed out of the lodge and made her way to the pterosaur and mounted the beast and directed it to launch itself from the edge of the cupola. Her mount refused to move!

She bullied the dragon with her mind and reluctantly it shuffled forwards, fighting her instructions sullenly and once he got to the edge still refused to spread his wings and fly. Exasperated Eloen drove into the reluctant beast's mind and found out why it would not fly. She had allowed the creature to overfeed himself. With a distended stomach full of bones and flesh he would have dived into the ground, killing them both! She would have no choice but to allow her mount to digest the gargantuan meal she had left with him. There was no chance that she could go after the fleeing gnomes and silence them. She realised that the chances of their survival on the Plains of Scion were slim and the time that they took to travel the many dangerous miles to Peterkin's castle, would give her plenty of time to get to where she needed to go.

Eloen wandered around the gardens laid out with precision by the housekeeping gnomes. It was obvious that this safe place was a stopover point for flying traffic going and coming from where the dwarves lived, to the elfin residence at the centre of the plains of Scion. She found ripening fruit and gathered some of the most durable looking. The Halfling tasted apples for the first time in her life and marvelled at the taste until she crunched down onto a green one. She spat out the bitter tasting pulp and washed her mouth out from her own water bottle. Carefully she selected a bright orange and red one and was rewarded by sweetness.

"I have still a lot to learn about this place and the world of the Ljo'sa'lfar," she thought to herself."

She walked back to where the Quetzalcoatlus was preening himself and climbed onto the joint between his neck and shoulders. Judging by the heap of dung he had left behind, he should be more than ready to take to the air than before, so she urged him forwards. This time the creature did not complain and took to the air, catching the last of the afternoon thermals that rushed up the mushroom stalk and splayed out at the edge. He swooped down to gain speed and flew straight into an updraft that took him up to the cloud layer. With another sweep of his wings the dragon took them up into the afternoon sun and once again headed towards the Great Gorge and the dwarves. With wings outstretched he made a long glide towards the mountains of the crater's edge.

Some miles in the opposite direction Lorena and Rassel were moving through the undergrowth and bushes seeking a tall tree to shelter in. the sun was going down and the things that hunted in the night were not to be tempted. They set their sights on a fern tree that splayed out at the top. There was an ominous rustling in the bushes to their left so they deviated to the right and picked up the pace. Sweat rolled down the gnomes' cheeks as they began to panic as they ran towards the giant fern. Still they kept hold of the few things that they had packed for survival and made it to the base of the fern. They climbed upwards in the failing light and made their way towards the top until they came to a large fork where a branch peeled out of the main trunk. There was a flat area big enough for both of them to lie down.

Rassel took a small hammer from out of his bag and hammered a spike into the branch at each edge. He put four spikes securely in position and then spread a rope between the four spikes in a criss-cross fashion. The two of them wriggled underneath this improvised net and tied themselves into the web along with their bags of provisions.

"I hope she eats the stew," said Lorena bitterly.

"I shouldn't think so my love. I think she would be far too clever for that," replied Rassel. Try to get some sleep. We should be quite safe up here for the night. Be thankful we are not down there amongst the night hunters!"

Just then the sound of a big meat eater roared and another creature screamed as it died. This was answered by other roars and more screams! The two gnomes held on to each other tightly and Lorena sobbed in terror while Rassel did his best to calm her.

"It's little comfort, my love, but had we stayed in the lodge, I'm sure we would have been killed by whatever that thing was by now!"

"I know, dearest. I know, but I am still terrified," she answered and stared into the pitch blackness that seemed to intensify.

The early morning sun began to drift through the fern leaves and Rassel shook Lorena awake and said, "We're still alive my dear. It's time to eat and climb down this fern tree. We must get on our way."

Lorena shuddered, but she kissed her husband and replied, "There is bread and jam in a pot. That will keep us going for a while."

"My dear it will have to keep us going until we find shelter for another night. We can't afford to stop for long. If we are going to make it we have to make a steady pace. Our best bet is to get as far as we can from the Lodge and deeper into the Plains. Somewhere out there are the raptors that helped Peterkin. If we can light a fire they will see and smell the smoke and they will come. So as we travel along keep your eyes open for kindling wood and gather some as we go."

Rassel uprooted his spikes and replaced them into his carrying satchel along with his hammer. The two of them made their way down to the ground and continued their journey. Every night they counted their blessings at still being alive and every night they climbed a fern tree and slept lashed to the branch. Every morning Rassel would search the plains for a tell-tale indication of a fire, but to no avail. Lorena never complained, but the two of them got steadily thinner and weaker as time went by.

They eventually made it to a higher rise of ground littered with large boulders that they felt that they could hide behind. Two of them were close enough together to provide a gap that they could squeeze into if pressed. They marshalled the collection of kindling that they had both gathered and lit a fire. Rassel foraged into the brush that grew in profusion and found some dead bushes with leaves still on them. He dragged them onto the fire and was rewarded by a whoosh as the oily leaves ignited, sending clouds of smoke into the late afternoon sky. The gnome quickly made his way back to where the dead bushes once grew and hacked off as many bushes as he could find with his steel hatchet, while Lorena kept pushing the outsides of the bushes back into the flames. Rassel pushed more bushes into the flames and had a pillar of fire shooting up in the darkening surroundings. He added several large dried branches to the fire and banked it.

"They ought to be able to see that, my love. If not we're in trouble. We have no food and I don't think that either of us can get any further on our own," Rassel panted and lay down exhausted.

Both of the gnomes were bleeding from countless scratches and their clothes were torn and filthy. Lorena threw another large branch on the fire and handed Rassel a biscuit that she had found in the bottom of her bag and broke it in half. They munched on the last of the food and wrapped their only blanket around them, leaning against the boulder at their backs. Out in the darkness the screams of the hunted and the roars of the hunters echoed in their terrified ears. Their only hope lay in keeping the fire alive from the small pile of dead branches that they had collected before it got too dark.

All that was left of the fire were dead ashes as dawning sun began to dispel the morning mists. Lorena and Rassel woke and tried to coax the fire back into life, without any success and fearfully scanned the mists for any signs of life. There was the sound of snapping dead bushes as something large began to scent them at the bottom of the hill. The two gnomes pressed themselves into the tight spaces between the boulders at the top of the rise. They were stood on stone and there was nowhere to go except into the gap between the rocks. Rassel drew out his hatchet and handed Lorena his hammer.

"It's coming up the hill," whispered Rassel, "with luck it might be too big to get its head into this tiny space. If it takes me, you must try and get to the raptors no matter what happens to me. The High King must know that evil walks the land again."

"You old fool! If it takes you then I shall be close behind you. I will never be able to find them on my own. If we are to die here then we will die together," Lorena grimly replied and gripped the hammer tightly.

The bushes at the edge of their camp were pushed aside

and a young allosaurus about twenty feet long strode into view, casting its head from side to side catching their scent. It gave a high-pitched screech as it caught sight of the gnomes trying to wriggle deeper into the fissure between the boulders. It hopped forwards and pushed its head into the crevice trying to force its nose close enough to grab hold of Rassel. The gnome brought down the hatchet down onto the teeth of the lower jaw and split the gums. The stench of its breath filled the narrow hole as it screamed in rage. Its three fingered hands scrabbled for purchase as it tried to force the rock apart. Again Rassel brought the hatchet down and split the gum in another place, losing the beast a tooth and was rewarded by a spray of blood that made his grip on his weapon slippery.

It turned to its side and tried to hook the gnome out by using its claws, just missing his chest by inches. Lorena lent over her husband and brought the hammer down onto the wrist of the maddened beast against the wall. She felt a satisfying crunch and wriggled back behind Rassel out of reach. The thing let out a scream of pain and jerked the injured limb away from further damage. They saw it stiffen and draw back away from the crack they were hiding in to turn around. They both saw a heavy spear jutting out of the beast's armpit and this was followed by another two into the gut. Something very fast rushed close in and disembowelled the creature. A rope was cast over its neck and pulled hard, making the beast fall onto its side and exposing its throat. A raptor buried a flint axe into the neck, opening up a main artery and quickly hopped aside out of the way. It did not take long for the beast to die.

Rassel and Lorena wriggled out of the fissure into view. They stared at the velociraptors that had saved their lives. They stood as high as a human with semi-winged arms and feathered tails, crowns and ruffs around their necks. The feet had an enlarged scimitar shaped claw that they carried pointing upwards, razor sharp. This was how the allosaurus was disembowelled by one of them as it leapt over its stomach. The colouration of the feathers was mainly brown and barred so that they were perfectly camouflaged against the undergrowth. The ridged tails stood out behind them with feathers sloping out along the horizontal edge of the limb. This worked like a rudder when they needed to abruptly change direction. One of them pointed at the fire with its three-fingered hands, curling its thumb into its palm to extend the claw and then at its eyes.

"They saw the fire, husband," said Lorena and clung tightly to Rassel.

She then slid slowly to the ground in shock and sat, sobbing with relief on the stony ground.

One of them beckoned to the gnomes and pointed toward the thick jungle that grew around the small hill they had made stand on. Rassel shook his head and sat down with Lorena fished out an empty water bottle and upended it to show that it was empty. A lot of chirruping took place between their rescuers and one of them took out a large egg shook it so that it sloshed before pulling a plug out of it. He handed it to Rassel who took a grateful swig and passed it to Lorena who also drank. It was the first drink they had managed to swallow since the last two days had passed. The raptors whistled and chirruped to each other again and turned to the gnomes and one of them gestured to the broad back of another. They unsteadily got to their feet and nodded, pointing to themselves and the back of the raptor. The leader bent forwards and picked up Lorena, placing her on the raptor's back amongst the feathery ruff. The gnome grabbed a handful of feathers and they disappeared down the hill. It then did the same for Rassel and all of them set out down the hill. Mounted on the backs of their benefactors the gnomes were amazed how quickly the creatures were able to travel. Every so often they would change mounts to share the load.

As it got dark in the late afternoon the raptors slowed the pace and called out some long hooting calls that were answered from in front. A palisade came into sight with a gate that had been opened. Inside was a large cooking fire that purposely drifted smoke around the compound. The big meat eaters had long ago avoided this area and the smell of smoke was enough to keep them away. Every so often the raptors would go on the hunt to thin down these troublesome predators and leave them to rot. They had learnt how to herd the vegetarians for their own purposes and kept some of them in enclosures. They had also learnt how to grow certain crops that they found useful and defend them from being raided by other dinosaurs. A strong stockade had been erected all around the village with sharp ends pointing outwards every so often, so that it was difficult to approach where the raptors lived.

Rassel and Lorena were helped off their 'mounts' and escorted into the safe area inside the stockade and were given a place to sit by the cooking fire where pieces of meat were roasting on spits erected over the fires. Both of the gnomes began to salivate at the smell wafting around them. One of the raptors that had saved them immediately sensed this and chirruped to those who were doing the cooking. A spit that had been skewered through a dozen smaller chunks was taken out of the flames and handed over to Rassel. He stripped off a number of them and handed the greasy lumps to Lorena who immediately chewed and swallowed several pieces. The greasy juices ran done the fine beard on her chin as she nodded to her benefactor who was extracting another spit-full of chunks. Rassel gratefully did the same and filled his empty stomach. He pointed to the food and his stomach and held three fingers up to the raptor, pointing at the skies. It had been three days since the two of them had eaten properly.

Water was brought to them in large egg shells with a hole knocked into the top and after the gnomes had drunk their fill they washed themselves and their filthy clothes. Upon seeing the scratched and torn areas of their bodies a raptor appeared holding a half egg containing pounded herbs mixed with some kind of grease. This it dabbed over a bad scratch on Rassel's shoulder and handed the egg to Lorena to finish the job. Its pain-relieving properties eased the many pains that were nagging at the gnome's body and he quickly took the bowl sized egg and applied it to his wife. A bed of fresh ferns with a skin of some kind of animal thrown over it had been constructed and a raptor gestured to it and the gnomes. Once they were laid on this bed another raptor spread another tanned skin over the two of them and sat by the side of it to reassure them that they were safe.

Exhausted the two gnomes fell into a safe and dreamless sleep.

Eloen hung onto her mount and urged it onwards towards the Great Gorge and this time she would not allow the Quetzalcoatlus to rest until she arrived at one of the dwarves strongholds. She examined the goblin's memories afresh about the two towns each side of the river that flowed through the gorge and on into the sea. The town on the right was called the Stormgalt and the one on the left was the Skaldargate. It was the one on the right that she needed, as it was just beyond the edge of the mountain range that was part of the crater wall, that Peterkin fought and defeated Abaddon. It was here under tons of rock that the Staff of Power slept. The goblin had been there when Peterkin had collapsed the Arch of the Dream-shifter, smashed the control chair and piled the rubble onto the shattered bones of Abaddon. He never come back to find Molock's Wand and left it buried there, as none but the

Dokka'lfar could use it. Eloen was a direct descendant of Molock and she was sure that she could resurrect its power, because just as Abaddon was his son she was his daughter!

Darkness fell over the world beneath her and still the Quetzalcoatlus continued to flap his wings and glide. He was quite capable of staying aloft for many days at a time and the addition of his rider, while it made flying more strenuous, he could manage. Eloen managed to get some uneasy sleep, strapped tightly to the creature's back as he continued to power along.

The cold light of dawn woke Eloen and she shivered inside her flying gear. She reached into her bag of supplies and found a water bottle that still had some cold herbal tea in it. She felt round and also found a meat and vegetable pie still wrapped in greaseproof paper. The Halfling broke it into manageable pieces and chewed her breakfast thinking to herself that the food in this world was far better than any she had eaten on Alfheimr. This did not stem the rage that she felt about having her whole existence turned upside down by the hated Ljo'sa'lfar. She would make them pay a blood price that they would never forget! She peeked over the flyer's long beak and around the vane at the back of his head and searched for the dark line of the mountains. At the moment the morning sun was shining over the tops of the crater edge and she couldn't judge the distance. At least it seemed that soon her long journey of revenge would soon go up a notch. She took another drink of the herbal tea, settled herself across the creature's neck and shoulders to fall fitfully asleep again.

This time Eloen dreamed about her stronghold that she had taken a century ago or more from the Dokka'lfar master that had in turn taken it from another. Sometimes as they grew older the Dokka'lfar became careless. This was when a younger one would take down an overlord and move into his or hers property. Eloen had ruthlessly kept down the degenerate Dark Elves by systematic culling. She only kept the ones who could speak and take orders; the others were butchered and fed to the rest. The Halfling had bred humans, but having seen what cocaine did to them and being half human herself, did not indulge in Dokka'lfar practices. The constant struggle for supremacy had kept her alert enough and the humans had tilled the soil for her and harvested her crops. What the degenerate elves found to eat was theirs to dine on, but they soon learned not to touch her produce as they were guarded by her 'pressed' humans. They had her permission to eat any that strayed onto her lands, so she solved the problem of having to feed the humans that she bred. If the harvest was good then she made sure that her humans were fed from the roots that were gathered and the greens that grew with them. It was little point having attentive slaves on the edge of starvation so Eloen made sure that they stayed as healthy as she could afford.

She moaned in her sleep as she relived the night of terror when the humans revolted with the iron around their necks. They had attacked and killed all of her able-thinking Dokka'lfar that was the ring of security that was stationed on the lower floors of the stronghold. The mindless they left for later. The sickness had raged for days before all this had happened weakening the mental hold that the Dark Elves had upon the humans.

She had managed to escape through a back window only to see her home go up in flames as the mob ripped it apart searching for her. With them were the giant dragons that she learnt were T Rexs that would only eat the Dokka'lfar. It had been a close run thing and had the sickness taken root in her body, she would have been torn apart just like her brethren. Eloen awoke with hatred refreshed as she shook off the dreams that had tormented her while she lay strapped down on the Quetzalcoatlus. The sun had risen and had passed overhead and now the mountainous edge of the crater wall could be plainly seen. Once again she drank from her bottle until it was finished and ate the rest of the pie. Now she desperately needed to go to toilet and if she landed down onto the ground below, the flyer would not be able to get off the ground with her weight. As the pterosaur approached the foothills of the mountains she could see a moat and palisade that stretched for a mile or so. Inside this were many buildings and tented areas. This was the Stormgalt that the goblin remembered and there were many people who had rushed out to see the flyer as she approached.

"Now for the next part of my plan," she thought and she scanned the crowd with her mind.

There were no Ljo'sa'lfar and no gnomes. All of the minds that awaited her were hers to imprint and control.

MOLOCK'S WAND

CHAPTER SIX

Eloen eased the pterosaur into a glide path downwards towards the crowd and generated an image of a Ljo'sa'lfar to all and sundry. She pulled back the hood of her clock and shook her head to release her hair, showing off her pointed ears. Anyone of the dwarves that looked into her eyes would see that her irises were slit like a cat's. Her hands were the only problem as she had the same number of fingers as the humans so she broadcast an extra finger projected from her mind. Her lack of wings was another problem, so she also needed to hide that deficiency from the dwarves. She had made up a bulge over her shoulder blades to imitate the way that the Light Elves tucked their wings out of the way. It would do until she gained control over their minds and then none of them would question what she was.

As she narrowed the gap between the dwarves and herself, one of them pushed forwards to stand waiting for her to alight. Eloen dropped the Quetzalcoatlus in front of the dwarf and slid out of the saddle before her. The Halfling entered the dwarf's mind and established her rank and name. While she was in there she installed a feeling of obedience to her also a false memory of her coming here before and her name.

"Good day, Hilden, daughter of Hildegard I have come here

again to seek your help in a matter of great urgency. I need refreshment and the use of a toilet before we discuss this problem," Eloen said and shook the female dwarf by the hand.

"My Lady Eloen," she answered, "where are my manners! Of course you need attention after such a long flight. Please come with me and you will be attended to. You, Hammer-fist, see that the flyer is stabled while I attend to our guest."

Hilden led the Halfling into a large building that was made out of stone and showed her where she could take off the warm, flying clothes. She pointed out the toilet and Eloen gratefully went inside. It had indeed been a long journey!

Once she had finished she exited after washing and asked, "Where are the guest quarters? I am tired and need to eat and rest before we talk."

A moment's confusion twitched inside Hilden's mind as she was sure that the elf had visited before. Eloen caught the stray thought and pinched it off. She rapidly absorbed the memories of the dwarf and took on the layout of the Stormgalt.

"Of course I know the way," Eloen added quickly, "It would be appreciated if food and drink could be brought to my rooms. We can talk while I eat and drink. I will change into some clean clothes while you sort something out for me."

Hilden nodded her head and quickly walked away to sort out a meal and drink for her guest while the Halfling entered the rooms allocated to visiting Ljo'sa'lfar. Eloen quickly closed the door and walked over to the wardrobe and stared at the cloths hung up there. She selected a baggy all-in-one dress that had the bustle on the back that would take care of the wings that the other elves were blessed with. In this cavity she stuffed another dress to make it seem as if she had something in there. Her mind control would do the rest and those who were close to her would not see that anything was wrong.

There was a knock on the door and two dwarves entered

carrying a tray of freshly prepared food and a pitcher of water with earthenware mugs. Behind them came Hilden along with a male dwarf that she recognised as Hammer-fist. Eloen sat by a table on the bench provided while the other two dwarves sat with her, while the younger ones left.

"Lady Eloen, when you have refreshed yourself, please tell us what brings you all this way on your own?" Hilden asked, as she too lifted a freshly baked cake to her lips.

Eloen took a while and spent some time altering the suspicious mind of the male dwarf and bending it to her purpose. She also looked into his memories of the surrounding area to see where it overlapped the goblin's recollection. It would not be difficult for a large band of dwarves to get to where Peterkin had defeated Abaddon. A day's march and they would be there. Eloen relaxed a little and carried on eating. When she had finished she drank from the mug and sat up straight.

She stared into the faces of her new servants and said, "Who here can remember the High King's battle against Abaddon? Peterkin needs something that was buried there many years ago."

Hilden replied, "My mother, Hildegard was there when the great High King brought him down. I will call her and she can tell you all about that wonderful day."

"Do so, Hilden," Eloen replied, "for it will be necessary for your people to dig it out from where it was buried. Peterkin has sent me to you for you to do this thing for him."

"It shall be as the High King commands, Lady Eloen," the dwarf replied, "I will fetch her, this very minute."

The Halfling relaxed and helped herself to another fruit - filled cake. For the first time in a year or so events seemed to be moving at a measured pace. She spent a little time reinforcing the protectiveness that Hammer-fist had for his leader and directed it towards herself. While she ate, she also sent her mind out amongst the descendants of the Neanderthals that the Ljo'sa'lfar had brought here thousands of years ago. They were even easier to control than she had found the humans to be. They were short and stocky unlike the humans that she had used in the past. It struck her that they were ideal for tunnelling and mining. She was sure that it would not take them more than a few days to uncover what she needed.

While she was thinking about this the door opened and Hilden slowly walked in with her mother. She was very old and bent with the passing of the years, but her eyes were clear and her mind sharp.

She shuffled forwards and stared at Eloen intently, "What are you!" she asked and her face was creased in horror.

Eloen paralysed the other two gnomes holding them deaf and blind where they stood. She concentrated her will on the ancient dwarf rooted to her stick before her. The Halfling slid into her mind and found a Ljo'sa'lfar block that had prevented Hildegard from seeing what she had projected. It crumbled under her probe and the old dwarfess now saw her as a Light Elf. She released them all from her thrall and stood to shake the old lady by her hand. The whole episode had lasted seconds and as Eloen radiated calm, no-one seemed to notice that anything untoward had taken place. The Halfling led Hildegard to a bench and sat her down and offered her a drink from the earthenware mugs.

"Are you alright? She asked. "You stumbled a little when you spoke to me. Do you need anything?

Hildegard looked puzzled and replied, "No! There was something, but I have forgotten just what it was. You wanted to see me about when Peterkin fought and destroyed Molock's powerful son, Abaddon just beyond the edge of the Great Gorge."

"I did indeed, Hildegard. I need information about that conflict and I believe that you were there that very day."

"I was, Lady Eloen. I was stood right next to the High King during his battle of wills with that spawn of evil. I helped to carry him to safety when he collapsed at the feet of Ameela."

Eloen smiled and asked, "Would you mind if I looked into your mind and replayed that day."

She knew that by asking in front of her daughter and making this a real memory rather than one inserted, it would bolster the illusion that she was Ljo'sa'lfar and quiet any suspicions that they may have harboured.

The old dwarfess smiled at Eloen and answered, "It would be an honour to share my mind with such as you again."

This time Eloen entered the old dwarfess's mind with care as she did not want to trip another block placed there by the Ljo'sa'lfar. She slid down the memories until Hildegard was a young woman and stayed with her as she entered the Spellbinder. She stood with the High King as he directed operations and locked minds with Abaddon. Eloen marvelled at the technology that the Elf King brought to bear and the force of the explosives. She was also respectful of the power of his mind as he drove Abaddon to his knees and had the humans reduce the arch to rubble. All of it fell upon the Dark Lord's body and he was crushed under slabs of elf-stone still clutching the Staff of Power as another missile hit and blew him apart.

She was also mindful of the amount of death energy that had been fed into the insane Dream-shifter due to the carnage that had washed over it. That energy had not been enough to allow the Dark Lord to beat Peterkin and that she was very aware of. Nevertheless the retrieval of the Staff of Power would grant her access to what remained of the Dream-shifter and it would augment what psychic powers she possessed to a far higher degree. As she retreated from the old dwarfess's memories she triggered a beacon that began to erupt from the very brain stem that would alert any Ljo'sa'lfar in the vicinity. Eloen turned it off before it got to any strength and cast around for more. This she did not expect when she slid into the old lady's mind. It was obvious that Peterkin had insured that if any Dokka'lfar survived and sought out Molock's Staff of Power it would trigger off a warning. She guessed that there was so much to do with rebuilding Alfheimr that the retrieval of Molock's Wand was something that could be done many years in the future and as he was sure that all Dokka'lfar had died soon after the conflict, then it was of minor importance.

Eloen opened her eyes and was aware of three pairs of eyes staring at her with some concern.

She smiled at them and said, "I have the information that I needed. Now I need you to organise a workforce to take me to where the wand is buried and dig it out. We must start tomorrow as time is of the essence and the High King is waiting for me to bring it back to him. I have seen in your recent memories that you have joined up the road that Abaddon almost finished from the Stormgalt to the sea, so it should not take long to get there."

Hammer-fist scowled and clenched his fists before remarking, "I did not give permission for you to enter my mind."

"Would you deny the High King his requirements? The fact that you live here without fear of the Dokka'lfar is all because he dared to pit himself against an overwhelming force! I give apologies if I have offended you Hammer-fist, but I can assure you that I did only touch you lightly," the Halfling replied and as she did so, she reinforced her earlier tinkering.

The dwarf struggled with conflicting loyalties that chased through his mind and flushed with embarrassment.

"I am sorry, my Lady," he answered and hung his head with

shame. "Of course whatever information you require must be available to you. I have no experience with receiving the Ljo'sa'lfar, so please forgive my bad manners."

"Hammer-fist, it was as if this never happened," Eloen smiled and added, "I shall expect to see you tomorrow at dawn with a band of strong miners and plenty of provisions. Till then, dwarf-friend, till then!"

Eloen yawned and stood, holding Hildegard's hand in hers while Hammer-fist exited the room leaving just Hilden and her mother together.

"Please forgive me, but it has been a long ride to get here," Eloen smiled, "I really do need to sleep."

"Of course you do, my Lady Eloen," Hilden replied and ushered her mother outside the room. "I will see you at dawn. You will not be disturbed."

She shut the door and as she did so, Eloen fixed in her mind that only she would enter the Halfling's bed-chamber and she would wait until she was acknowledged. The last thing that Eloen wanted was the dwarfess to see her unclothed, sleeping and wingless.

The Halfling awake to a timid knock at the door and Hilden crying out, "Lady Eloen it is time to get dressed, the sun will soon be up. I have breakfast with me."

"Come in," cried Eloen and set down my breakfast tray. Close the door behind you as you enter and draw the curtains wide. You may help me dress."

She filled the dwarf's mind with the wings that she expected to see, as she stretched her arms wide and rolled out of bed. Eloen washed her face and hands at the wash basin and looked out of the window. Already at first light she could see that the dwarves were organising themselves for a journey. Waggons were being hitched to young Iguanodons and loaded up with foodstuff and tools. Eloen quickly finished washing and began her breakfast as Hilden helped to dress her. She once again picked out a baggy dress that she could pack something in to look as if her wings were tucked up inside the bustle. With her raven hair pulled back into a pony tail it allowed everyone to see her ears while she hid her hands inside a pair of mittens. Anyone from a distance would 'know' that she was a Ljo'sa'lfar Lady and would think no more than that.

With Hilden by her side she strode through the visitors complex and out into the morning sun. A thin mist was creeping around the many buildings of the Stormgalt and the early morning sun began to disperse it as she watched. A place had been left on the front of the waggon for her to sit and take it easy while the young beast was urged on by a dwarf sat at the base of its neck. She climbed aboard and settled down for what she thought would be uneventful journey.

Flanking them were other dwarves mounted on a more nimble dinosaur that ran on its hind legs and stood twice the height of a dwarf. It had an elongated neck that supported a long mouth filled with small pointed teeth. The arms were long enough to reach the ground if it bent forwards and they ended in three fingered hands capable of grasping they prey. Its back legs ended in powerful four toed feet, quite well adapted to its upright gait. How could these forerunners of humanity get these dangerous creatures to do their bidding? Eloen entered the mind of one of the dwarves mounted on a beast and found that it was quite simple. Each one of these creatures had hatched with a dwarf present and had imprinted onto a different creature that fed it and lived with it as it grew. She felt a moment's admiration for the dwarves as she bumped along the road that led around the mountains to the sea.

Once the sun was well up in the sky all traces of the early mountain mists had long gone and the view was clear. They were travelling along a well-trodden road that had been well and truly flattened by the passage of large dinosaurs. She recognised that from the goblin's memories that this had once been the secret tunnel that Abaddon had constructed out of slabs of stone. Down to her left was the vast estuary that had once been clogged by the poisoned brier preventing the Dokka'lfar from entering the plains of Scion. Around the side of the mountain would have been the quarries that Abaddon had put to use, to hew out the blocks of stone. A shiver of excitement went through her as they travelled along. Soon she would have what she wanted. She could then be as powerful as the cursed High King and bring him down. A shudder of concern soon followed that thought and she determined then that she had no need to hurry, once all that she needed became hers.

The dwarf called Hammer-fist rode up on one of the two legged beasts and leaned over to say, "We shall soon be there, my Lady Eloen. We need to stop a while and allow the draught-beasts to drink and eat or they get fractious. Once we clear the bend in the road you will be able to see the area that you are interested in with another half-day's journey."

Eloen smiled and replied, "Well done Hammer-fist, I shall be sure to remind the High King just how helpful you have been when next I see him. He will be well pleased that you have made it possible to unearth this ancient artefact."

The Halfling lightly touched the dwarf's mind and reinforced the pleasure that he had experienced in pleasing the High King. Moulding the minds of these creatures was so easy that she sat and prowled through those that were in the surrounding area. A little touch here and a withdrawal of any suspicions wherever she found them, all helped her to appear as Ljo'sa'lfar to their malleable minds. It was inherent in all the dwarves to look upon the Light Elves as their benefactors, so this made it even easier to make them do her bidding. While she sat and ate, she trawled through Hilden's, mother's memories. Her adventures with the High King and her association with the humans that Peterkin had brought back from Earth fascinated her. It was Hildegard's memories of the weapons that intrigued her the most. This was a place that she really needed to visit and to do that she had to master the Wand. Now she began to feel impatient and restless.

The caravan stopped and the dwarves fed the iguanodons bundles of greenery that were inside the waggons. Buckets of water were dragged round to slake the creature's thirst. When that was done the dwarves stopped for a rest and fed themselves from the supply cart, eating cold meat and bread rolls.

Eloen wriggled about on the cushion as she thought about what she needed to do and did a telepathic sweep of the area. She connected with the mind of what the dwarves called an 'eater' and realised that it was the mind of a T Rex! It was stalking what it thought was a small herd and was keeping pace with the caravan slinking through the heavy brush on the banks of the estuary. It was a big one, all of forty feet long from nose to tail and weighing over seven tons.

Eloen realised that she would not be able to control her and turned to Hilden and said, "There is a large 'eater' moving in on our left hand flank. It's a really big one and she is very hungry!"

Hilden stood up and blew a whistle. Three sharp blasts split the air. That got the attention of the outriders. One long blast confirmed that they were dealing with a large meat Eater.

The dwarfess turned and asked, "Where?"

Eloen pointed to the far left where the beast was steadily catching up with the waggon train and said, "She's in that direction walking along the edge of the estuary. I can't turn her. She is just too big and far too hungry to influence very much."

"That's ok," she answered, "fire will stop her. Up here on the road there is little to burn, but lower down the bush, it is tinder dry."

Several of the mounted dwarves reached down for their powerful cross-bows that were strapped to their mount's harness. They selected a special arrow with the head soaked in pitch and oil and cocked the bow. They then focussed the sun's rays through a magnifying glass on this small bundle of oil-saturated fibres that rapidly began to smoke and burst into flames. These they loosed into the air down towards the dry bushes along the estuary banks. There was an audible crackle and gouts of flame erupted from the bushes with clouds of smoke.

Eloen caught hold of Hilden's arm and said, "That did the trick! She has panicked and is running back towards the plains with the fire close behind her. I can see through her eyes that the brush has given way to wet marsh, but that won't stop her from putting as much distance between herself and the fire as she can."

"It was thanks to you we were warned with good time, my Lady Eloen. We have learnt that of all things, even the largest of the 'eaters' can be driven off by fire," Hilden replied and on impulse she kissed her hand.

An odd feeling of wrongness flooded her mind as she held a far smaller hand that she should. There were four fingers and a thumb instead of five fingers! She looked up into the elf's eyes and met a blaze of fury in the slit eyes. All at once it seemed natural that the hand that she held was a Ljo'sa'lfar hand and no other. The elf radiated serenity and kindness. The thought that anything could be wrong was taken from her and discarded. After all, the lady Eloen had saved their lives with the early warning.

There was a cry of, "Waggons HO!"

The iguanodons were persuaded to stop their mid-day chewing of the foliage brought with them in the waggons. There were a few ill-tempered snorts, but the dwarves were insistent and the big animals leant into the traces and soon got the caravan moving. After some time they rounded the long bend in the road and Eloen caught sight of the sea and began to recognise some details from Hildegard's memories that tied in with the dead goblin's. She could see that it would take all of the afternoon to get to where she needed to be so she relaxed in the knowledge that tomorrow morning a start would be made to begin shifting the rubble that had entombed her father's Staff of Power.

The hours steadily passed by and the other edge of the crater wall began to slope down to show the foothills of the outside of the huge crater. The area showed no sign of the battle that had been fought here. All that remained was a large mound that had been grown over by the rampant vegetation. The waggons stopped as the late afternoon sun began to dip down towards the horizon of the sea. Eloen slipped off the seat of the waggon and approached the mound. The dwarves drew the waggons round into a circle and built a fire in the centre and began to establish a camp. Hilden saw that all was being attended to and joined the Halfling as she walked towards the mound. The closer they got to the knoll the stranger the vegetation seemed to be. Nothing had grown straight. Every tree-like growth was twisted as if the plants did not know where the sun was and tried to find it. Vines grew in profusion strangling any tree that they touched. Nothing animal lived here! During the journey along the foot of the gorge things had scurried out of the brush and the sides of the gorge. Eloen and Hilden were aware of how vibrantly alive this world was. Here there were no butterflies or creeping insects. There was a silence about the mound that could almost be tasted.

Hilden drew back in apprehension as the atmosphere clung to every nerve-ending in her body.

"This place is cursed!" She cried and turned away to face back towards the cheerful fire that had been lit at the camp.

"Nonsense! There is no such thing as a curse," retorted Eloen and strode on and up to the mound.

She lent forwards and placed her hands onto a large piece of rubble and thrust her mind into the recesses inside the mound. Deep inside she got an echo! Something woke, she was sure of it! Eloen examined the piece of rubble that she had put her hand upon and could see in the fading light that it was a green stone that had a shattered edge. It was elf-stone, she was sure of it. Oh yes, what she had come for was buried here underneath this hillock. All she needed to do was to get the dwarves to dig it out and dig it out they would, no matter what lives would be spent doing it!

Eloen walked back down the hill, clasped Hilden on her shoulder and said, "What I seek is here. I have told Peterkin that soon he will have the Staff of Power in his hands and he can put his worries to rest. He will be well pleased by the help that you have given me and will be in your debt."

Hilden still shuddered as she quickly walked back to the fire and the safety of the circle of waggons, but to aid the High King was reward in itself.

MOLOCK'S WAND

CHAPTER SEVEN

The raptor's stockade swirled with early morning mist as the sun began to rise. Rassel and Lorena awoke as movement began around them. As they began to move about on top of their leafy bed and emerge from the warm skins laid over them, they were aware of the velociraptors sat patiently around them. Large golden eyes were fixed upon the bed and as soon as they began to move one of them whistled several load notes and a smaller one came running to the side of the 'bed' with an egg filled with fresh water and a woven basket full of food. Rassel stared into the basket and fished out a baked egg that he broke apart and dropped the hot chunks back onto the large broad leaves that had been provided as plates.

Lorena grabbed a chunk, chewed and swallowed gratefully, drinking from the eggshell provided. There was also fruit that had been gathered and softened by rolling in the embers of the communal fire. To their amazement there was also unleavened bread made from ground seeds that had been baked at the edge of the fire on flat stones. Once the edge had been taken off her hunger, Lorena felt the need to use a toilet. Knowing that the raptors must have some arrangement she stood up and pantomimed her needs. This was immediately understood and she was shown to a suitable place where she was soon joined by her husband.

When they had finished the two of them walked back to where the elders of the raptor village waited for them. Rassel picked up a pointed stick that had been fire hardened and had fallen out of the fire. He smoothed out the ashes that had fallen to the edge and began to draw a circle that had a large break on one side. He drew a line that went through the gap and matchstick-men each side to represent the dwarf towns of the Stormgalt and the Skaldargate. He then picked up a flat stone and placed it on top of several smaller ones halfway between the dwarf towns and the centre to represent the Tower of Absolom. In the centre he built a pyramid of stones and place small stones around the base and a larger one part of the way up to signify Peterkin's castle. He pointed to the raptors and then to the two gnomes, marked out a place between the Tower and the mound in the centre. He drew two matchstick figures there and a number of crosses, again pointing at the raptors. Rassel looked up at the ring of intent faces and could see that they understood. He sighed with relief and drew a line from where they were on the map and to where the Ljo'sa'lfar lived. Rassel again pointed to them and to the mound in the centre and slapped himself on the chest. To make quite sure he indicated at his pointed ears that were similar to the elves and directed their attention to the mound.

A great deal of whistling and chirruping took place within the group of raptors as they discussed the idea. The one with bags of tools hanging from her belt turned to the gnomes and held out her three fingered hand for the stick. She pointed up at the sun and crossed the line to the mound with three slashes, physically turned Rassel around and pointed him in the direction that they needed to go and tapped him on the shoulder three times.

"They understand! It would seem that we are three days journey away from the foothills of the Ljo'sa'lfar," he said to Lorena and gave her a hug.

He felt a tap on his shoulder and turned round to see the tool carrier smooth out the map and draw in the ashes a large dinosaur. She then scratched two matchstick men and a lot of crosses on the top of the creature's shoulders. The raptor stared into Rassel's face to see if he understood and was relieved to see the gnome nod his head.

Lorena heaved a sigh of relief and said to Rassel, "Thank goodness for that. It looks as if we are going to be given a lift. Three more days of walking through that wilderness would just about finish me!"

They heard some loud whistling and chirruping from the raptors and something began to move towards the village from a large stockade. A booming call answered the raptors and several heads peered over the top of the points of the stockade as the iguanodon group stood up on their hind legs to see their masters.

Rassel gasped and said, "They must be fully grown! They must be over thirty feet in length. Stood up like that, every one of them has to be five or six times our height! Once we are sat on one of those I am sure that most of the other smaller meat eaters will give way to a herd of those. This should be an interesting three days!"

The raptors soon wound a harness around the chest and shoulders of the surprisingly tractable beasts and joined them to a strap that went around the hindquarters. There were now two parallel leather straps running down the huge creature's sides. A velociraptor rapidly climbed up a hanging strip of knotted leather, sat herself astride the neck and beckoned the two gnomes to climb aboard. Lorena reached up to the knots, but just did not have the strength to heave her weight aboard. She suddenly felt a strong clawed hand fixed into her belt and she was lifted onto the shoulders of the iguanodon before she could protest by another raptor that climbed the knotted strap with ease. Rassel was also 'helped' aboard and took his place behind Lorena. The raptor sat in front gave some sort of command and swaying from side to side they plodded out of the stockade and into the wilderness. Once they were pointed in the right direction, the raptor gave another command and the beast stood up on its hind legs only. Once upright it began to run with great strides at a steady speed flattening anything in its way. The two gnomes held on tightly for dear life as the miles flashed by and the rest of the small herd thundered across the Plains of Scion towards the home of the Light Elves.

The morning had dawned bright and sunny and the sea mists had soon given way while the dwarves had breakfast while Eloen fidgeted with impatience. She could not keep her eyes off the mound, covered in green elf-stone. Eloen could feel the call from what was buried there. She knew that her father's Staff would be genetically keyed to her, just as it was to her half-brother Abaddon and it was an ache in her very soul.

She could see that the dwarves were clearing away so she said to Hilden, "Gather your people round and I will speak with them."

The dwarfess climbed to her feet and blew on her whistle. As the heads turned round Hilden beckoned them closer. They were soon assembled in a half-circle around the waggon and Eloen stood on the seat so that she was much higher than them.

"Listen carefully to me," she called out, "what I seek for the great High King is here. It lies under that mound of rubble covered in that twisted vegetation. You will need to pull away those blocks of green stone and I feel that what we seek will be buried underneath them. I will leave it to you to devise the method of removal, but I urge you to get to work as soon as you can."

Eloen chose that moment to urge on the dwarves with a

mental reinforcing. All of them were compelled to work with a great need that would not be satisfied until dirt began to move. Those of the dwarves that were skilled in mining took control of the others and assessed the situation. Strong ropes were fetched from the waggons and hitched up to some of the large green stones. These were then fixed to the harnesses on the larger iguanodons and they were urged to pull. The great beasts lent into the taut ropes and strained, encouraged by their masters. One of the slabs began to pivot upwards and turned right over. It slid down the mound and was pulled clear. Underneath was a veritable boneyard of crushed Dokka'lfar remains.

Teams of the beasts pulled other slabs from away from the top and slid these down to the foot of the mound uncovering more bones. The sun began to climb into the sky and still the labour went on, driven by the Halfling's mental goading. By late afternoon the top of the mound had been cleared of the large green-stone slabs. The edges of these blocks had razor sharp edges and many of the dwarves had been cut by them, but did not seem to notice due to Eloen's constant mental urging.

As the late afternoon sun began to set Eloen realised that little could be accomplished during the hours of darkness, so she let the exhausted dwarves rest. Once she had let the workers relax they became aware of the many cuts and bruises they had sustained during the day. They were also aware of the deadly silence around the excavated mound as nothing moved around the twisted trees. The iguanodons became fretful and edged away from where they had been made to work. Sensing their unrest the dwarf beast-masters led them away and back to the camp where the wagonloads of food would soon ease their hunger and temperament. While this was going on Eloen returned to the excavations and extended her senses down into the soil that had been uncovered. Again an echo of an imprisoned mind ricocheted back at her. Deep beneath her feet she could feel the Staff of Power reaching out to her and responding to her searching mind.

She returned to the waggon that she shared with Hilden in a fever of excitement as the sun slipped down over the plains of Scion. The leader of the dwarves had prepared food for her new mistress and had laid the food out onto the waggon driving seat. Even though she was bone tired, she had made sure that her 'guest' was well looked after and wanted for nothing.

"Is everything to your liking, Lady Eloen? I have prepared food and drink for you," the dwarfess said, pointed to the earthen-ware plates and bowls.

"Everything is fine Hilden," she replied and stretched out her arms, yawning as she did so. "I am pleased with what we have accomplished today. I think tomorrow the miners will be able to start digging down below where the slabs of Elf-stone have lain for many years. What Peterkin needs will soon be in our grasp."

"There is a wrongfulness about this place," Hilden remarked and pointed to where the mound used to be. "I have not seen so much as a butterfly or any kind of insect near that mound. Do you not find it strange, my Lady?"

"What I seek in the name of the High King shuns life that is not tuned to it. We are in no danger, Hilden! No danger at all! You will see. Another day's digging by your people and I may yet find what I have been sent for," Eloen replied and bit into a cold meat pie.

She sent her mind out of the circle of waggons and into the wilderness beyond and could sense no dangerous beasts in the vicinity. The smell of smoke coupled with the unsettling atmosphere around the mound was enough to keep even a hungry T Rex at bay. Feeling quite satisfied she crawled into her sleeping roll and soon fell asleep.

The chill of the dawn woke her and she opened her eyes to see that the camp was on the move. Fires were being stoked up; strips of meat were being grilled and placed into bread rolls. Jars of relish were opened and spread over the greasy meat to add to the flavour. Those that had eaten were pulling shovels and spades from out of the waggons and checking that the handles were good. Wheelbarrows were being unpacked and tools laid into them. Eloen relaxed and ate from the rolls that Hilden had prepared for her.

The lightest mental touch was enough to get the dwarves to speed up and put more effort into the day's task. Gangs of workers made their way to where the green elf-stone had been dragged away. Blocks of rubble still needed to be excavated and dragged away before they could dig downwards. Hour after hour the dwarves toiled in the heat of the tropical sun, dragging every obstacle out of the widening hole. As they worked so they uncovered even more Dokka'lfar bones. These were cleared away and discarded.

Eloen strode round and round the deepening hole in the ground feeling the pull exerted by the Staff. She was so intent on the search that she failed to notice that some of the dwarves had fainted from exhaustion from the heat and the endless toil. Eloen even stepped onto one of them and pulled up, suddenly recognising that her workforce was dying around her. She relaxed her iron control, allowing them to rest and drink for a while.

Once she was sure that the dwarves could continue to dig she drove them relentlessly until the sun went down. Furious that the lack of light had ended the excavation she let go of the compulsion to dig and watched her workforce slump to the ground. Those that could still walk fetched water for those who had collapsed. Slowly they made their way back to the waggons not quite sure why they were in such a state of exhaustion. Some were too tired to eat and dropped onto a blanket, slipping into a weary sleep.

Eloen sat with her back against the waggon and chewed a piece of cold meat and fidgeted with impatience. The leader of the dwarves lay at her feet, deeply asleep, her hands still covered in dirt from where she had also toiled for the Halfling all through the day. Moonlight illuminated the camp with a silvery light allowing Eloen to see quite clearly with her pupils dilated. There was still a respectable amount of wood on the fire to keep it burning though the night, but Eloen became uneasy. She sent her mind out into the wilderness searching for the definitive signature of any 'eaters' that might be on the prowl. There were two of them slowly moving towards the camp. They could smell the iguanodons, but they could also smell the smoke from the large camp-fire. This caused them to be uneasy, but hunger had made them bold. Eloen made contact with one of the beast-masters that was asleep next to his charges.

"Wake," she screamed into his mind. "Get up. Get up now."

The dwarf got to his feet and stood unsteadily as Eloen took control of his limbs. His eyes were open, but his mind was still fuddled. The Halfling made him go to the stockade fence and undo the ropes holding the gate closed. She then made him swing the gate open so that the beasts inside could wander out. Several of the younger ones made their way through the gate and into the wilderness. The atmosphere from the excavated mound was a constant pressure on the iguanodons to want to be somewhere else. It was only the training of the dwarves that kept them here and the open stockade was all they needed as an incentive to go. Eloen took the dwarf back to his sleeping place and sent him back to sleep. The dinosaurs were tiny brained at most and needed very little persuasion from her to make their way towards the two meat eaters that were downwind. They could smell the meals moving towards them. The kill was quick and easy so they gorged themselves where they were and slept by the carcass to re-join it in the morning. As this would keep them miles away from Eloen's excavation, she was quite satisfied and went to sleep.

When the sun came up the loss of the iguanodons set the dwarves into a state of panic. These were prime beasts that had spent years in training and were very difficult to replace. Some of the beast-masters wanted to mount a search party to find them and bring them back. Eloen had no time for this and gathered the dwarves around her, standing once more on the driving seat of the waggon.

"Listen to me," she called out. "We are very close to what your High King needs. Once we have Molock's Wand, it will be easy for me to bring back all of the missing beasts. This day we will definitely find what I have been sent to retrieve. Once I have it in my hands we can all rest. You have done so well, Peterkin's people. Now is not the time to let him down!"

At the same time as she filled their ears with lies, she added incentives into their minds. Soon they would be impatient to start digging and this time she would drive them until they dropped or she laid her hands on her father's Staff of Power. She stood tall and watched as the mental coercion began to do its trick and the dwarves began to once again pick up their picks and shovels. Soon a long line of workers were pushing wheelbarrows towards the excavation loaded with tools and water. Eloen was too impatient to allow them to eat this morning, but she realised that they would need to drink to keep working. She munched on a cold meat pie while she walked back to watch, as the miners pressed timbers into the soft ground to prevent the soil from rolling back. Buckets of earth were lifted on ropes as the dwarves dug deeper and deeper beneath where the slabs of elf-stone had dropped onto Abaddon. Soon their hands were bleeding from where the razor-sharp fragments of the shattered, green stone, had cut into them. The ropes on the buckets began to get slippery, but all Eloen would do was to allow different people to change places. All the time the Staff called out to her and the ache in her soul was as persistent as toothache.

As the sun passed overhead and the afternoon began a shout rang out from the foot of the hole.

"Lady Eloen, is this, what you seek for the High King? I see a hand that is clutching a wooden staff," one the dwarves at the bottom shouted.

"Lower a bucket," she ordered. "You down there pull the Staff out of the soil and place it in the bucket by using the bones of the hand. Do not touch it on any account. Tie it in place so that it will not fall out."

The dwarf pulled the Staff out of the mud by gripping the long dead wrist of Abaddon's hand that was still gripping the wand. He carefully laid it into the bucket and tied a rope over the shaft of the staff. On the end of the staff was a dirt encrusted knob that swung round as the bucket began to lift upwards. It caught the miner a glancing blow and he fended it off with his bare bloody hand. A terrible scream of agony wrenched from the dwarf's throat and he went into convulsions and died at the bottom of the pit amongst the others. It took every amount of mental coercion to make Hilden and the other dwarves to continue to pull the bucket out of the pit. The dwarfess's face was contorted with terrified fear as she pulled the Staff into the light of day.

Eloen felt the song of the Staff increase as it rose out of the pit. It called to her with the voice of Abaddon and deep under that was the strength of her father, Molock, the first of the

Dokka'lfar. She stepped forward as the bucket rose into view, laid her hands onto the staff and kissed the filthy, dirt encrusted knob on the end.

"Mine," she screamed. "Mine to command. Mine to serve and mine to feed!"

She snatched the water bottle from Hilden and cleaned the faceted jewel that was fixed onto the top. She wiped the dirt from the Wand and gripped it by the shaft a third of the way to the centre on both sides. The power flowed through her from the staff and reached out to the dwarves and took all the life that she needed. The dwarves around her fell like desiccated leaves as Eloen pulled the life energy from them and fed it back to the Staff of Power.

She gave the command, "Dream-shifter, reassemble!"

The ground began to shake as the green elf-stone began to boil out of the ground and head to a common area. Blocks began to fuse together as bits and pieces migrated into contact. Razor sharp shards became bonded into strange shapes that sank into the fabric of Abaddon's reality bending ship. The whole area seemed to be on the move as the Dream-shifter re-assembled in front of Eloen's eyes. More dwarves fell to the ground as the ship drew life-energy from them. They shrivelled as they gave up their lives to feed the Halfling's need.

Slowly a command chair built itself out of the rubble and around it formed an arch of stone that seemed to pulse. At the top of the arch great discs swivelled to greedily suck energy from the sun. Eloen could feel the power flood in as the Dream-shifter re-assembled itself and basked in the late afternoon sun. The long dead mind of Abaddon slid into hers like a hand into a glove as soon as she sat in the chair.

"Welcome little sister. I have been asleep for a very long time. I am here to guide you. The strength of your father will aid you. The powers of the Dream-shifter are yours, for you are the daughter of Molock. Anyone else that touched the Staff of Power would have died. The ship and memory banks are genetically tuned to Molock's blood-line. I must warn you that we suffered great damage when the High King defeated us. It will take time for the demolition of my systems to heal. There is one place that we can go to allow this to happen. I can transport us to where we first collected the slaves that served us so well. May I advise you to do this now? The Spellbinder will sense my resurrection if we are here too long. We are not strong enough to stand against Peterkin's powers. Not yet, my princess. Not yet!"

Eloen had protected Hilden and Hammer-fist from the draining of life energy and drew them to her side, where they stared out in horror at what the Halfling had done to all of their people. They were now Eloen's puppets to do exactly as they were bidden.

"Take us to the Earth, Dream-shifter," she commanded and the view of the estuary became full of swirling mist as the ship warped reality and crossed into the parallel universe.

By the time Eloen had dug into the mound and was a day away from excavating Molock's Staff of Power, Rassel and Lorena reached the foothills of the elven kingdom and had contacted Ljo'sa'lfar who were living in that area. A telepathic summons to the castle and two dragon riders made their way from the castle to the farm where the raptors had left the gnomes. Once they were sure that the gnomes were safe, they made their way back onto the Plains of Scion and towards their home.

It was late afternoon when two Quetzalcoatlus circled the farm and dropped out of the sky. Eduardo and Calando had urged their mounts to fly at top speed as the reptiles would fly during darkness, but were reluctant to land. The two elves were Peterkin's most trusted lieutenants and were also his inmost friends. They had been guards to Waldwick the mad High King and had transferred their allegiance to Peterkin. Waldwick had been infected with the virus he had intended to infect Ameela's daughter, Mia and left mindless at the mercy of the Dokka'lfar. He had initially spread the plague amongst the Dark Elves and started the beginning of the end. I did the rest by visiting Alfheimr, spreading the petulance and the 'pressed' T Rex's wherever the Spellbinder touched down. It took some time to spread and eradicate the evil spawn of Molock's loins. The main thing was that the head had been cut off and the driving force removed. Now I was not so sure that all had gone to plan. The telepathic cry for help could not be precise as the elf concerned could not read the gnomes' mind. All he could say was that the two custodians of the Tower of Absolom had appeared on his doorstep with a band of velociraptors. Whatever had happened was important enough for them to flee the Tower and try to get to me on foot! If the raptors had not seen their signal bonfire we would never have seen them again.

I had used the attribute of the gnome's fuzzy minds to my advantage when they had travelled on the Spellbinder, masking my presence from the powerful mind of Molock. Now I would have to wait until tomorrow to find out what had made them risk their lives in such a way.

MOLOCK'S WAND

CHAPTER EIGHT

Morning had eventually arrived and I had spent most of the night staring out of the windows and listening to the arguments in my head. There was nothing that I could do until they arrived! It was the lack of knowledge that worried me, what could possibly happen at that remote stop-over point to the dwarves? I had lost track of the years that had passed since I had cleansed the Elves home world. All my human friends had long ago passed away and their children had grown up and had grandchildren of their own. My own son, Elthred had slowly grown into a fine young elf and Mia was a beautiful creature with her mother's tallness. Seeding Alfheimr with the virus and transporting programmed T Rex's and allosaurus had gone on for years until I was sure that every Dokka'lfar had been exterminated.

The last places that I had visited with the Spellbinder were what would have been Ireland and Britain. Europe and the great continents had been allocated the double hammer of the genetically-modified virus and the meat-eating dinosaurs first. It had taken a century to cleanse Europe and what would have been America on the Earth. Even the hordes of the Dokka'lfar found the Amazon and African jungles too much to take on, but everywhere else they had spread in their billions, eating anything and everything with no thought of conservation. The Gobi desert had spread into China and had buried vast areas of good ground under sand. Everywhere that the deserts on Earth had been held back by the ingenuity of mankind, the Dark Elves had just moved to where there was food until famine struck.

The mutation that had brought Molock into existence did not repeat itself. When he mated with the female elves that he dominated by his superior mind control, the offspring became the Dokka'lfar. The problem began when these mated amongst themselves and their offspring were often mentally retarded. Some were capable of speech, but the majority were not and they were incredibly fertile. The first generation controlled them by telepathy and used the mobs as armies. All of them had the long lifespan of elves and their numbers continually multiplied. Fortunately they were all susceptible to the virus and those that lived became sterile. We could show no mercy and I made sure that it was a decree that governed every elf, goblin, gnome and human. As the humans had been bred for centuries for food and sport, they needed no urging once the mental control was turned off. Once the manufacture of iron collars had spread throughout the communities and the humans found out that the iron prevented the Dokka'lfar from mentally controlling them, they went on a killing spree.

I watched the sun come up from behind the mountain and the long shadows of the castle spread out upon the foothills beneath me. What little sleep I had managed to have was from sitting in the chair and I ached in every muscle. I was still dressed in yesterday's clothes and my skin felt itchy and in need of a wash. There was a discrete cough from behind me and I turned round to see a gnome with a jug of hot water and a bowl. Over his stubby arm was a towel and on top of that was a cake of soap.

"I believe you could do with a wash sire," he said and placed the bowl onto a table. He poured out the hot water and stood ready to help.

"Thank you Razzmutt," I replied. "Will you help me off with my shirt?"

I bent forwards and my friend pulled the shirt over my head after undoing the straps that that fastened over my wings. As the shirt came off I flexed my shoulders and extended my wings to their full. My back still bore the branding iron marks where Waldwick has sliced my wings off and cauterised the stumps. Had it not been for the Dokka'lfar's incredible healing ointment I would have remained flightless all of my life. That long time that I was unable to fly, taught me many things about the limitations that all the other people came to terms with. I knelt down on the floor while Razzmutt applied a soapy flannel to my back and then rinsed me down. He ran the cloth along the outstretched wings and inspected each joint and fine feathers for splits and damage. Satisfied that there were none he handed me the cloth to do my front while he dried me off at the back.

"I know Rassel well my liege and he would not have put Lorena at risk unless there was real cause. The tower of Absolom is a long way on foot across those plains. Particularly if you are a gnome! Had they not been found by the raptors and brought here by them, they would have disappeared down the throat of some beast!"

"I know that, Razzmutt and that is what has kept me up all night!"

"Two of us can watch the sun rise, husband! If you could not sleep, you should have woken me," Ameela said from behind him, sliding her hands under my wings and around my chest.

I kissed her hands and asked, "Razzmutt can you get me a

clean shirt and organise some breakfast for the two of us?"

The gnome nodded and dragged off the dirty shirt putting it into a basket, retrieving a clean one for me. Ameela helped me put it on and assisted me to tuck up my wings back into the dormant position.

As she did so she reminded me, "Even if they left at dawn, the dragons would not arrive here until at least mid-day. There is nothing that you can do, husband except wait until they get here. Be patient my love and come away from that window. Razzmutt has brought us breakfast and you might as well fill your empty stomach if not your mind!"

I tore my gaze away from the empty skies and sat down at the table where my faithful gnome had filled it with morning goodies. There was toasted bread with a selection of fruit preserves along with freshly boiled eggs. Also there was butter made from goat's milk to spread upon the toast. The smell was enough to make my mouth water and I tucked in.

Already the castle was beginning to come alive with people coming and going. There were a number of humans here studying in the laboratories under one of John Smith's descendants. They enjoyed working with the goblins that were of the same technological bent. What they were trying to do was to duplicate the Spellbinder so that the reality-shifting abilities of this sentient ship could be used by others. Deedlit had built only one reality-shifting ship completely. The other vessel he had named the Dream-shifter and had begun construction of it to lighten the load on the Spellbinder. The advance of the Dokka'lfar towards the last of the Ljo'sa'lfar had been far quicker than was realised and the partially built vessel was left behind. Molock and his son, Abaddon had spent over a thousand years trying to get the ship to work for them and had finally succeeded. Abaddon was given the task to find the whereabouts of the Light Elves and tracked them to the Earth, only for the Spellbinder to disappear into another parallel universe. By the time that the Dark Lord had found them again on Haven, the ship had deteriorated so much, that all Abaddon could do was keep the Arch open as a gateway from Alfheimr to Haven. Fortunately for us the Dream-shifter had carried the Dokka'lfar outside of the Great Gorge and the crater walls that were so high it was impossible to breathe. We managed to seed the poisoned brier and fill the gorge with our people safely inside, but the dwarves paid a heavy blood price to keep them out until the gorge was impassable. Abaddon kept the arch open for centuries by feeding the life energy of the mindless Dokka'lfar into the dream-shifter. It went insane!

So far the only other elves that could operate my ship had to be genetically keyed from my bloodline and that meant only Mia and Elthred could command the Spellbinder. This tied the three of us to an agenda that was quite irksome at times. My geneticists were also working on a way to transplant the gene that gave us the longevity into humans and dwarves so that they too could count on centuries instead of decades.

Mother and I would sometimes catch a morning thermal and rise up the mountain above the castle to our private tomb high above. It was here that the remains lay of those brave human beings that had elected to come here with me, to rescue Ameela and my daughter Mia from Waldwick's evil plan. We came here together and spent a while remembering dead friends. My mother had taken Henry Spencer as a lover after a long period of celibacy full in the knowledge of the few decades that they could be together. His coal-black skin made him look like a Dokka'lfar and made those elves that did not know him very uneasy. She had ridden on the back of what we called dragons, armed with a Kalashnikov AK47, sat behind Spencer and spraying the Dokka'lfar with bullets from the air.

At the moment she was living on Aifheimr, helping to rebuild the Elven civilization on our old world along with the humans who had been slaves there. Now there were goblins and gnomes living there once more. Native animals were returning from the more remote areas and re-establishing themselves now that the Dokka'lfar had disappeared. Once the grasslands and woods had spread and flourished, I worked my special magic. I took various herd animals from Earth and dinosaurs from Haven in the Spellbinder to the empty world. The Earth was in ruins with small pockets of civilization hanging on. Some areas were poisonously radioactive and empty of life. The final Jihad had taken place with no winners in the struggle. There were square miles of glass where the deserts of the Middle East had once been. The Dead Sea was now fused glass with mile after mile of what once had been irrigated farmlands. The Mediterranean Sea was entirely dead and the shoreline pushed back by the tsunamis that had flooded along the land. The area around where Acme Engineering used to exist was now melted into a vast glassy hole where the city used to be. Fortunately I had closed all of the portals on the Earth so there was no leak-over effect from the bombs. I evacuated all of my people and resettled them on Alfheimr where they had built a new city complete with its own power supply. They called it New-New Los Angeles! Or just New-New!

I could see it coming and was helpless to prevent it from happening, so I did my best to transport as many self-reliant groups as I could to the Elven home world of Aifheimr. In the end I hardened my heart and would not travel there again. The brutality of life on that world was so bad that the people left there would bring nothing but violence and trouble if they were transported here. The weight of that decision was heavy on my soul, year after year, as I fully realised that I was condemning many innocent lives to a short and miserable span. Surprisingly enough the humans that I had brought to both Elven worlds agreed to the decision. I did not interfere with any of the communities that were scattered across both worlds. My rule over all of them was light and there was very little that I forbid except the weapons that the humans had developed and I used, to destroy the Dokka'lfar. Now as the Earth lay in ruins the possibility of ever finding ammunition for the projectile weapons made it a surety that the only rifles and guns in existence would remain locked away in the cellars of my castle coated in grease. I hoped that I would never need to use them.

Time passed slowly as the morning dragged on as I hunted in the skies for two large dots. I ate another hasty meal, still scanning the cloudy heavens in the direction of the Tower, when I heard Eduardo's voice inside my mind.

"Sire, we will not be too much longer. The dragons are a little tired carrying a double load, but we should be with you very soon. We are above the clouds and can see the mountain quite clearly, so we are about to drop through and then you should be able to see us."

I reached for the pair of binoculars that had belonged to my friend, Sam Pitts and searched for the returning dragons and their loads. Soon two great winged shapes drifted out of the clouds, gliding downwards towards the height of the castle parapet that jutted out from my quarters. My two friends held onto the harnesses and the gnomes, as the Quetzalcoatlus stalled in front of me and both dropped onto the flagstones at my feet. The first thing that I saw was that the gnomes were still hanging onto the harnesses with grim death, eyes tightly closed and almost part of the beast that they were riding. At a muffled word from Eduardo and Calando they slowly unclenched their fingers from the leather straps and stared about.

"Welcome Rassel and Lorena," I said. "You have come a long way to see me and have risked your lives to get here, so please dismount and then you can tell me what has brought you here!"

My two elves helped them to slide down the legs of the dragons and onto the parapet. They rapidly moved away from the edge as there was no balcony to prevent them falling off. This always bothered the humans who lived and worked here, but to us a winged race, it was no problem.

Razzmutt appeared from behind me with two hot mugs of herbal tea laced with honey and gave one each to our visitors. The gnomes gratefully drank from the mugs cupping their hands around them to draw out some warmth. I gestured to the table that still held hot food from our lunch-time meal. There were a number of chairs a little higher than the rest so that gnomes could sit with elves at the same height. My new guests gratefully climbed onto two of these and sat down, still cradling the hot mugs.

Lorena spoke first and said, "We have come here to warn you. Something evil has come here and I do not know what it is."

"What do you mean?" I asked.

"We had a visitor some days ago," Rassel explained. "I have lost track of the days so I cannot be precise, High King. She rode a dragon to the lodge and we gave her shelter as is our duty and our pleasure. There was something about her that was different. She looked like a Ljo'sa'lfar, but there were things we noticed about her that were different. She had four fingers, not five and she wore her hair in a fringe, but occasionally Lorena saw that she had no antennae on her forehead. Also we are sure that she had no wings! Whatever she had stuffed into the back of her robes I can tell you it was not wings. The thing is if she could control a dragon with her mind, what else could she do? She had the ears and eyes of an elf and the telepathic powers, but there was a ruthless feel about her. There was one other thing that Lorena sensed and that there was a wisp of gnomish about her. It was as if she had killed a young girl and held the essence in her mind. Why she needed that I have no idea, but occasionally we both felt the icy hand of death about her. She spoke about Alfheimr as if is she knew it well and described what was being done there. The other thing that we felt was odd, was that she did not seem to know anything about the castle of the High King and fended off all inquiries. She said that she was on her way to visit the dwarves at Stormgalt. So we fogged our minds and escaped from the Tower whilst she slept and we spoiled the food that was left there. If you go there, please make sure that all the supplies that were left behind are destroyed and fresh brought in."

I listened to Rassel's account with a sinking heart as a great disquiet filled my mind. What could it all mean? I would have to go and find out myself in the Spellbinder, but there was something I needed to do first.

"Lorena as you were the one who was the most sensitive to whatever this was, I have to ask a favour of you," and I stood up and walked round the table to where she was sat. I need to enter your mind and see what you saw."

"Great High King, I am honoured. Please allow me to order my thoughts and concentrate on what I saw," she replied.

She nodded when she was ready and to make it easier for the two of us I laid hands upon her forehead. I gently slipped into her mind and was able to work my way through the cloudiness and into her memories. There I caught my first sight of Eloen and could see why she would blend in. Her face was elfish except for the lack of antennae and her hair was ebony black. Then I was shocked to my core as the wisp of gnomish identity floated in front of my searching mind. There was a residue gradually evaporating from this female's mind. She had murdered a young gnome on Alfheimr and tied the essence in place over hers. There could only be one reason! I had brought her here inside the Spellbinder! She had used the young girl's fuzzy mind as a shield to escape detection.

I surfaced from Lorena's memories and sat white faced in shock at what I had found. I passed the information on to Ameela and gathered my thoughts, deciding what to do.

"What would be so important that she would murder her way onto this world and seek out the dwarves?" asked Ameela.

A cold shudder went down my spine, as I knew what it was this elf-like creature wanted.

"It's not the dwarves she is after, Ameela, its Molock's Staff of Power she seeks! She must be some kind of Dokka'lfar that has escaped the annihilation of her kind," I cried.

I walked over to where the command chair had been parked by the parapet, sat down and I reached for the Staff of Power that was keyed to my bloodline. I gripped the staff with both hands and concentrated my will, pushing it into the socket. "Spellbinder; activate!"

The next thing I did was to call Eduardo and Calando to collect a dozen more elves and a number of gnomes to make sure that whatever was at the site of Abaddon's grave had no knowledge of our coming. The parapet soon filled up with people including several goblins and the humans that were studying with them. They rapidly walked into the soap bubble that was the outside force field of the Spellbinder and the screen snapped shut.

"Spellbinder, take us to the Tower of Absolom and make it fast," I thought and watched as we detached from the parapet and began to speed over the foothills of our home mountain and across the Plains of Scion.

Very soon the inverted mushroom shape that stood on the pillar came into sight. The Spellbinder gently dropped onto the ground in front of the Lodge and we all got out. Quickly we searched the place and found it just as Rassel had told us. Whoever had been here had not been stupid enough to raid the cupboards of food before she left. While we were there we dropped off some gnomes to settle the lodge again and clean up, leaving with them sufficient supplies to keep them going before the gardens produced.

I sat in the command chair and gave the order, "Spellbinder, take us to Stormgalt."

Once again the walls of the soap bubble hardened and we were on our way across the home of the dinosaurs and I marvelled at the herculean task it must have been for Rassel and Lorena to have walked across them. Had they not been found by the velociraptors when they did, they would never have reached me alive. So much time had elapsed from the destruction of the Dokka'lfar that I had become complacent, so sure was I that the scourge had been removed. The forward view soon began to change as we coasted over the foothills of the crater's edge and I could plainly see the stockade and moat that kept the dwarves' town safe from the meat eating predators of the plains. A crowd soon gathered as the Spellbinder came into sight. I looked through the binoculars and soon picked out Hildegard.

We landed in front of her and I sprang out of my chair and walked quickly towards the extremely old lady. It always hurt like a hammer-blow when time took my mortal friends away and I was so pleased to still see that she was still quite spritely.

"What brings you, Long Shadow? Are you following the Lady Eloen? She is at the site of your battle with Abaddon searching for Molock's Wand as you asked!"

"What did you call her? What help have you given her? Tell

me what help have you given her? Oh Hildegard I fear that a terrible thing has happened here. I must read your mind and look at your memories," I cried and without giving her the courtesy of asking I plunged into her memories and held her tightly by her frail arms.

It was all there! These brave and gentle people had done everything that this creature Eloen had asked. The truth was that she had not asked! With lies and mental coercion she had wound them up like a clockwork set of toys. She had managed to control hundreds of the dwarves and make them believe she was Ljo'sa'lfar and on an errand for me. I hung my head and wept for the inevitable death camp that I knew I would discover.

I held the frail old body of my friend and asked, "When did they go from here?"

"Four days ago, my King. Your face! It is so full of sorrow. Please tell me what has happened, I beg you! Tell me," she cried and stepped back to stare up at me.

"Hildegard I fear a strong Dokka'lfar has entered this world. She will use your people to retrieve what I should have destroyed many years ago. She must be a direct descendant of Molock and has escaped the plague I unleashed upon them. Somehow she has managed to stow away on the Spellbinder and remain hidden, by killing a young gnome girl and concealing her mind under hers. I brought her here Hildegard and I fear for what she has done to your families and friends," I said and held her tightly in my arms.

"Great King, you could not know. How would any of us guess that one of that devil's spawn would survive? There must be something very different about her to make it so that she lived when all the others died," Hildegard replied.

"There is, Hildegard! I believe that she may be an elf-human hybrid, with all of the ruthless brutality that the Dokka'lfar wallow in. I must go to the site right now and see what has transpired. Do you want to come with us?"

"Yes, but others must come too," she answered and blew a whistle hanging around her neck.

Immediately a number of dwarves ran up to her and she rapidly gave information and instructions to them and a half dozen entered the Spellbinder with her.

"Let us go 'Long-shadow' and find the truth of what we must face," the elderly dwarfess grimly said.

I gave the command to lift and the Spellbinder began to fly parallel to the edge of the Great Gorge around to the other side of the crater wall. As the Spellbinder followed the bend in the gorge the all too familiar area of my battle of wills against Abaddon began to open up. I saw the beach where the estuary of the river that flowed out of the Great Gorge emptied into the sea. There was a camp of waggons drawn into a circle, but it was completely empty. The iguanodons were all missing and the stockade open. As the Spellbinder followed the curve around the seaward side of the crater, the rest of the old battlefield opened up and I remembered that my Uzbekistani friends had reduced the Arch of the dream-shifter to rubble. There was no trace of the destruction wrought. Every green elf-stone had attached itself to others of its kind and had re-assembled to once more become the Dokka'lfar's sentient ship.

The first things that I noticed were the bodies of the dwarves that lay where they had dropped. Already the scavengers had started to pick the corpses apart. The mound that had buried the Abaddon and his father's Staff of Power had been torn apart by the resurrection of the Dokka'lfar ship. I lowered the Spellbinder to the ground and released the force-field to allow the dwarves to disembark and search amongst the bodies for any who had survived. Humans, goblins and gnomes assisted in the terrible task. None had survived Eloen's need for power to bring the Dream-shifter to operational status. Hildegard examined the dead, looking for her daughter and her mate. The old dwarfess wiped tears from her eyes as she had the bodies turned over by her helpers.

"High King! They are not here," she cried. "That thing has taken them with her! Where can they have gone?"

I felt my psychic power go off the scale as I gave the next order and the Spellbinder connected to the Dream-shifter. I slammed into a wall of hate.

A cold voice echoed in my mind, "Too late, Great King. You can clean up! I am done here."

MOLOCK'S WAND

CHAPTER NINE

With those cold tones ringing in my head I stood and watched helpless as Hildegard's frail, ancient body sank to the ground. We had managed to extend the dwarves years of active life for over two centuries, but no longer. Hildegard had lived beyond two hundred and thirty years with her mind still sharp. The loss of her daughter and her husband was just too much for her to take in along with so many of her people scattered around in lifeless bundles. I knelt by her side and folded her into my arms and felt her faint breath against my cheek.

"Find them Long-shadow and bring them back," she gasped and staring into my eyes, she died.

I held the bundle of lifeless bones against my chest and felt the stillness of her heart as it bumped twice and stopped. Again time had robbed me of a good friend. I found myself ringed by dwarves waiting for me to instruct them.

"Gather the dead and put them into the Spellbinder," I said. "We will take them back to the Stormgalt where they can be returned to the earth from whence we all came."

I turned and shed tears over my old friends face and carried her into the Spellbinder myself. I laid the ancient dwarfess gently down by the side of the command chair and opened my mind to the Spellbinder.

"Where did she go? I thought that you emptied the memory banks of the accursed vessel when we fought Abaddon," I grimly said as I closed the eyelids over Hildegard's sightless eyes.

"I have secondary memory banks, High King. The Dream-shifter would have been constructed in the same fashion. It has had a long enough time to shed the mindless energy that made it become insane. Buried deep beneath the ground and shattered into so many pieces, that energy has leaked away. Did you not see the twisted shapes that the vegetation had grown into and the fact that there has been no life creeping about that area? Even the dead bodies of the dwarves had only just begun to draw the carrion eaters to this place! Send your mind into the area and understand what I am telling you," the Spellbinder whispered into my mind.

I did what the Spellbinder suggested and found an eerie silence where there should have been a hum of semi-mindless activity. There were a few insects that had wandered into the vegetation, but little else. I expanded the radius of my search until I was a considerable distance from where the arch of the Dream-shifter was buried before I began to pick up life-signs. I shuddered as the implications hit me. I had never re-visited this place, due to my continual involvement in re-settling Alfheimr by transferring humans, seeds and animals back and forth the three worlds. My journeys to Earth were kept secret and I made sure that the powers that be on that violent world knew nothing of my activity. Had they known how to travel from one parallel world to another it would have led to disaster! Had they known of the existence of such a fact they were clever enough to have worked at it until they solved the problem. The thought of humans loose with their weapons and warlike attitudes into our peaceful society horrified not just me, but also those who I had re-settled. This was another reason that I would not return to Earth. Now I might have to, with my search for this Halfling Dokka'lfar and her two captives.

Ameela shook me by the shoulder and said into my ear, "They're all inside Peterkin, so take us back to the Stormgalt and let us be rid of this awful cargo!"

"Spellbinder is there anything more to be learnt here before we take these bodies to their final resting place?"

"There is nothing, great King. The Dream-shifter left no trace for me to follow. The only thing that I can tell you was that in that moment of contact I caught the fleeting touch of Abaddon's mind as they winked out of existence on this plane. It makes sense that as he died with the Staff in his hands his psyche was absorbed by it and has become part of the Dream-shifter."

"What other minds have been absorbed into your sister ship? Do you have anything else that you can tell me?"

"It would be logical that Molock himself would have generated an alter ego to be the bedrock of the Dream-shifter's personality. Whatever else is in there you had best regain that moment that you defeated Abaddon and search your memories for the answers," the Spellbinder replied.

"Then take us to the Stormgalt and get us there as soon as you can," I commanded.

The bubble of the Spellbinder swung into the air and the ground beneath us became a blur as we returned to the dwarves' township with our sombre cargo. The sun was setting fast and the Great Gorge was soon shrouded in darkness. This made no difference to the spellbinder as its senses did not rely on just light. Soon the ship rounded the bend and settled onto the ground outside the large stone building that Eloen had been staying in. There were oil lamps lit and once the Spellbinder had been seen, a crowd soon gathered to see what had transpired. Once the walls of the ship had evaporated and the grim cargo seen, bitter sobbing rent the air as the full impact of the horror took place. Fortunately some of the dwarves that had travelled with us were deputy leaders of the community and were able to take charge. The lifeless and desiccated corpses were stacked in lines to be identified by family, but they were so dried out and twisted up that this would become very difficult. Eloen had sucked every scrap of life energy and fed it to the Dream-shifter. This time it had been fed on functional minds and would not be driven insane! The only corpse that was easily identified was that of my friend, Hildegard. At least her face had softened and she looked at peace, but I knew different.

Her last words echoed in the vey depths of my soul.

"Find them Long-shadow and bring them back," she had asked and I had little idea as to where I could find them.

I was aware of a dwarf stood in front of me and vaguely recognised his features as someone I ought to know and said, "I feel that we have met before somewhere."

"No great King, but you knew my grandfather well. His name was Mellitus Hammerhand and he stood at your side. I am known as Aradun Hammerhand and I would do the same. There is a blood-debt to be paid against the Stormgalt and I would be part of the paying of that debt. Thorin Hammer-fist's son is here with me and would also accompany you wherever you choose to go."

I looked at the muscular dwarf that had quickly put himself at Aradun's side and asked, "What is your first-name, Hammer-fist?"

I am Thorinson, my King. That creature has my father and my mother in her power. I will have her dead in repayment of that debt."

"You may come with me, but I will decide whether she dies or lives, not you Thorinson! Do you agree?"

"I agree, my King. My emotions overcame me. I am sorry. It will not happen again," the young dwarf replied, struggling with his grief.

Ameela put her hand upon my shoulder and said, "We should go my love. We need to get back to the castle and you need to gather a band together to hunt her down. This is not the place to be right now. Let these people do what they have to dispose of their dead while we make our way home."

I regretfully agreed, said my sorrowful goodbyes to the people of the Stormgalt and returned to the Spellbinder accompanied by my two new bodyguards.

As I walked back to my vessel the surroundings were lit by the funeral pyre that the dwarves had quickly piled their dead. They burnt very quickly, as Eloen had drained them of all energy and the desiccated corpses were bone dry. My mind was in turmoil as I re-ran the events that I should have foreseen and dealt with long ago. My only thin excuse was that the combination of the virus and the meat-eaters had proved successful to the knowledge that I had at my disposal. All that I could reason out was that Eloen was a hybrid between elf and human. This was something that had never happened before. The Dokka'lfar had used human women for sexual gratification for a thousand years, but there were no offspring between them. This was a freak of nature and unfortunately I would guess that she would have the enhanced abilities of Molock himself. If that were so, then she could be a greater adversary than Abaddon had been. I would bear that in mind and take no chances when we eventually met.

I had a lot to think about on the return journey home and the voices in my head argued amongst themselves incessantly. I alone had used technology in my war against the Dokka'lfar and basically it was against an easy foe that had not progressed from simple weapons, thinking that sheer numbers were enough. Enlisting the six mercenaries from Earth had tipped the balance. I could do with the redoubtable Sam Pitts and the agile and adaptive mind of John Smith. They had become dust nearly two centuries ago. The last time I had dared translate to the Earth I found that it had been reduced to barbarism in the few pockets of liveable areas left untouched by the destruction. There were still surviving towns away from the rubble of the big cities that were wresting a living from the war-torn land. The people that lived there were distrustful of strangers and relied on weapons that would never be manufactured now. Ammunition was difficult to get and exceedingly difficult to produce with dwindling resources. What armies had remained viable propped up war-lords and sustained dictatorships.

When they ran out of bullets I was sure they would beat each other to death with sticks! Yet as I turned things over in my 'minds' the surety came to me that this was where Eloen would go, to take over the easily malleable minds of human beings. If she was clever enough to stowaway on the Spellbinder and remain hidden, I was sure that she would surround herself with a well-equipped army. She would turn Hilden and Thorin Hammer-fist into restrained puppets that would willingly die for her if necessary. If her mental powers equalled those of Molock, controlling an army would be quite easy for her. All she need do was to concentrate on the steps of command and the lower ranks would do as they were told. A general reinforcement of subservience to her leadership would be all that it would take!

My mind was on fire by the time that the Spellbinder arrived at the castle. I had not slept properly in days and it was beginning to take its toll. Ameela called Razzmutt to her and directed him to mix a sleeping draught that would send me into a deep sleep against my protestations. In the end I could see the wisdom of my wife's insistence and drank the spicy brew, undressed and fell into the folds of our bed. It did not take long for the potion to take effect and I released all hold on consciousness. My sleep was not dreamless! Time and time again I held Hildegard in my arms and watched her die.

"Find them Long-shadow and bring them back," I heard her gasp.

Find them indeed!

Unbidden, the face of the Halfling thrust herself before my face and I heard her mind close like a steel trap over mine and say, "Too late, Great King. You can clean up! I am done here."

The words, "Too late, too late," burned into my mind and I awoke with clenched fists and my eyes streaming tears.

How many non-elves would die in this conflict as well as my own people? I had buried the weapons we had used to exterminate the Dokka'lfar deep under the castle, packed in grease, never thinking that they would ever be used again. I would have to turn some of my gentle people back into killers again. I would have to make them like me! In my bloodline was hidden the ability to kill another elf. We held all sentient life to be sacrosanct and that is why my people the Ljo'sa'lfar, had merely moved away from the cannibalistic Dokka'lfar, instead of wiping them out when their legions were small and manageable. Now I would have to hunt down this aberration and if necessary terminate her followers.

The weeks to come must be carefully planned and I needed people that I could rely on. There were none living under my rule that were well versed in weapons. I had no Sam Pitts to rely on to help plan a campaign, or a John Smith whose scientific mind had always been there to apply his unique way of thinking. I had the wisdom of all the previous High Kings, but none of them were founts of knowledge about hunting and killing. I had been the one who had bent the peaceful minds of my people into slayers of the Dokka'lfar. I still had nightmares about the way I had changed them. Now two centuries later I had to do it all over again. If I could not be as ruthless as the Halfling in my dealings and plans then she would infect my realm with death and destruction.

The fact was, I needed these two human beings that had died so long ago and there might be a way to bring them back. As we flew through the night back to my castle and home I dug into the memory banks of the Spellbinder. There had been a wisp of thought from the original builder, Deedlit, buried in the multi-mined sentient creature that was the essence of my ship. Also I was sure that Freyr was aware of this very secret piece of knowledge and I plunged into the deepest of the memory banks. The original High King was reluctant to discuss the subject as it was as an abomination to him that Deedlit had included this lost art into the construction of the Spellbinder.

I would not let the matter drop and argued the point against the other three kings. I had an unexpected ally that surfaced in this unequal battle of wills. My long dead father came into the discussion from the back of my mind! He had been there all along ever since he had died at Waldwick's hand. He too was of the stuff of kings and would have been genetically keyed to command the Spellbinder. It was a shock to me to realise that he had been there all the time, looking through my eyes and listening to my thoughts, but bound not to interfere in any way except to lend me his strength when things got tough. I had got used to the others that lived in my head and also in the fabric of the Spellbinder ever since that day I had inserted the Staff of Power into the connecting hole in front of the command chair.

Freyr maintained, "It was an eldritch thing to do, raising the dead in such a fashion. I do not approve! It must not be attempted!"

My father, Peter replied, "If this is not done, who will advise my son in the evil arts of war and killing? We the Ljo'sa'lfar have never had to deal with a creature like this Halfling! She is clever, ruthless and I am sure is bent on revenge on our race if not our family. We took her race and exterminated it like the vermin that it was. Billions of them where almost mindless and we did nothing, but ran away."

Auberon insisted, "In those times we held to the principal that no elf would raise their hands against another. The idea of causing death was abhorrent! How many of us died on Alfheimr to preserve that dictate? When that evil spawn found us on Earth long ago, we fled again, leaving that world to become the plaything of Molock and his children. It was only the widespread use of iron that forced them to give up that world. They took enough human beings to be able to breed them for food and sport. We left them to rot under a terrible legacy. Peterkin freed them all! Now he has tried to settle two worlds with humans and our own kind that evolved on the home-world. Would you have this entire emerging civilization tumble around our ears? I say that when the Spellbinder returns to the castle, Peterkin sets in motion the necessary actions to bring back from their rest, those two human beings that did so much to destroy the Dokka'lfar!"

I felt two cool hands upon my brow that flattened my antennae to my forehead and a voice in my mind, "Enough! Quieten your strident tones. Would you drive my husband mad? Cease! Cease now and give him rest from this debate. He will do the right thing even if it seems abhorrent to you. He will do it because there is no other way! Do you think that he would do this lightly? Be still!"

I turned and held my Ameela in my arms and sobbed against her shoulder as the awful reality of what I was going to do hit me like a hammer blow. I was going to call the souls of my deepest friends and entomb them back into mortal flesh. What right had I to do this? What dark necessity had driven me to even think of such a thing? I cursed Eloen for what she was forcing me to do and sat sombre and still in the command chair as we winged through the night.

By midmorning we had docked with the castle parapet and I had sent Eduardo and Calando into the depths of the castle to start removing the weapons from storage that I had packed away so long ago. Now I needed to take the Spellbinder much higher up the mountain to the tomb that I had interred my human friends bones after they had died of old age. There was one other friend that I had placed there and that was Mellitus Hammer-hand, a dwarf with great courage. He too had stood by my side and his bones were also buried in that tomb.

Elves have few customs on dealing with the dead except to have respect for those who have gone before us. We tend to bury or place in tombs all the bones together in a common receptacle. I realised that as all the bones of my friends were together, than all of them would be resurrected, as I could not possibly sort through the jumble inside the sarcophagus. This also was not something that I could share with anyone else as it would need the High King's blood to affect the 'calling' and give life to the recipients.

Ameela insisted on accompanying me and had the practicality of mind to bring cloaks and undergarments for them to wear. What I was about to do had only been done a very few times before tens of thousands of years ago and it was very dangerous for the resurrector. It would be very easy to lose my mind while casting a net into the afterlife and become trapped there forever. Ameela would be my anchor along with the Spellbinder. I had only managed to snatch a little sleep whilst sat in the command chair, but it would have to do! I ate a hasty meal to make sure that I would not fail through bodily weakness and sat once more in the chair flanked by Thorinson and Aradun whose part in this was to be the muscle that would peel back the cover of the sarcophagus to allow me to do what was necessary.

As if the heavens knew that there would be a need for energy, the clouds were dark anvils of seething electrical energy. Lightning split the air as the Spellbinder climbed upwards towards the tomb I had, had built for my friends. Now I was about to do more than disturb their rest, I was going to tear them away from whatever the after-life was to become mortal again. The weight of that awesome responsibility lay heavy on my heart and mind. All too soon it seemed the Spellbinder docked with the edge of the tomb. It was hewn into the very rock of the mountainside and open to the elements. The dwarves had scooped out a disc shaped recess that used the stone-face above as the roof. They had hammered pillars into the base and ceiling to make sure that the tomb was securely placed. The stone sarcophagus had been dragged into the farthest end of the recess and placed on cubes of black granite. A polished green-granite lid lay on top of a red, rosy black-flecked square box that contained my dear friends' bones. Leading up to this was a polished set of stone steps that I climbed with a swiftly beating heart.

Aradun put his shoulder to one corner, while Thorinson pushed against the opposing side. The muscles on their stocky frames stood out in knots as bit by bit the lid began to swing open as the flat square grudgingly slid to one side. With a resounding crunch, the lid fell off the right hand side.

I stood looking into the box at the skulls and bones that had been stacked inside. Reaching in, I held the skull of Mellitus in my hands. There was no mistaking those pronounced eye-ridges and that long brain-case at the back. I kissed him on his forehead and placed his skull on the wide ledge, stretched in and did the same with each skull, making a connection to each person that had once lived inside these bone cases.

Carefully I placed them all back inside, reached for my obsidian knife and cut deep enough into the heel of my hand to drip my blood steadily onto the pile of bones, so that the flow splashed onto each skull.

Now I reached out for the composite mind of the Spellbinder and drew on the strength of the minds of the High Kings that I carried deep inside my psyche. I also made contact with Ameela as she provided me with an anchor. She then telepathically joined to the race mind of the elves scattered about the castle and forged the link that would bring me back.

The Spellbinder and I spread the mental mesh into sub-space and those who had ascended into the afterlife existed in whatever state they did. The power of Kings flowed through my very substance and held me steady. Here was the universe of the rifts that bound together all of the parallel universes and provided the gateways that I had travelled, using the Spellbinder's abilities. There were trillions of souls that swirled this way and that uninterested in what I needed. I saw an infinite number of Earths that waxed and waned. Some were blue and full of life and some burned with molten intensity. I ignored them all! 'Behind' me was a thread connecting me with Ameela and I swam along paying it out. Somewhere in that scattered mass were seven that I desperately needed. As I instituted the 'calling' I steadily bled over the bones of my friends.

My mind became a beacon spread over this multi-verse and in a timeless instant a recognition occurred. Then another and another as soul after soul was caught up in the Spellbinder's net until all seven were with me inside the tomb poised over the blood spattered bones. This was the very moment that the

Spellbinder spun time back and the bones inside the crypt began to be covered in flesh. The bodies began to writhe around collecting parts and building on what was rapidly assembling before my eyes. They separated and each soul lodged itself into its old home. At this point I closed the link between us and severed the bond to my kin.

I stepped back and closed the wound on my hand, as seven men stood unsteadily on their new feet and faced me. All of them looked as if they were in their early thirties and were as clean as a newly-washed baby. What blood I had shed over the bones was now inside them and part of them. The lightning flashed outside and the rain came hissing down making the temperature outside the sepulchre drop rapidly. Great claps of thunder rent the air, but left the fabric of the Spellbinder unscathed. We were sealed in from the elements and were untouched by all of this. Ameela walked forwards and presented the clothes to the naked men, who rapidly put them on. So far no-one had spoken and I held up my hand to get their undivided attention.

"Welcome back, gentlemen. Much has happened since you all died. This resurrection was not something that I would have done lightly. I desperately need you and all your skills. There are none alive on Alfheimr or Haven who have the skills and knowledge that you possess. Believe me my friends I had to do this for the safety of millions of mixed souls and our uncertain future."

Sam Pitts was the first to speak and said, "I remember nothing of where we have been except for my death! I can hear your mind; old friend and I quite understand that we are here because of some great crisis that you cannot handle alone. All that I know is that I have a warm healthy body that is not quite the same as my old one!"

John Smith flexed his muscles in almost disbelief at what

he could feel and gave Peterkin a hug that took him off his feet. The others also came forward and joined in the group hug, passing the High King from one to another until Mellitus stood before me.

"You are my King," he said and held me by my shoulders, lifting me again off my feet. "If you needed to call me back from the afterlife, then so be it. I am here! Whatever it is you need, it is my will that it be so. I too remember nothing of where I was and what I had become. I would ask one question of you Great King."

"Ask old friend, just ask," I replied.

"Why do I have pointed ears and why is it I can see quite plainly in this half-light!"

"All of you have been given life by me and my blood now courses through your bodies. You will find many changes to how your living bodies work. All of you are part elf and have been resurrected as such. I could not ask for better brothers or sons. Come, I have much to explain to you. It is time that you entered the Spellbinder and we were on our way back down the mountain to my home."

MOLOCK'S WAND

CHAPTER TEN

With the Spellbinder docked, it was time that I brought my old friends up to date and also to give them their first meal since they had once again regained the mantle of flesh! Aradun and Thorinson had been very quiet during the quick journey back down the mountain. What had taken place in front of their eyes had shaken them to the very core. So far Aradun had said very little, but kept staring at his grandfather in awe and disbelief of his senses.

Eventually Mellitus turned to him and said, "I too can hardly believe it, grandson, but I am here! Honestly, I can remember nothing of what has passed on the 'other side' and all that I know is that there was a calling. I heard that calling as did all of the others that are here with me. I am now flesh and blood. I can die again as easily as you can, so remember that when things get tough! Standing next to Peterkin can be a chancy business so keep all of your wits about you in the future."

The table was laid with an abundance of fresh bread rolls, goats' butter, smoked meats, cheese and salads of all descriptions. I had taken off the menu anything alcoholic as I could not be certain how these freshly made bodies would cope with the flagons of ale usually consumed by my mortal friends.

"Eat slowly and sparingly as these new bodies that you now

inhabit may not cope if you tax them too much. I have never done this before and although the knowledge is in the annuals of Elven lore, much of the after effects have not been inscribed. While you eat I will fill your memories with a pertinent selection of my own so that you all know what I have gathered in the short time that I have had," I instructed them.

While they carefully ate, I told them about the Halfling and what she had done to the members of the Stormgalt. I left nothing out although I could see that it affected Mellitus greatly. Because of the elfin touch about them their mastery of telepathy was greatly improved since they were once completely human. They began to feel other's thoughts and were able to receive mine with ease. There was one other thing that I was aware of that had edged into Henry Spencer's mind, that would not go away.

"She is not here, Spence. She is with my son on Alfheimr working to re-establish elves on the home-world," I told him. "Also my dear friend, she has no knowledge of what I have done. How my mother will re-act I cannot say, to find that you are alive again. All I can tell you and I say this to all of you, your lifespans are no longer a known quantity. There is Elven blood and flesh supporting your life processes, so if you are careful and we destroy this aberration, then there is no reason that you will age as quickly as a normal human would."

"In that case High King, I will quite happily enjoy the pointy ears and cat's eyes," laughed Hoatzin, "and make sure that I do not fall off a flying dragon. It's a pity you could not run to a pair of wings old friend! Now that little goodie would really make a difference!"

The twins, David and Steven, both turned their heads towards me and spoke in unison every other word, "The only thing is, High King that we are not sure who is who! Am I David or Steven? Or are we both each other?"

This I had not been prepared for and could only stare horrified at what I had done. The expression on my face was in the end too much for the twins who burst out laughing and nearly choked on the food they were chewing!

"Human humour! I will never understand it," I cried and threw a bread roll at the grinning face of David, who dodged it to allow Steven to catch it easily.

They had always had this ability of acting as a corporate being so it was no wonder I had been fooled as it would have been the next logical step! I must admit that with my old friends around me again, I felt that I could relax somewhat and take some respite from events. For the time being it was enough to see all seven of my companions just sit and eat.

This did not last very long as Sam soon pushed himself away from the table and said, "First things first, Peterkin and that is to do a weapons' check on the ordinance that we buried here long ago. I shall feel a lot better when I have a working M16 in my hands and I am sure that everything we put down into storage, works!"

"Everyone here knows what I have done and although you will be subject to some stares and even a few questions, you will find that your previous statute has been restored," I assured them. "Wherever you need to go and whatever you want to do, you will find that my authority goes with you. I need to sleep for a while to restore my energy levels and my sanity!"

Ameela and I retired to our sleeping chamber and I sank gratefully down onto the softness of our bed in a state of exhaustion. I lay with my head in my Queen's lap as she 'laid hands' upon my forehead and drew out the anxiety and pain from my mind. Within a short time I slipped away into dreamless sleep, but not for long.

Once again I was poised above the abyss calling for my long dead friends, only this time the thread connecting me with the living world snapped! I was drawn into another existence.

Now I was laid in the bottom of a deep grave where the entrance was so far above me that all I could see was a silver rectangle of light. The stench of death was all around me and I choked. I knew that to survive I would have to get to the top and the hole was so narrow that I could not spread my wings. I dug my fingers into the clay soil each side of me and pulled myself upwards. Both hearts beat to an uneven rhythm as I climbed up and upwards. For the first time, in it seemed eons, I was alone in my head. There were no kings to advise me. No voices, just me! Above me could be the twisted soul of Molock and his favourite son, Abaddon. Gritting my teeth, I vowed that as I had defeated them once, then I could do it again.

I was bathed in light! My wings could extend and I could once more fly. All the voices were with me again and a silver tether stretched behind me all the way back to Ameela and the rest of the Elven Kingdom. I was no longer lost! Purpose once again flooded my soul and I could feel the warmth of my resurrected friends restoring my being. The terrible thing that I had accomplished would stay with me until that day that I would agree to enter of my own free will, that beckoning call. In accepting this I once again swam into sleep and found myself in the company of a young Hildegard.

"Listen to me Long-shadow. It was prophesied long ago that a wingless elf would destroy the Dokka'lfar. The revelation did not say how long it would take! That does not mean that you will be totally successful against this new threat. You will have difficult decisions to make, so assume nothing! You are that Great High King, make no mistake in that, but make the wrong decision and all will not end well. The responsibility rests upon your shoulders and yours alone," Hildegard insisted and was gone.

This time I awoke still with my head in Ameela's lap with

her hands still cupping my forehead. My face was awash with her tears and I realised that she had been with me in my 'dreams,' unable to help me or influence them in any way. She had maintained that connecting thread that I had momentarily lost and had re-forged the link between us and Elven-kind. She lifted my head to the height of her lips and gently kissed me.

"I would not let you go into that place alone, my love. I would not let you go! We are twin souls not to be parted in life or death. These people that you have torn through the veil of the beyond will stand by your side as ever they did in life. What you have given them will not be treated lightly. While you have slept they have been down to the armoury and have been checking out the weapons you stored there centuries ago. Already gnomes have flocked to the berth where the Spellbinder sits to give you mental cover. Goblins have removed certain items from the laboratories and stored them in crash proof cases to be loaded into your ship, should you need them. Other humans have left their studies to join with you and to learn how to operate the weapons, by being trained by Sam Pitts and the others. Give them a week at least before you attempt to track this Dokka'lfar down and to clear your head, my King," Ameela implored and wrapped me in her arms and wings.

Eloen basked in triumph as the Dream-shifter slipped through multiple realities heading for the Earth that her forefathers had plundered eons in the past. The sentient vessel was brim-full of fresh energy and had its receptors extended to catch the power of the sun to add to the storage banks. Fully awake and functioning far better than when Abaddon had driven it into madness the Dream-shifter was hers to command. She listened to her half-brother intently as she began to learn just what this vessel could do. A copy of his mind resided in the memory banks along with aspects of Molock himself. There were other lesser minds that operated mundane tasks within the scope of the ship, but it was the addition of Abaddon that gave the Dream-shifter stability.

They broke through the last rift and floated above a planet that radiated concentrated death from where once great cities had stood. Now vast areas of fused glass covered what had once been the Sahara desert, around a poisoned sea. The Dream-shifter quickly rose well above these deadly areas and hovered for a moment waiting for instructions as Eloen tried to take in the awful destruction that unfurled underneath her. She could see that a long narrow sea had a fused hole that joined a larger sea and separated the continent from the Eastern side. Nothing lived in the lands beneath her or could for many millions of years.

"Dream-shifter, go West," she ordered, "and keep away from anything that looks like these lands beneath us. I can sense nothing here that lives! It is as if my head were encased in iron! This place is no use to me. We must find human beings that have weapons that I can use, that have healthy bodies and some kind of technical civilization."

As the reality-shifting vessel travelled further away from the fused glass area spots of green could be seen and slowly life began to re-appear but not in significant volumes. As the vessel left the coast a chain of islands were volcanically thrusting themselves from the ocean depths and once again the Dream-shifter registered deadly radiation. Eloen stared down at the scene of bubbling lava that was still flowing down to the sea. The volcano had exploded and a vast area had split away from the wall of the caldera and sunk into the sea exposing the heart of the beast. This had to have been engineered by an atomic blast because of the radiation that was still leaking out of the area. It wasn't until she saw what the tsunami that the landslide had produced had done, to the coastline of the continent on the other side of the sea that they were crossing, that she understood.

"What extremes of hatred could have unleashed such desolation?" she thought and quizzed the memory banks of the Dream-shifter to see if it had any information.

She found that there was very little evidence to be gleaned about this world at all, except Abaddon's slaving trips when he gathered humans for the breeding pens. The increasing use of iron made it more and more difficult for the elves to manipulate human beings on Earth so they concentrated all of their efforts to find the Ljo'sa'lfar. The humans had certainly built an extremely technological civilization that in the end had proved to be too much for them to control. The Dokka'lfar had found little use for the advancement of science and had concentrated on the pleasures that a life of complete dominance could provide. It was only the discovery of the incomplete Dream-shifter and the Light Elves escape, which had motivated Molock to press his favourite son to finish the construction of the sentient vessel.

Eloen sat quiet in the command chair as the empty miles of sea was crossed as the Dream-shifter made its way towards the ruins of what had once been the American sea-coast. As the ship tacked northwest she was soon able to see what the nuclear explosion had done when it precipitated the landslide into the deep sea around what had once been the Canary Islands. A wave two hundred feet high had surged over the coastal towns and cities penetrating over twenty miles inland. Then the wave had collapsed and drained back into the ocean carrying with it anything that floated. Only the stumps of what had been skyscrapers remained, covered with rank vegetation after the centuries had passed.

As she passed over the destruction she began to feel life-signs, but with little organisation. What she wanted was some sort of civilization and the further west the Dream-shifter travelled the more organised the survivors seemed to be. Her two 'pressed' slaves still sat quietly on the floor beside her command chair unable to move until she partially released them. They were beginning to smell as their bodily functions continued to work although their minds were still in induced sleep. Eloen had been so immersed in the journey that she had forgotten about them.

"Dream-shifter can you form a shower room and clean these dwarves? Their stink is becoming offensive to me. Also make sure that they are able to drink.

She watched as a new wall sprouted from the floor and formed a cubical against the side of the vessel. Eloen released Hilden and Thorin from their induced sleep. The two dwarves gave a moan of agony as joints that had set needed to flex and they rolled over on their hands and knees. They stared at each other in horror as both of them were caked in filth. They stood unsteadily to their feet and faced their mistress. A rush of hatred filled them as they realised who had done this to them, but Eloen stopped that feeling with a small amount of mental manipulation and replaced it with a feeling of gratitude that they were able to wash. She then sent them into the cubical and the Dream-shifter drenched them in water until all traces of the mess they were in was gone. Their clothes were similarly treated and dried and the vessel absorbed the excrement around the command chair.

Before they had escaped from Peterkin's grasp, there had been enough time to grab plenty of food from the waggons and load it on board. There was also time to strip some of the corpses of their clothes and weapons. These too were added to the Dream-shifter and made available to the passengers.

Eloen made certain that the mind control she had over the dwarves was well in place and they were no danger to her before she too entered the cubical and enjoyed a shower. They could hate her all that they liked, but it was impossible for them to even think of harming her.

"The two of you have a look through the food we loaded on board and prepare me something to eat. If you are quick I may allow you to eat as well," the Halfling stated. "Remember that I am inside your minds at all times, so be careful what you prepare for me!"

The two dwarves obeyed their orders and searched through the hastily looted provisions and found smoked meat, bread, cheese and chutney. Their mouths watered at the sight of the food, but neither of them dared to help themselves before Eloen allowed them to eat. They quickly prepared chunks of bread spread with the pickle and slices of the meat. There were apples as well that were un-bruised as well as some dried fruits.

By the time they returned, Eloen had instructed the Dream-shifter to produce a table close enough to the command chair for her to remain seated and comfortably reach the food. Hilden placed the open bread chunks in front of Eloen while Thorin picked over the best fruit and placed it next to her plate. He had also found some flasks of herbal tea and earthenware mugs to drink from.

Eloen smiled at them and said, "You may eat. You will be no use to me if you are not fed and kept healthy."

The two dwarves stood at the edge of the table and helped themselves to the food that they had prepared, still drying off from the welcome shower. Eloen caused two stools to rise behind them so that they could sit at her table. They gratefully sat down and tried not to eat too fast as both of them knew that to do so would to invite vomiting, after such a long time without food. They both drank plenty of the herbal tea to rehydrate themselves. Their muscles still protested about the length of time they had sat forgotten by the Halfling and they were still subjected to cramps.

"I want the two of you to go through everything that we picked up and loaded onto the Dream-shifter and stow everything away. Check the clothing that you stripped from the bodies of your people to see if it will do for yourselves and have it washed. The ship will make an area available to you to do this. You will find that my vessel will have constructed cupboards to stow things away. If you need anything from it, just ask and it will accommodate you. Now I am going to rest for a while as we travel west to find what traces of civilization are left on this continent," Eloen said and yawned. "One more thing before I sleep! Do not touch the Wand, or it will kill you."

With that said, Eloen instructed the command chair to flatten out so that she could sleep.

Over a thousand miles away from where the Dream-shifter was speeding towards them the community of Twenty-nine Palms Marine Base was totally unaware of the abrupt change that was about to engulf them. These were the descendants of the marines stationed here when the world fell apart. In a world of looting and chaos they had stood firm and had maintained order. With their superior weapons and training they had quickly put down any criminal elements that had cast envious eyes upon the food stocks and farmlands surrounding them. They had only one penalty during those times and that was swift execution of any resistance or looting. Power stations were maintained and food production carried on while all around this enclave, township after township failed. Vital skills were cherished and schools maintained over the centuries that passed. A manufacturing industry was able to turn out what was needed and all metal that was found was dragged into the furnaces and melted down to be stored for future use. Here civilization had stood firm.

Eloen awoke to find that both Hilden and Thorin were fast asleep curled up on the floor next to her command chair. She smiled to herself as she was sure in her own mind that the dwarves conditioning had kept her safe. These two willing fools would sacrifice their own lives to save her; such was the hold that she had on them. Every day that she had contact with her father's Staff of Power her mental powers grew stronger. Her use of the Dream-shifter had triggered something deep inside her mind. The two of them fitted together like a hand in a glove. She cast out her mind to the sentient vessel and contacted the mind of her half-brother.

"Abaddon have you counsel to give on my next task. Is there more that I need to know about how the Dream-shifter works? What protection does the vessel have against outside forces?"

"Great Lady Eloen there is no outside force that can penetrate the walls of this vessel," Abaddon replied. "We cannot be seen unless you wish it. If you step outside the walls of this vessel I can extend my protection around you as long as you have the Staff of Power with you. I am genetically keyed to your person so where you go, I go! I will forever live inside your thoughts to give counsel!"

"Does Peterkin have this same protection with the Spellbinder?" asked Eloen.

"He does."

"How can I kill him?"

"You can't! He is far more powerful than you at the moment," the Dream-shifter replied. "You must seek other ways to have your revenge on him."

Eloen sat and thought about what she could do to exact a

measure of revenge against the High King as the long miles sped below them. Then she smiled and 'called' Hilden to her side.

"Hilden, tell me what you know about the High King and his family," she ordered and with that question ringing inside her mind the dwarfess was powerless to stop the information flowing though her mind.

Within a few minutes Eloen had all she needed to know about Peterkin so she 'called' Thorin to her side and asked him, "Have you been to the castle where the High King lives."

"Yes my Lady. Many times," he replied, struggling to think of something else.

"What weapons does he possess? Tell me what you have seen," she insisted and laughed at the pathetic attempt of resistance that the dwarf tried, to hide his knowledge.

The sweat ran down his face and into his beard as Eloen squeezed his mind for every drop of information about the defences that were in place. To her incredulity there was nothing there except cross-bows. The dwarf had seen nothing else during the visits he had made there. The palace was totally unprotected! He had no knowledge of the weapons that the goblin Jolene had seen used, when Peterkin smashed the Dream-shifter and killed the mortal body of Abaddon. That, she found very interesting and she wondered to herself what had happened to those weapons after all this time. What she did know was that this world had plenty of weapons, as the humans were obsessed by them. As the Dream-shifter travelled along she was increasingly aware that the concentration of human thoughts was becoming more frequent as she travelled west. They passed over a vast canyon situated in the desert still heading west and chasing the sunset.

The terrain began to change as the desert turned into arable land and farms began appearing along with small townships.

Whatever disaster had befallen the planet seemed to have left this area alone. Much of it was intact and what Eloen did not know was that it was under the control of the descendants of the marines stationed at Twenty-nine palms. The one thing that Eloen became sure of was that this was the right area for her to stop. This would make a good temporary base for her to gather what she needed before going on her way.

She brought the Dream-shifter to a stop, hovering over the military establishment and sent her mind out to find out if what she needed was here. It was! Not only was this place well-armed with weapons that she could not easily understand, but was full of young men well versed in the use of them. She picked on one human being that was cleaning his 'rifle' and began to pick up his knowledge of what it did and how simple it was to use! Eloen picked up the names of the weapons and all sorts of other terms that allowed her to see why the rest of the world had so easily been destroyed! From him she learned the command structure of the base and who was the person in sole charge.

Slowly she made the Dream-shifter float over the buildings until she was positioned in front of the main building. Eloen settled the vessel down onto the hard parade ground and increased its size until it was a bubble the size of a football arena. She would keep the Dream-shifter unseen until the morning, then and only then, she would begin the next part of her plan. Now it was time to sleep and rest as she would be very busy when the sun came up.

MOLOCK'S WAND

CHAPTER ELEVEN

As the sun came up, the military base became active. The first thing that was noticed was the strange distortion that sat in front of the building. It was possible to see right through it as if looking through a heat haze. When the first man tried to touch the distortion he was repulsed and fell back onto the ground. He panicked, drew a pistol and cracked off a round that came straight back at him, killing him instantly. Immediately several others fired at the distortion and fell to the ground bleeding from the self-inflicted wounds.

"Stop firing! Whatever goes into that thing comes back in exactly the same vector," an older man shouted. "I think this is an elf-ship! There are records of something like this operating here centuries ago before the Great Fall happened. Do nothing offensive towards it. You there, pick up the wounded and get them attended to."

"Yes Sir, General Price," answered several soldiers and busily picked up the injured men.

"The rest of you put your firearms back in their holsters and wait and see what happens next. Do nothing hostile! Be assured whatever is in that thing can see us and is deciding what to do. If we stand at ease and show no animosity, whoever is inside may come out. Whatever it looks like, do nothing that might be construed as a threat. We are out matched!"

Eloen allowed an hour to go by and the sun to beat down upon the ranks of soldiers before she made her move.

"Dream-shifter, open a portal to the outside world. If any of them makes a move towards their weapons flatten them. The man at the front is the one that I seek. I will go and escort him inside," Eloen ordered and walked through the now visible door.

The men lined, up saw an area in front of them lose its semi-transparent surface and become solid. Through this hole stepped a female humanoid with long dark hair, her ears came to points and her eyes were split just like a cat's. Her height was no more than to the shoulder of any of them. She was slimly built, beautiful to look at and moved with a cat-like grace. She wore a short pleated leather skirt with a loose blouse and knee-high boots. In her hand she carried a wooden shaft, topped with what looked to be a large faceted gem-stone, held in place by a clawed mounting.

Eloen was inside James Price's mind the moment she stepped through the portal and had all of his memories. She found his language very similar to the humans' on Alfheimr.

She stood for a while assessing the information that the general possessed and said, "Follow me!"

As Eloen walked back to the portal, James found that his body had become a puppet operated by the woman in front of him. To his mounting horror he found that he had no choice. The soldiers continued to stand still under the climbing sun not knowing what else to do except obey the last order of their general unaware of his situation. They watched as the portal closed and their commander disappeared from sight. From inside the building came Lieutenant colonel, Curtis Jones. He had just seen his commander walk inside whatever had landed in front of the headquarters with what seemed to be a young woman. He called the soldiers inside and quickly de-briefed them. Three of the men who had fired on the distortion had died from their wounds the others were being patched up and would recover. The lieutenant ordered the men to arm themselves with M 16's and take up positions inside the building facing through the windows, but on no account to shoot unless he ordered them to do so. Faced with nothing to do but wait, they waited!

Inside the Dream-shifter, General Price was astonished at what he could see. The inside of the vessel appeared to be made of a green stone. It was much cooler inside the vessel and the sweat on his body made him feel quite clammy. He found that he now had control of his limbs and could walk about, but the presence of two other strange people made him uneasy. They were not quite human. They had pronounced bony ridges over their eyes and their skulls were longer than what he was used to seeing. Both of them came up to his shoulder and each of them was bearded, although he was sure that one of them was female. The 'elf' if that was what it was, sat confidently in a large green chair holding the staff she had taken outside.

She stuck the pointed end into a socket before the chair and said, "Get the General a drink of water, Thorin. It's quite hot outside and he would be feeling quite uncomfortable."

James turned to Eloen and said, "You speak our language! What are you? What you did to me out there was not the way to make friends."

"It was the easiest way to get out of the heat and I have no time for arguments. As for what I am, let us say that I am just someone that you are going to obey, or a lot of your people will die! There are things that I need and you are going to supply them," she insisted.

The general stared at the diminutive figure in the command chair and asked "What sort of things are you asking for?"

"I want men and weapons! It's quite simple really, General Price and if you do as you are told no-one needs to die just yet," Eloen replied. "Ah here is your drink of cool water. I suggest that you calm your temper and drink. Whatever you feel you might be able to do, I can stop you dead. I can read your mind at any time and at quite a distance, now that we are acquainted. In fact just to be sure I will alter some of your values so you will be a lot more obedient."

General Price became a little dizzy for a few moments and found that the women sat in the chair needed his help. It was of the utmost importance to him, that everything she needed, the military base would supply. He also thought that it would be extremely beneficial for a number of his personal to accompany this great Lady on her travels. He could hardly wait to get outside and give the orders to stock the vessel with what the Lady Eloen wanted, so he quickly drank the cool water provided.

Eloen cast her mind towards the building looking for another mind in charge and connected with Lieutenant colonel, Curtis Jones. She quickly made him receptive to her will and looked through his memories. He would be ideal to select the soldiers that she needed and the weapons they would need. She connected the situation to her captive general and he agreed the decision was excellent. She sent the general outside to organise what she needed and sat back in the command chair.

"Prepare me some food Hilden, while I have some alterations to do with the Dream-shifter."

Abaddon and Eloen reprogrammed the Dream-shifter to produce storage capacity sealed off from the control chair. An entrance formed in front of it and became opaque so that the soldiers could plainly see that part of the ship. In here would be stored the arms and provisions that Eloen's 'mind pressed' army would require. A dormitory was formed next door, capable of housing a hundred men and women.

Over the passing of three days the constantly active military base continued to load the Dream-shifter with arms and provisions. None of the soldiers questioned the orders given by General Price and Lieutenant colonel Jones. The energy requirements of the Dream-shifter exceeded the amount that could be harnessed by the solar collectors so Eloen decided that she would 'tap in' to the recourses available. She loaded the hundred hand-picked men and women into the dormitory and instructed the Dream-shifter to send them to sleep. She then opened a portal into the ship and had the general march a hundred more men and women into her vessel. These souls were absorbed by the Dream-shifter and all of their life-energy stored into the reserves. Crossing into another reality took more energy than could be gathered by sunlight. Abaddon and Molock had not attempted to further design something that worked! Life had been cheap on Alfheimr with plenty of Dokka'lfar at hand to feed the fuel banks. The absorption of so many mindless souls had contributed to the Dream-shifter's insanity and burn-out. The refinements that had been built into the Spellbinder had never been attempted by the Dokka'lfar. Eloen was beginning to understand the workings of the Dream-shifter far better than Abaddon ever did, when he was alive. The fact that a copy of the Dark Lord's mind now controlled the Dream-shifter's functions made her total control much easier to practise. The down-side of her control, was that not being a true elf, she aged a little each time she used the systems. Already the boost she had got from killing the gnome girl was fading away and weariness occasionally showed.

Eloen called to the Dream-shifter, "Isolate two of the women from the inductees and put them in a holding cell. I will join them soon."

The sentient vessel opened a portal into the dormitory and selected two sleeping figures that lay upon the 'sleeping slabs'. The elf-stone began to move and the sleeping women lay very still as the portions of the Dream-shifter moved out of the chamber. Once the slabs were outside of the sleeping quarters they became encased in the green stone walls. The ship stopped the sub-sonic signal that kept the two women asleep and waited for Eloen.

The Halfling had noticed actual wrinkles on her hands and walked quickly to where the Dream-shifter had incarcerated the two women. She was conscious of a great hunger within herself and was quite edgy. She removed all of her clothes and laid them on a tidy heap. As she neared the cell she opened the minds of the two women and paralysed them before she stepped through the wall. They were young and healthy. This was just what she needed to replenish her energy levels. This would not be the first time she had fed on a human and she was going to enjoy the richness of their life-force. She could feel the puzzlement of the two women as they lay immobile on the floor as to what was going to happen to them. Eloen soon showed them.

In full view of the other, the Halfling cut the throat of the dark haired one and filled her stomach with warm blood at the same time as she drank her victim's life-essence. The body of the woman began to shrivel as the very cells gave up every joule of energy. Now the other woman began to scream inside her mind as Eloen reached for her. She feasted on her terror and delicious fear, cradling her head in her hands, purring to herself. The Halfling could make this one last, as her first hunger was sated. Slowly the woman began to weaken and desiccate just as her companion had. Within an ecstatic five minutes she too was dead and Eloen no longer had wrinkles on her hands.

"Dream-shifter, wash me down and appropriate these two creatures into your substance," she ordered.

She was bathed in fresh warm water from the ceiling and was soon clean again. Eloen walked naked through the wall leaving the Dream-shifter to absorb the withered remains of the two women and discard the bloody clothing to the outside.

Eloen connected to Hilden and Thorin ordered them to sleep while she made her way back to the command chair. Now that her body once again shone with health she could take the next step in her obsession for revenge. Her mind was invigorated by the excellent nourishment that she had taken and she could think clearly again.

It was time to journey to Alfheimr and take the next step.

"Dream-shifter take us home," she ordered and the distortion disappeared from in front of the military compound.

Peterkin sat at the round table in front of the twin thrones and listened to his friends' reports about the weapons he had asked them to put in storage centuries ago.

Sam Pitts laid an M 16 rifle on the table. He had cleaned and tested the rifle along with many others. The six of them had recovered the entire ordinance that they had all carefully packed away. A crash course on operating these instruments of death had been given to all the various beings that were coming with them. It does not take very long to learn how to operate an AK 47. Accuracy with rifles like the M16 take a little longer. Mellitus was quite happy to get his hands on his beloved Kalashnikov, as close up, he felt that this gun would do what was necessary. His grandson and Thorinson had agreed with his logic and soon were able to use one as well as him.

"We have checked out all of the weapons that we may need," Sam insisted, "and I think that any more training is wasted time. I am sure that everything we may need has been loaded onto the Spellbinder and it is time to go!"

John Smith, my scientific friend who had altered many things inside the castle with the use of solar panels that supplied electrical power, then took the floor.

"My descendants have developed a means to follow a warp in reality through the rifts. The Spellbinder and the Dream-shifter leave tiny distortions in space-time that remains for some time. If we take the Spellbinder back to where Eloen disappeared with her ship, my operators are sure that we can track her from there. If we connect their minds to the Spellbinder through you they say it should work," John insisted. "We should go now while the trail is still there. It will be far easier to follow her than to try and find where she has gone by going straight to the Earth and looking for her there."

I laid my hands upon the Staff of Power and asked, "Spellbinder, are we all set? Is everything loaded on board that we may need?"

"This mission needs to be 'go,' High King," the sentient ship replied. "Let us be on our way. I am eager to meet the Dream-shifter and to put down this last of the Dokka'lfar."

There was a murmur of assent from the minds of the Kings that I carried.

"Very well gentlemen, let us get on our way. Everyone get on board and let us hope that all of us will return!"

We made our way into the Spellbinder and I inserted the Staff of Power into the socket and we disengaged from the castle. Our fuel cells were filled by solar energy that the ship had been collecting for days. It had also tapped into the life-force of all those living in and around the castle. Taking such a small percentage from the elves, goblins and gnomes did not leave them depleted of very much energy, as their life-spans were very similar to ours. Ameela stood behind my chair and placed her hands upon my shoulders. Eduardo and Calando also placed their hands upon hers and we merged with the Spellbinder. Now the combined entity rose high in the sky and hurtled towards the crater's rim, aiming for the departure point of the Dream-shifter.

I sought a rift and opened it. Everything outside became that place you could not see and we flipped out, over the hole that the dwarves had dug under the lash of Eloen's will. We hovered over the hole while John and his 'students' operated the seeking console sifting through the realities for a trace. John's mind connected with the gestalt and pointed the way. Again I sought the correct rift and closed Haven's reality behind us. I had never asked so much from the Spellbinder as now and we brutally bullied our way through a dozen rifts, emerging over a land of fused glass. The ship elevated high above the radioactive area and we all looked down in horror.

Sam was the first to find his voice and said, "The whole of the Arabian states including Israel has vanished! Africa is now separate from the rest of the Middle East. All I can see down there is what was once molten glass. This had not happened when we were alive! Did you know about this Peterkin?"

"I knew," I sadly replied. "There was nothing that the elves could do to stop the madness. I have not been back here since what your people called 'The Great Fall' occurred. We rescued what we could and I became so afraid of the damage to the Spellbinder that I declared the Earth to be out of bounds. There was so much to do, re-settling Alfheimr and Haven that I had to economise and leave the Earth to find its own way to ruin or salvation. Now John, in what direction do we go to pick up Eloen's trail?"

"Due west," he replied. "Chase the setting sun."

Once again we joined our minds to the Spellbinder and forced it to accelerate beyond its designed capability. As we passed over what had once been the Canary Islands we could plainly see what had happened, as once more, radiation poured upwards from the volcano that was still erupting beneath us.

There was a collective stifled sob from my friends as they realised what had been done here. A vast chunk of crater wall had been purposely blown into the sea. It had been known for some time that the tsunami generated from this land-slip would devastate the eastern coast of both North and South America. Someone had deliberately detonated an atomic device to cause this. The damage would have travelled northwards as well, swamping the coast of Europe and the British Isles. I could feel relief that not enough ash had been sent up into the air to generate a nuclear winter!

Once again we flew on over the Atlantic Sea, towards what my friends knew would be a destruction path that would have drowned every seacoast city along that shore. Sure enough we soon approached the demolished skyscrapers and the rank vegetation that had soon reclaimed what civilization had built. The sea had reached over eighty miles in places, into the interior. There were no signs of intelligent life to be seen. As mile after mile flashed by, with the Spellbinder travelling at beyond its safe limits I began to wonder what we would find on the west coastal areas. It was ironic that we were heading towards what had been Los Angeles where I had first made contact with humans. I had got to like that area of this planet and I knew that all six of my friends had lived there before I took them away to rescue Ameela and Mia. They had chosen to live on Haven until their death and had never returned to the world of their birth.

I had been with each of them when old age had finally

taken its toll. I had caught their last breath and felt the passing of each personality from my mind's embrace. Each death had cost me greatly and I personally interred their bones after all the flesh had been eaten away by maggots and beetles in the crypt. Never did I think to see them ever again, except perhaps in dreams or that place beyond life. I had 'called' them and they came. They were far more than friends to me! Now, my blood pulsed in their veins and the very cells that made up their flesh were copied from mine and blended with their own. They had become my Halflings and more like my children to me. They were the children of the Spellbinder too and were bound to it.

We passed over the Colorado canyon with the sun now high in the sky as we had caught up with the passing hours. Now we could see signs of life as the dessert gave way to the mountains and on the other side lay California. The instruments continued to track Eloen's movement towards what appeared to be a military base some miles out from Los Angeles. It was here that the trail finished on this world and I bid the Spellbinder stop.

It was early afternoon and yet the place seemed deserted, but we got the impression that we were being watched by fearful eyes. We four elves separated from the gestalt and released the Spellbinder from our insistent need for speed. Sam Pitts and his men had got the Spellbinder to create a military uniform for each of them so that the humans here would feel that there was order. At this point we had little idea of what Eloen had subjected these people too and wanted to defuse the situation as far as possible.

Just to be sure, I made the Spellbinder extend a bubble of protection in front of us and Sam and the twins walked out of the portal that I opened. They walked forward and stood at ease without weapons waiting for a response. I made the entire Spellbinder visible so that the men and women inside the building would perhaps feel more at ease. Several minutes ticked by until the main doors swung open and a number of well-armed soldiers stepped out in formation with an older man at the front.

He held his hands up and wide and said, "You're the second elf-ship that has come our way. I'm begging you please don't kill any more of my people!"

I could feel his fear of the consequences from inside the Spellbinder and in moments I had the whole evil story in my mind. The responsibility I felt due to her actions shrivelled my soul. While I was shuddering over the deaths that she had used as fuel for the Dream-shifter, Sam had stepped forwards and had given the General a salute. Slightly behind him the twins did the same and the situation mellowed somewhat.

"You may come aboard sir and meet my superior officer. He would like to de-brief you. Please feel free to bring your men with you. What you have encountered was not a Ljo'sa'lfar vessel, but an abomination run by a rouge Dokka'lfar. You may bring your weapons with you, but be prepared to see things that are far more different than anything in your experience," Sam instructed. "I would advise you all to make sure all safeties are on as we do not need any more accidents!"

General Price turned and barked the order, "Company, disarm! Company, follow me into the vessel." He stared into Sam's strange eyes, noting the pointed ears and said, "We have learnt to our cost that our weapons are no match for an elf's mind. All I can hope for is that your leader is not like the creature that was here a few days ago."

"General Price I can assure you that the elf you are going to meet is far more different than Eloen could ever be. He is the High King of the whole Elven Kingdom and he cares about every soul willingly under his command," Sam declared and led the general into an amazing wonderland.

The inside of the Spellbinder that the humans could see, looked like a great hall with a round table, surrounded by seats of different heights. Sat down were achingly beautiful creatures that were winged and had to be elves. Sat with them were much shorter beings that had beards, pointed ears and the cat's eyes that the elves had. Seated with them were skinny green skinned people with long spidery hands whose ears and eyes were just the same as the elves. In amongst these sat what the general had seen only in prehistory books; they had to be Neanderthal men.

I left my seat and walked towards him. He could see that I was nothing like Eloen and a different creature altogether. I spread my wings and let him see the shimmering gold feathers that gave me the power of flight as did my elfin companions as they too stood for a moment. We folded them behind our backs and tucked them away. He looked in awe at the sight of us and I held out a six fingered hand clasping the general's in mine.

"General Price, welcome to the Spellbinder," I said and led him to a chair. "My name is Peterkin and I am the High King of the Elven Kingdoms. I just wish that it were better circumstances. Tell my people what has happened here. Later I will introduce you, but first things first. Tell us all about the atrocities conducted by the Halfling and then I will tell you a little of the history that has brought us here."

As the general talked, those of us that could read minds suffered to see the awful pictures of Eloen's depredation of this peacekeeping base. It was when the general reached the point of departure and the discovery of the one hundred uniforms that the Dream-shifter had discarded when it left, I bid him to stop.

"My heart is full of sorrow General Price at what has been done here to you and your people. You have suffered the indignity of being 'pressed' and controlled like a puppet! The people that she took will have had their minds altered and would gladly die serving her whims. I know that you will not feel that you can trust me, but I must assure you that you can. I am going to enter your mind and give you an edited set of memories so that you can understand what has happened here and many years ago.

With that, I gave him the terrible story of the conflict between the Ljo'sa'lfar and the mutant race that sprung from one 'Dark' elf, producing the Dokka'lfar.

After he had sat quietly and assimilated this information he asked, "The people that left their uniforms behind when the Dream-shifter disappeared. Is there no hope for them?"

"None," I replied.

MOLOCK'S WAND

CHAPTER TWELVE

The General sagged in his seat as I passed on the awful fact.

"The Dokka'lfar have no concept of compassion and look upon all life as something to be used and discarded when it suits them. They are pure hedonists and completely selfish. My ancestors found it easier to leave them on the home-world and move on, rather than do what was unthinkable for them and that was to fight back, committing violence. My family line has that ability and I took the decisions that wiped them out, or so I thought. One survived! She is a Halfling hybrid born of Molock's line and a human woman. That is why she survived the virus that destroyed so many of the Dokka'lfar. She is clever and resourceful and managed to stowaway on this ship, by murdering a young gnome and keeping her mind alive inside hers. Gnomes have fuzzy minds and can shield their thoughts from elves. I carried her to Haven where the ship she now travels in, was turned into debris by my people. She made it to the site of that destructive battle and made the dwarves dig up the Staff of Power. Once she had that Wand in her hands, she drew the Dream-shifter back together, using the very life energy of those who retrieved it for her. She has two of them with her to be her servants," I explained to General Price.

"I met these two people when I came aboard. One was

called Thorin and the other was called Hilden," the human said.

Thorinson stood away from the table and gasped, "They are alive! Those two people are my mother and father. Were they well?"

The General shrugged and replied, "As far as I could see they were, but they were her willing servants and I have no doubt after what your King has said, that they are completely in her power."

Thorinson became ashen faced when he heard that news and he sat heavily down at my conference table. He put his head into his hands and visibly struggled to contain his emotions.

General Price turned to me and asked, "This ability to control minds. Do all elves share this?"

"They do," I answered.

"Then if you can do that, what proof do I have that you are not controlling me and what I see is what you want me to see?"

"That comes down to a matter of trust," I replied. "You are free to go as you please from the Spellbinder and none would stop you from leaving. The Ljo'sa'lfar have a strict code of ethics that binds us to the people that we both serve and rule. I administrate over two parallel Earths and am doing my best to re-settle many very different people on both. These men you see before you aided me at my time of need and are my friends and advisers. They are not elves, but human-elf hybrids and no, I will not explain any more, other than to say listen to them. They will tell you about what we had to do over two centuries ago."

John approached the General carrying a small box with a switch on the top and put it down in front of him.

"This is both a beacon and an alarm. All you have to do is

to make sure that it is left in sunlight for a few hours a day and it will continue to put out a signal that we can home in to, should Eloen return. Flick the switch and it will alert us to her presence here or if you are in need. We will come," John insisted and returned to his seat.

I rapped on the table to get the General's attention and said, "There is one resource that I am short of General Price and that is well trained soldiers. The problem will be that the men that Eloen took will be conditioned to fight for her. That means that your men will have to be willing to kill their friends as they will have no compunctions about killing them! Will you give this some thought before we go? It must be quick, for every hour I spend here means that she is further away and closer to what she will do."

"How many soldiers do you need?" the General asked.

"As many as you can spare. And yes General Price, I would be honoured if you would accompany us and lead your soldiers," I replied. "As for the beacon I suggest you leave with instructions to your next in commend, just in case you do not return!"

"I must leave a peace-keeping force behind sufficient to carry on if we do not return, as many hungry eyes stare down at Los Angeles and the territories that we control. I can bring with me at least two hundred without putting the base at risk and I have another lieutenant colonel that will fit the bill. Let me go back with my men and I will organise an ordinance drop into this vessel. I have no doubt that you will be able to accommodate what I will bring back," James Price answered and rose from the chair.

"There is one more thing that I must ask of you my friend and that is to enter your mind to look for something that I might need."

The General flinched but he nodded to me and I slipped

into his mind. I quickly scanned his memories about the weapons capability and found what I was looking for.

"Bring it, but bring it hidden," I projected into his mind.

He stared at me and his face went white as he comprehended the lengths that I would go.

Still in his mind I said, "It is part of being High King, elf-friend James. The responsibility is always mine," and I let him go.

I spent the next few hours altering the Spellbinder to accommodate our new guests and keep them comfortable. We constructed a storage facility to keep the weapons safe and instantly obtainable. The next thing we did was to set up a low temperature stockpile of perishable foodstuffs along with other rations.

My dependable John Smith took over the loading of the device that was my ultimate chess piece along with the control system that it needed. Hoatzin and Spencer soon made themselves known to the descendants of the Marines who had maintained law and order during the 'Fall.' They told them a little of the elf worlds where settlements had been made and the fact that they were parallel worlds to the Earth that they knew. The main thing that was different was the vastly different histories on both worlds and the creatures that had evolved there. When they were told about the fire and tool using Velociraptors that had aided in the destruction of the Dokka'lfar they were amazed. My re-stocking of the home world Alfheimr with dinosaurs from Haven and the many uses that they were put to made them look at me with astonishment. The question that they all asked was, how?

There were some things that I deemed were on a need-to-know basis. The adaptability of the Spellbinder was something that I was not too keen for them to know, just in case any of them found themselves under Eloen's brutal mind probe. The less she could know about the parallel secrets of the Dream-shifter, the less able she would be.

The sun had begun to set and darkness deepened the area in shadows as the soldiers continued to load on board supplies. Some of the electronic control systems were spirited away by the goblins on board and stripped down to the basic parts. They reassembled the parts, blending them with some of the equipment that was taken from the laboratories from the castle on Haven.

I knew better than to ask what they were up to, as when they were content with the results of their labour I would be told. Goblins have always had a far more inquiring nature than elves and have delved into strange places. It was a goblin called Lilliant that discovered the rifts that led to the parallel worlds. It was his association with Deedlit that eventually led to the construction of the early Spellbinder. Both of them had merged their minds with the consciousness that they had woven into sentience. Now there were the minds of the long dead High Kings also blended into the mix. I knew that when I died a copy of my essence would also enter the mix, as both an individual and part of the blend. It was my connection to the Spellbinder that gave me access to the memories and advice of those that had been its master, but it was far more than that. I had become accustomed to the voices of the Kings and I needed that council at this moment.

I called them to me now, Freyr, Auberon, Elweard and Peter, my father, all swam uppermost into my mind.

"The instruments say that she has gone to Alfheimr. Where on that world would she go? That is the question that nags at my mind. Unlike Molock who was aggressively male, she cannot spread her progeny throughout the kingdoms." I asked the long dead minds, "What is it that she wants?"

My four descendants mulled over the problem and then my father spoke to me and said, "I did not rule the elven kingdom, so I have not grown up in the disciplines of kingship. I think that she is not motivated by the urge for power as were Molock and his favourite son, Abaddon. I believe that what she wants is revenge. So think, Peterkin, about what exists on the home-world that is of spiritual value to you."

"My son, Elthred and my mother are settled there at the castle we called Homecoming. They are re-building on the ruins of our old central home. Also Mia is there working on a settlement on the other side of the world. That's where we will have to go, but what about the trail that the Dream-shifter leaves? If we do not stay on it and she goes somewhere else we could lose the scent! Also there is the fact that wherever she travels the Halfling will do unspeakable harm. We must know what she does and the reasons behind it."

Eloen sat back in the command chair and relaxed, attended by her two loyal dwarves. She had discovered all manner of sweets in the stores that the humans had loaded on board and had for the first time tasted chocolate that had been hoarded over the years in deep freeze. All kinds of sugary cakes had also been stored and she found that she enjoyed them all. She found it difficult to ration herself when there was so much to choose from. It was the same problem after the taking of the two women's souls. After a while she felt the hunger again and fought against the soaring need. The Dream-shifter was carrying a heavy load and the knock-on effect was that the ship was drawing on her life-force.

Suddenly they were through the last rift and New London appeared beneath them. Immediately the hunger subsided and she felt much better.

She 'called' for Lieutenant colonel Jones and he appeared at her elbow.

"When we touch down I want you to take your men and capture as many gnomes that you can find. Kill anyone who resists except for the gnomes. I want them alive! I have a space reserved for them once you can get them aboard. Should you manage to lay hands on a winged elf, bring it to me alive! Wound it if you must, but do not damage the creature beyond incapacitating him or her," Eloen insisted and daintily scrunched up another small cake.

Once the Dream-shifter landed on the grassy area kept for the comings and goings of the Spellbinder a crowd quickly gathered. Eloen opened the Dream-shifter and her 'loyal' troops marched down the ramp onto the green.

Lieutenant colonel Jones was flanked by his men who stood at the ready and called out to the puzzled crowd, "We have come here to take on board gnomes. You will either fetch them here or tell us where to look for them or I will shoot some of you to show we mean business."

There were incredulous murmurings from the people gathered round and a man stood forth from the crowd and answered, "What are you doing here and what do you want with the gnomes?"

"I'm not here to answer your questions! You are here to answer mine," the Lieutenant replied. "Shoot him in the leg, sergeant Peters."

There was a crack of pistol fire and the man went down clutching his leg in agony.

"Corporal Smith, take hold of that young girl and put your pistol to her head," the Lieutenant ordered. "Blow her brains out at my command."

Several gnomes pushed their way to the front and stood in front of the now terrified girl, who had been forced to her knees.

"Please stop this! We will come with you and do whatever you want. I will stay here and my brother will run into town and call the rest of my people to come here. You have my word that there will be no trouble or resistance," the old gnome implored.

Eloen chose that moment to make her appearance and the old Gnome sagged at his knees when he saw her.

"You were here when my granddaughter died in the mill-race," he said.

"Hello, Master Hewit, we meet again. I have need of your people, so gather them up and direct them to enter the Dreamshifter. Yes old man it is the Dokka'lfar ship and your granddaughter helped me to find it. You can answer a question for me while your people gather. Are there any elves here? Do not think that they can interfere if they are, because each of my armed men wears iron around their necks and cannot be controlled."

"You can go back to whatever hell you sprang from," Hewit replied.

"Blow her brains out, Corporal Smith," Eloen answered.

There was a sharp crack and blood and bone shot out of the back of the young girl's head and she dropped to the grass.

"Pick another," Eloen ordered, "from the children that are gathered here."

Without question the soldiers pushed into the crowd and grabbed another three children and brought them in front of Eloen for her to choose.

The elderly gnome fell to his knees in horror and grasped onto the long blades of grass for support.

"Do as she says," he cried. "Don't give her the excuse to kill a child!"

The inhabitants of New London had never experienced such savagery and were frozen in place terrified of the consequences of moving. Only Hewit's brother, ran into the town as fast as his short legs could carry him. He was not gone very long when a procession of gnomes made their terrified way to the Dream-shifter. Walking with them was a white haired Ljo'sa'lfar leaning onto a carved stick made from ironwood.

Eloen smiled and said, "What is your name? If you do not do exactly as I command, you will be responsible for the deaths of these human children."

"My name is Nekadien. I will do as you ask. I see you wear the iron as do your soldiers so I cannot coerce you in any way. Please release the children unharmed," the elf replied. "I can do you no harm, so what would you gain in hurting them?"

"Lieutenant Jones, collar this winged freak with iron and chain him to one of your men so that he cannot wander off," Eloen ordered. She looked at the group of gnomes assembled before her and continued, "Sort the gnomes out and leave the old ones here. Keep the ones that still have colour in their hair and discard the rest. I want a mix of male and female gnomes that can still breed. If they have children with them, take them as well."

Eloen's 'pressed' soldiers rapidly sorted out the younger gnomes from the older ones and shepherded them on board the Dream-shifter. Having seen what happens to anyone that protested, the crowd remained resentfully quiet, nursing their grief.

Inside the mind of Lieutenant colonel Jones there was turmoil, as he unhesitatingly carried out any of Eloen's orders. Any thoughts of disobedience were rewarded with an intense migraine pain that made him sweat and want to vomit. She had complete control of him and with his troops. Every time Curtis carried out her orders he was satisfied with a thrill of pleasure. The more time that passed, the more conditioned he became and his will weakened.

Once she got the gnomes and her soldiers on board, she turned her attentions to the elder Ljo'sa'lfar.

"Dream-shifter, prepare a restraint chair for my guest," she ordered.

The fabric of the ship rose opposite her command chair and became a seat with snap action manacles at wrists and feet. Eloen forced Nekadien back into the chair's embrace and allowed the chains to be released from the human.

"Allow your people to eat and rest lieutenant, by returning to your quarters. The Dream-shifter will administer to your needs. When they are satisfied you will all be put into a deep sleep to await my next need of your services," the Halfling declared and turned to look at the elf restrained by the chair.

Nekadien stared at Eloen with puzzlement and asked, "What manner of elf are you? You are certainly not truly Ljo'sa'lfar or Dokka'lfar. Yet you have some of the attributes of both!"

"My mother was human and my father was the great Molock himself. I am a Halfling, Nekadien, but in heart I can assure you I am pure Dokka'lfar! I intend to have my revenge on your High King, Peterkin and I will make him suffer."

"Why? Can you not see that there is all around you a far better world now that those diseased kindred of yours are all gone? Can you not take a part in it and forsake this idea of revenge? How many lives have you taken to get this far, besides the one you took outside this abomination? It is still not too late to turn your back on this foolish enterprise," the elf replied.

Eloen's answer was to slap his face so hard that it split his lip and drew blood. She followed it up with a punch to the side of his ear that filled his eyes with tears.

"Now listen carefully and listen well. Peterkin's son is here on this world. You are going to tell me where! I want the location of the castle that he is building that they call Homecoming, for that is where he is."

Immediately Eloen entered his mind with Abaddon's backup with all the finesse of a mental sledgehammer. The two minds peeled apart all the defences that Nekadien tried to put in place. Each time they prised apart a block they seared it open so that it could not shut behind them. Bit by bit they hammered and stretched until everything that the elder elf knew lay before them. Nekadien's mind was broken and he sat soaked in vomit and faeces, dribbling down his blouse. He had been here on Alfheimr when Molock's hoards had driven the Ljo'sa'lfar to leave this world and flee. Now Eloen cupped his forehead in her hands and drained him of every drop of his life-force.

"Absorb him, Dream-shifter and take us to the castle," ordered the Halfling. "Hilden, get rid of his clothes. I need to take a shower while we travel to the next stop. This has been a good day!"

The Dream-shifter became a distortion in the air above the grassy landing spot and disappeared after it had spent a little time dropping some of the cargo that Lieutenant Jones's men had loaded on board. Fire took hold amongst the stone and wooden buildings. People began to form bucket chains from the river to try and put out the fires.

Once the fires had been put out, only now did the people react to Eloen's visit. Gnomes and humans gathered together in their grief over the young girl's death. The man who had questioned her was carried off to the hospital to have the bullet removed from his leg while the parents of the three children that the soldiers had taken stood paralysed with fear. It would be some time before New London recovered from this day.

I decided to follow the trail left behind the Dream-shifter in the knowledge that I might have to undo some of the harm that may have been doled out by her Dokka'lfar methods. Once again the elves on board joined minds to give the Spellbinder that extra turn of speed. We ripped through the rifts at breakneck speed and shot out of the sky above New London and looked down on desolation! It was dawn and we were by my estimate three days behind her, but I was honour bound to stop! These were my people and judging by the fire damage, they needed my help.

Sam Pitts stood at my side and said, "That's explosives damage, Peterkin. Look at the way that the buildings have been torn apart. This is pure malicious destruction! Why would she come here? What would this re-built town have to offer her?"

"There only one way to find out, my friend. Spellbinder, take us down," I ordered.

When we sat down on the grassy landing spot there were no welcoming crowd, but we knew that we were being watched. I could feel the aura of fear and apprehension spreading out over the field.

Eduardo placed his hand upon my shoulder and insisted, "I will go outside with Calando and we will extend our wings so that the people can see that we are not Dokka'lfar. No arguments High King, you must stay safe."

I could see the strength of the reasoning and opened the Spellbinder to its ancient home. The moment that I did this, the smell of the still smouldering town hit the nostrils like a blow.

I heard Hoatzin mutter to himself, "Phosphorous and napalm! No wonder it still stinks!"

As my two loyal officers walked down the ramp with wings extended a shift in the mental atmosphere became apparent. People were exiting buildings, still carrying cross-bows, but no longer cocked. Several gnomes pushed their way to the front of the gathering crowd and made their way towards the Spellbinder. In the lead was a face that I knew well.

I stood and made my way down the ramp towards him, "Master Hewit, what has happened here. Come into the Spellbinder and unburden yourself to me. I fear that much evil has been done."

"Indeed High King," the old gnome said, "Truly, much evil has been done. I will make my mind clear and you must look inside."

I knelt before him and placed my hands each side of his forehead and looked at the terrible memories that he bore. I saw his great, great granddaughter brought out of the mill-race and laid upon the grass. This was done by the very creature that had killed her living body and stolen her mind to hide beneath. Then everything else came tumbling out and I saw Eloen's reason for coming here. She would hide herself from my superior mind-skills by surrounding herself with gnomes. She needed to be able to remove her iron collar to operate her own mental skills, but on who? Then I saw the elder Ljo'sa'lfar Nekadien, led in chains into the Dream-shifter. I knew deep inside me that he would not be able to resist the combined power of Eloen and her half-brother, Abaddon, linked with the ship. They would now know where Homecoming was located, in the vast mountain ranges of Earth called Sierra de Guadarrama in Spain. This had been the ancestral home of the Ljo'sa'lfar for hundreds of thousands of years. The Dokka'lfar had driven out Freyr and my people and had destroyed much of what had been built. They had no eye for beauty and were driven by one thing only; dominance and hunger!

I dropped my hands away from the old gnome's forehead and said, "Master Hewit, you have suffered much, along with this new town. I am afraid to tell you that I have no easy answers for you and all who dwell here. This day had passed badly and if I do not succeed in stopping this abomination she will return and take what she wants. Those people that she came with have been mentally altered to defend her at all costs and do her bidding no matter what she asks of them. These humans that have accompanied us to this place in pursuit know well enough that they will have to kill people that were once their friends. So do not feel that you sorrow on your own!"

I shook the old gnome's hands and walked back inside the Spellbinder. Inside my living ship I sat heavily down into the command chair and one thought dominated my mind. She was already there at Homecoming. Whatever she had decided to do was already done and revenge was her one driving force. My mother and my son were living at the rebuilding of that ancient castle. With a ship full of gnomes they would have no idea or warning of her approach.

MOLOCK'S WAND

CHAPTER THIRTEEN

Eloen sent the Dream-shifter back across the sea towards what would have been Spain on the human Earth. She had the ship send to sleep all of the soldiers on board, but left the gnomes awake in the large cell she had prepared for them. The floor was tipped enough that no matter what they tried they could not get comfortable enough for all of them to sleep except for a few bed spaces that were level. This gave their minds little rest and filled them with anxiety. She had kept the lieutenant awake to study his knowledge of warfare and to see what she could learn from him.

What military campaigns had been carried out to ensure peace-keeping, had ranged far and wide around the area around Los Angeles. They avoided the radioactive remains of the city that was placed about one-hundred and forty miles from the base. Fortunately the day that the guided missile fell on the city, the prevailing wind was off-shore due to a hurricane that had torn across the country, due to the freak weather conditions caused by the conflict. It had been the last of the limited nuclear arsenal possessed by the terrorists. The return strike had totally destroyed whatever capability they had acquired. Nothing lived there now.

Elthred had felt uneasy for several days, as he oversaw the work that was going on, restoring the ancient castle that they had re-named Homecoming. His grandmother, Dawn, had mentioned the evening before, that there was an air of ominous expectancy that hung just out of reach. Even the goblins that were working on the restoration had said that they felt uneasy. It was as if hidden eyes were watching their every move. In the last hundred and fifty years the work had gone on at an unhurried rate with an elfin eye for ascetic detail keeping the work on track. Saplings had been planted, grown, harvested and cured into oaken planks and the process was still going on at this time. The old road to the castle had been repaired so that the loads could be more easily lifted and transported by waggon or sled. The heavy hauling had been done by iguanodons fully thirty feet long and massing ten-thousand pounds. The elves found that were easy to control and very docile. The young ones were very good eating and so were the eggs, so that evening, the two members of Peterkin's family sat at their table eating an egg salad with smoked meats, along with a mixture of other elves, goblins and gnomes.

Peterkin's mother and son were sat at one end of the long table watching the sun go down, waiting for the food to be dished up by the castle gnomes. The smell of fresh baked bread hung in the air. All looked normal, but there was still an aura of unease that seemed to intensify by the hour. The gnomes kept looking about the hall as if there were something just out of sight that was putting them off their food and gnomes were well known for a good appetite.

Elthred turned to his grandmother and asked, "Do you still have that strange feeling that we are being watched? I have probed the inside and outside of the walls of this castle with my mind and I can feel nothing," he said and continued to eat his salad.

Dawn put down her fork and concentrated her mind to pick up anything odd that would make sense of her grandson's uneasiness. She met a wall of gnomish fog! A strange emotion of excess misery flooded her mind and she shut down her receptivity.

"Elthred, I am more than uneasy," she said. "There is something wrong and it is here, quite close."

The hall that they were eating the evening meal in was well attended by goblins, elves and gnomes. There were also a large group of human carpenters and masons that were working alongside the Alfheimr people. It had a panoramic view over the countryside and had the usual parapet that would allow the elves to come and go by wing as they pleased. Suddenly a great darkness enveloped the hall as the Dream-shifter anchored itself to the edge of the parapet, cutting off the outside sunlight. Solar panels fed more energy into the lighting system, triggered off by the absence of light. At the same time forty, well-armed soldiers ran out of the Dream-shifter and took up a horseshoe position around the hall with weapons pointing inwards.

Dawn recognised the guns for what they were and shouted out, "Stay in your seats and do nothing to aggravate the situation."

An elflike female carrying a 'Staff of Power' emerged from behind the soldiers and stared thoughtfully at her. It was obvious to the elves that she was wingless and slightly different to them as she had no antennae on her forehead. She was dressed the same way as her soldiers in green and brown, camouflage battle-dress. Her raven black hair was cut at shoulder length and she carried an obsidian knife hanging from a sheath around her neck.

"Very sensible," remarked Eloen, as she walked over to them. "And who might you be?"

Dawn saw that every man and woman wore an iron collar around their necks as did the strange elf-like creature before her. There would be no mental coercion possible against this force.

Elthred slowly stood with his hands held above his head and replied, "This lady is my grandmother, 'The Silver Dawning Light' and I am the High King's son. What do you want here?"

"Collar him and the elf-queen and take them to the entrance of the Dream-shifter," Eloen ordered. She waited until they were behind her and gave the next order, "Shoot the rest of them. Leave none of them alive."

True to Eloen's directive the soldiers opened fire with automatic weapons until there was no movement to be seen. Those that ran from the table were soon dropped to the floor by a burst of automatic fire. Anyone still alive after the first discharge was shot in the head at close range.

"Block the doors and barricade them shut," she ordered. Set the charges so that this hall is sealed in from the inside of the castle."

Both Dawn and Elthred stood paralyzed with horror at the carnage that had taken place so quickly. They were both swathed in chains and handcuffs that had been looted from the marine base and could do nothing, but stand and wait for the Halfling's next move. There were several muffled explosions from the doors and the masonry collapsed, sealing off the hall from within. The Halfling approached the table and sat on the edge looking at the carnage that her visit had left behind. She helped herself to the remains of the evening meal and gestured to her soldiers to help themselves to whatever they wanted.

Eloen gave a throaty chuckle as she smoothed the blood from the face of one of the fallen elves and licked her fingers clean. She walked around the table and looked closely at the body count. Her raven dark hair swirled about her shoulders as she bent forward to stare into each dead face making sure that there were no survivors. Eventually she did the circuit of the hall and stood in front of the only two beings left alive that had sat and ate here, only a short while before.

She looked into their eyes and said, "One of you is staying here and one of you will come with me! Oh don't worry; I shall not leave you here alone, mother of Peterkin. You will have company while you wait for your son to arrive, but he will have a fight on his hands when he gets here. I shall leave some of my people behind to make it as difficult as possible for him to rescue you!"

She turned from the two elves and pointed at the carved panels at the back of the hall.

"Sargent, you and those men, strip her naked and drag her over to that wall. Stand her on that bench and hold her tightly against the panels. Use the iron nails to pin her to the wall and spread her wings wide to help carry her weight. Make sure that you miss her arteries. I do not want her to bleed to death."

Elthred struggled in his chains and shouted at Eloen, "Leave her alone. If you have to do this, do it to me, not her!"

Eloen whirled round and slapped him around his face hard enough to draw blood from his nose. The soldiers holding his chains pulled him to the floor and stood on the loose chains to hold him still; while Dawn had her clothes ripped from her body and was dragged across the room, struggling to get free. They spread-eagled her against the wall, hoisting her upon the bench and nailed her through the wrists and her wing-joints to the carved panelling like a giant butterfly in a display case.

She watched the High King's mother wriggling about on the spikes as she tried to take the weight of her body on her legs and feet by pushing up from the bench and smiled.

Eloen pointed at the men who had nailed her to the panel

and said, "You will stay here and make it as difficult as you can for Peterkin to rescue his mother. Shoot any elf that tries to get in from outside. Do not kill him and do not allow his mother to die. Make sure that she lasts and give her water at least once a day. Once we have left this place, take off her iron collar, but make sure that yours are secure. Now then, drag this one inside the Dream-shifter and tether him into the restraint chair that will be provided."

With that Eloen turned away from the Peterkin's mother and led the way back into the ship. The Sargent watched the Dream-shifter become a distortion and then disappear from view. He walked over to the chair that Dawn was stood upon and climbed up to face her so that he could undo the iron collar. Even in her agony, she spat into his face and was rewarded by an open handed slap that made her hang on the nails, making her scream.

"Be thankful I have left you the bench to stand on," he said and squeezed her breast as he got down. "Take up defensive positions men and sell your lives dearly. I think we will soon see action now that she can cry for help! We die for Eloen!"

Dawn concentrated her mind and sent a telepathic shout clear across the world to New London where Peterkin had parked the Spellbinder and was clearing up the damage left by Eloen's visit.

It was several days after we got there that the damage that Eloen had done was under control and I was anxious to make my way to where I knew she had gone to. When it came, my mother's anguished mental cry reverberated through my skull. The pain that she was enduring, we both instantly knew would have to continue until I could set her free. I was at least a day's travel away from the castle. I reached out and shared her pain combining her body with mine. Instantly I began to bleed from where the nail wounds would have been, on my wrists and wings. Feeling the awful pain, Ameela joined the gestalt and added her strength to my mother.

I gave what comfort that I could to her and sent out a mental shout to board the Spellbinder to my people and stop whatever they were doing. Within an hour we were 'locked down' and making our way across what would have been Europe on Earth heading for Spain. I had been to the ancestral home of my people many times during the rebuilding program, as we had hauled all manner of goods and tools to the ancient castle, so I knew it well. It was several hundred thousand years old and over the years constantly added to. When the Dokka'lfar drove us from this world it had been left to decay. Re-building the place was a labour of love.

Sam Pitts and the others that I had called back from the afterlife had given the situation a great deal of thought. They had laid out a plan of action that I was sure would be far better than any I could have decided to do.

Sam, his men and the dwarves would be dropped off on the roof behind the parapet to make their way to where they could pick off as many of the defending force silently by crossbow. This would be done simultaneously by linking minds. The soldiers that Eloen had left behind would be expecting a full frontal attack and would be concentrating their firepower outwards to cut down anyone who tried to storm over the parapet. They would not be expecting an attack through the roof of the hall. Henry Spencer would make his way to where my mother was nailed to the panel and remove the spikes from her flesh. Unfortunately the use of tear gas was out of the question, as the effects on anyone crucified would have been an agonising death of suffocation before they could be taken down.

Thinking that my mother could have pierced through the

pain and given us a picture of where the defending force were located, the sergeant had thought of that and put a cushion cover over my mother's head so that she could not see, but elves have other powers!

Using the pain of her body as a leverage, my mother 'stepped out' and detached her soul from her flesh. Instantly she had a three-dimensional view of the hall and a sharp vision of every human that was hidden from the parapet entrance. This she relayed straight to me and continued to do so as we approached the castle from behind the mountain range. Just to be sure I made the Spellbinder just a distortion in the sky and approached slowly after the forced speed that the elves on board had channelled into the receptive energy banks. We would soon recover naturally, unlike our foe, who would be weakened by the effort of slipping through the rifts. She would just channel through her own body and mind, the energy required, by taking it from the humans on board. That of course would result in their deaths. This was why she had taken so many humans on board and drained half of them immediately.

Ignoring the shared pain from my mother, I brought the Spellbinder to a stop over the rooftops of the castle. Here Sam and the others 'jumped ship' and dropped onto the tiles crawling over the crests of the roof over the main hall. Their new elfin heritage gave them extra strength and balance. I had impressed what knowledge I had of the castle and its many turrets and rooms above where the humans waited in ambush. Sam, Hoatzin and Thorinson began to remove tiles from the roof to the right of centre. The twins, David and Steven worked with Mellitus to the left. Spencer was frantically digging his way in at the centre over the top of my mother, aided by Aradun. Eduardo and Calando were there in case of anyone falling off the roof and had wings extended, ready.

John Smith and his descendants were aboard the

Spellbinder putting the final touches to the sapphire laser that the goblins had 'improved' on the journey here. The one thing about a burst of light is that it can easily pass out from the Spellbinder's outer membrane, but not be returned inside. The solar panels had charged the batteries to maximum fullness and would channel every amp collected into the laser discharge through the goblin's diffuser lens mounted on the front of the laser.

I took the Spellbinder to the front of the parapet, but hovering below the edge. There were dead elves scattered about the bottom of the ramparts. They had been easily picked off as they had tried to crest the parapet to try a rescue. My mother had pinpointed the large mirrors that were used to reflect the sunlight around the hall. I was also well aware of the body count in the hall. There were clouds of flies busy alighting on the corpses. It was slippery with the blood of the slain and hidden in amongst these poor souls were some of Eloen's delaying force, waiting for us. They were well trained and were prepared to die, so lying in this stench was accepted. Even though they had no knowledge of our arrival they lay still, preferring to be in their own mess than move, such was the mental programming that Eloen had planted in their heads.

I warned my mother, "Take refuge inside your body. The bag over your head will save your sight, but keep your eyes shut! In your astral form, I have no guarantee what you would see and how it would affect you. Embrace the pain, mother. We are still connected to you through me."

"No, my son! I can bear the pain. You will all need your wits about you when you take me down from this living hell. These poor souls are expendable and they all wear the iron collars that prevent us sizing their minds. Eloen has thought it through. She is piling on the anguish that you must bear. Remember, it is revenge she seeks. She intends me to live and suffer with you. Do what you must and do it as quickly as you can. I shudder to think what she has done to your son."

I did as my mother insisted, withdrew mental contact and the bleeding from my limbs stopped, healing over in an instant. I contacted my friends on the roof who had wriggled through the gaps and now had made entrance into the gallery behind the hall. I relayed the positions of the living amongst the dead. There were no doors to open up here, as elves have always favoured 'open plan' in our homes so they crawled along on their stomachs carrying the crossbows, primed and ready. They took up their positions, keeping their eyes tightly shut. Each one of them had a plan of the hall and the enemy positions firmly in their minds. The soldiers hiding amongst the dead bodies would be no problem, as I had a way of dealing with them.

When I was sure that we still had the measure of surprise I lifted the Spellbinder and as soon as we were over the parapet edge, the laser pulsed a diffused cone of light that reflected off the mirrors around the hall. The great hall lit up much brighter than the sun, with a brilliant cold light. There was nowhere to hide from the penetrating beams and the humans that had been slow in closing their eyes rolled around in agony. Even closing their eyes did not stop the beams of light from penetrating their eyelids. Those that had concealed themselves burst out of hiding and were felled by crossbow bolts from the gallery. Without thinking, Spencer jumped over the balcony and landed lightly on his feet in front of my mother. Without hesitation he stood on the bench and pulled the spikes out using a pair of grips, with his bare hands. As she collapsed into his arms, she stared into his face, taking in the differences and wept tears of joy.

"You wouldn't believe how far I came to find you," Henry said and straightened his back to hold her in his arms, cradled like a child.

"I never expected to see you again, Spence," she said. "I was with you when you died! What has my son done?"

Henry Spencer walked steadily to the Spellbinder ignoring the bodies of the humans that Eloen had left behind. The marks that the iron spikes had made were already beginning to knit together and the bleeding had stopped from my mother's wrists. She was however drenched in her own blood that had dribbled down her body and stunk from her own excreta. Spencer didn't care at all and carried her aboard and into the shower that the Spellbinder had formed. There he stood like a great black statue as the water rinsed off the mess from the two of them. Dawn opened her mouth and drank gratefully as her body re-hydrated from the days spent crucified. Every moment she felt stronger and suddenly realised that Henry Spencer was flooding her with his own life energy!

"Stop that you fool," she said. "That is plenty. I am and will be fine now. I can eat and drink quite soon. What has my son done to you? You are not human any longer and what I can see is an awful lot of elf blended in. Tell me as we dry."

Henry told her what Peterkin had done, calling the souls of the dead back from the hereafter and blending his blood with theirs as he resurrected them.

"So you are all here then? I must say my son is resourceful! I would never have thought of doing what he has done. He is indeed the High King, beyond any of his ancestors! I need clothes, Spence so while I continue to dry in here, go and get me something to wear."

I was waiting outside the shower room with a gown, as he appeared and handed it to him. Henry just smiled and returned to help my mother dress.

My wife and I now turned our attentions to the living men and women that Eloen had left to fight to the death. The members of the rescue team had taken off the iron collars from around their necks and had handcuffed them to one another. All of them were still blinded by the laser flash, but would recover, given time. General Price was anxious to speak with them and discover who remained alive of the people that Eloen had taken and what information they could give us about the Halfling's intentions.

Those people taken out by crossbow were all dead. We had no choice in the matter, as they had all been 'pressed' to kill us. The crossbow is silent but no match against an automatic rifle. I lay my hands upon the first one's head and dived into his mind, cutting myself off from the general hub-bub of unreasoning hatred that was coming from the others.

Eloen was incredibly skilled in mind manipulation. She had conditioned these poor souls to be willing to die for her and protect her at any cost. We were portrayed as infinitely evil and not capable of mercy. All of them expected to die at our hands. Turning these minds back to how they once were would take a very long time. I did not have the time to devote to this task, but I needed them to be rendered inoperative.

I summoned General Price to my side and said, "There is nothing that I can do with these people, as their minds have been turned by Eloen to such an extent that it will take far too long to remedy. I do not have that option so I will have to pass them into your care. They will remain blind for some time if they regain their sight at all. When this is over we will do what we can with elfin mind science. At the moment it would do no harm if you tried to reason with them in the meantime. Try to impress on them that we mean them no harm. Speak to the Spellbinder and tell it what you require and it will extend the ship to accommodate our new 'guests' and keep them out of the way. We will have to stay here for some time and it would be appreciated if your men could help unblock the doors to the hall and clear the dead away."

The General stared at me in disbelief and asked, "What about your son, High King? Surely you need to pursue this fiend from Hell and retrieve him?"

"James Price, I have duties that extend far beyond my family. These are my people and they need us. My son will endure. Eloen will not kill him yet, as she will need him alive to inflict more vengeance upon my family. What she has in mind to do, I have no way of stopping at the moment. My responsibilities lie elsewhere!"

MOLOCK'S WAND

CHAPTER FOURTEEN

"Peterkin! What are you going to do now old friend? Sam Pitts asked.

"I will do what a High King has to do at all times, look after his people first," I replied and looked round at the group around me. "The dead must be interred and this blood-bath cleaned up. The doorways into the castle must be made safe and the masonry cleared away so that the re-building can be started up again. There are many others in this castle that are on their way to the other side of the wall as we speak. They were told to keep away until I came with the Spellbinder. There will be time to mourn in the future, for those we have lost."

Sam stared at me, shook his head and said, "I would not be High King for any reward. Is there no way that we can chase after Eloen from here without you?"

"None! The Spellbinder is genetically keyed to me! The only other elf on this planet would be Mia and she is on the other side of the world. Besides we are just chasing a shadow! Always we go to where she has been. I need to go to where she will go! To do that I need to go deep beneath the roots of this castle and find the Troll Drottning and ask for her help. Some of the females have a unique gift, they can see forwards. It is why the Dokka'lfar could never find them and why the trolls always ambushed the Dark Elves without ever being taken. We need the services of a Spakr-Kona if they can be persuaded to allow one of their 'wise-women' to accompany us. We must go unarmed, deep beneath this castle to where they live. All we can hope for is that they still thrive down there."

"You will not go down there alone," insisted Sam, "We will come with you. All of us that you brought back from wherever we existed, would not let you wander off on your own."

"Some of you will come, but not all of you. Too many would look like a threat. I will take Mellitus, Thorinson and Aradun as they are used to burrowing in dark places. Sam you may pick two others that are not bothered about exceedingly dark places."

The twins, David and Steven spoke up, "We have no problem with dark, enclosed spaces and Hoatzin and Spencer will be better up here, working with John and your mother to sort out the terrible mess that Eloen left us. They also have General Price and his people to lend a hand. Besides we have this enhanced eyesight that you gave us. This will be a great time to find out how well it works!"

"Very well my friends we will be on our way, but first collect as much unspoiled food as you can from the table and pack it away in a sack or two. The castle gnomes have been busy at my bequest and have been baking for me, so contact them. We will present it as a small gift, when we meet the trolls who live way down underneath us. They seldom manage to eat what they refer to as 'yfir-grunnr-matr' (above ground food) particularly baked bread and cakes. They cultivate fungi of many kinds that in turn feed both them and other insects that are part of their food chain. They hunt bats and fish in the cave systems and forage for food after darkness outside. Trolls also hunted Dokka'lfar when they came too close to the concealed entrances to their caves."

Without another word they did my bidding and systematically stripped the tables of all unspoiled food, mainly fruit. By this time, the rubble had been cleared away from one of the doorways, giving us access to the rest of the castle and the people trapped below us. Soon everyone who had tried to rescue my mother by unsuccessfully digging out the collapsed doorways from the other side began the task of clearing away. We made our way past the throng and started to descend into the depths of the castle carrying sacks of the gnomes baking skills.

"Be careful, my son," said a familiar voice in my head. "We have had no dealings with these people since we left, many thousands of years ago. They may feel betrayed by us as we left this world without them and left them to the merciless Dokka'lfar!"

"I am well aware of that fact, mother. Yet I do not feel that there should be any animosity from them. We have been here for several centuries now and no contact has been made between us. Now that we need them, I will have to offer something that they will want in exchange," I replied as we continued to descend what seemed to be endless steps.

The walls glowed with bioluminescence and my old friends found that what would have been almost impenetrable darkness became a soft light that could easily be navigated in. Only Thorinson and Arundel found themselves at a disadvantage so they trusted the others to lead them by holding onto a sleeve. As their eyes adjusted they found that the gloomy aspect did in fact become a little brighter, but they still kept a tight hold onto their better sighted companions. After many hours the stonework became cave face and the fungi began to grow in great profusion leaching water and minerals from the rocks. This made the going easier as it became noticeable brighter. We had lamps with us, but the moment that we used them, we would lose our 'night-sight' and it would take some time to re-adjust to the darkness.

Several times the roof had fallen in and the tunnel downwards became blocked. Time and again we carefully moved chunks of stone and wriggled through small gaps, always downwards. In places the floor was uneven and wet, as water constantly dripped from the roof. In places the stalactites and stalagmites joined together to form pillars that was far more ancient than the elves themselves. We had been travelling downwards for what seemed many hours when at last I called for us to stop to rest for a while. We did not sit, as the floor was slippery with groundwater and we ate a little from the sacks of food.

There was the sound of water in the far distance, which was a relief to me as we had brought just a few bottles of wine with us and we soon drank that as we rested. I stood up and looked deep into the tunnel that stretched before us. I was sure that I had seen movement! I opened my mind to feel for the Trolls that I was sure were in front of us.

"We mean you no harm," I sent allowing my mind to generate friendship. "We have no weapons, but we do bring, 'yfir-grunnr-matr' as an offering of amity and goodwill."

"Long-shadow, welcome be," answered a troll clothed in darkness. "Many years has it been since our two elder races have met. The peace of this world has breached been, by something left over from your cleansing. You bring new life to this empty world and much good have you done. Now something of ours would you seek?"

"You speak truth. I would be a friend to the Trolls just as I am friend to many species of sentient. There is a force of evil abroad that can travel at will from one reality to another. She has the Staff of Power that was Molock's, used by his son Abaddon to control the Dream-shifter. Now that abomination serves her. She is a force of death and must be stopped at any price."

The troll-maiden slowly walked into sight and looked down onto my face. She was easily two heads taller than any of my companions. Her body was covered in black curly hair and she wore a leather tunic with a large tool belt. Around her neck was a thick golden chain with a scabbard hanging from it. Inside the scabbard was an obsidian knife crafted onto a golden handle set with diamonds. Her ears were elfin, but quite larger than ours and she had the six fingered hands that all of the Elven races had, along with the cat-like eyes that we possessed. The eyes were twice the size of ours however and would be at a great disadvantage in daylight in full sun. Platted braids hung to her shoulders, held together by gold wire at the ends.

"My name is No'tt-mjool or in your tongue, Night-flower and I am also what you seek. I am a Spakr-Kona. I can see ahead. My people have sent me to you, Long-shadow to guide you to what you seek and to lead you to my people. Follow me!"

Sam Pitts sucked in his breath and turned to David to say, "I always understood that Trolls were ugly! She is the most beautiful creature I have seen in a long time!"

"Man, you are strange," laughed David and nudged his twin, Steven to add, "You've been an elf-human hybrid for a little while and already your tastes in women are changing. "What next I wonder?"

Night-flower stopped, turned round and was next to David without seemingly to move! She lifted him effortlessly up to her eye-level by his upper arms and said loud enough for all the others to hear, "Shall I fix you up with an ugly one, David? Would that be, 'what next'?" She turned and looked more kindly at Sam who had flushed with embarrassment. "Thank you Sam for your comment. I too find you attractively different! I have very good hearing."

With that she put David back onto his feet and ruffled his hair with a huge hand, before taking the lead again. After another hour or more the tunnel widened out to become a cavern that could have housed New London easily. Here the light was much better as the air and walls were full of flying luminescent insects in their millions.

To my amazement I could see many thousands of trolls lived here beneath the ancient Elven castle. It was a thriving community that the Ljo'sa'lfar had never ever been involved with, although we had lived so close, long ago. I felt awkward that only now that I needed their help had I made any attempt to seek them out.

A male troll easily a head taller than Night-flower walked towards us accompanied by another female, decked in gold and leather. There was grey in the curly hair of their bodies and also in the braids that both of them had arranged. When he spoke the voice was deep and of a musical quality.

"I am Gramr for my people," he said, "Something like your title of High King amongst the elves. Welcome I bid you, Long-shadow and your friends. Awaited, have we for you, many, many years. My name is Moon-flower and my Drottning or queen is called Sees-far (Vita-fjarri), mother she is, to Night-flower and is also Spakr-Kona, which is where the gift comes from. Not all of the Troll-Folk are blessed with this ability. She has seen many threads branching into the future. Only with the aid of my daughter does any chance of success auger into the weft of time. A great price, will you pay and that is not for knowing at this time. Come, she it is that you have come to meet.

"I would speak to the dwarf known as Thorinson whose mother was Hilden, daughter of Hildegard. The gift of seeing forward was in your female line. It was your ancestor that foresaw the coming of the Long-shadow and the finish of the Dokka'lfar. Come you to me," Vita-fjarri commanded.

Thorinson walked forwards and stood in front of the troll queen and asked, "What would you have me do Wise woman?"

"I would speak to your grandmother through you, young Thorinson. There may be things that I need to know that only she can tell me. Place your head between the palms of my hands, by which I may enter into the Svefnhus that carries her spirit within you."

Thorinson edged nervously forwards and stood obediently still while Vita-fjarri held his head gently within the palms of her hands. She brought her forehead down to his level and touched his brow with hers. The two of them remained so still it bothered me and I began to wonder what would happen between them. Strangely the air about them began to cast a pearly glow as something swept over them. It was as if two giant butterflies had entered the two of them and enfolded them in their wings. Nobody moved or dared to speak as the glow encapsulated them and abruptly faded by going somewhere else.

I however felt the presence of my dear friend Hildegard quite strongly and one other that was in some way was bound to Thorinson. I was briefly touched by a strong female mind of a dwarfess named Cailleach.

Her powerful mind overcame mine in seconds and said, "Long-Shadow. You still have much to do. As I saw your coming and the end of the Dokka'lfar, so I was aware that there would be more than the one struggle. There are many paths to take, so heed what Vita-fjarri tells that you must do. Pay the bride-price for her assistance. Take heed of what No'tt-mjool will ask of you. Do not hesitate to do what she says whatever the cost!"

I was overwhelmed by the power, behind the voice in my mind. I also felt the reluctance to be involved with mortal struggles. This information had come at a great price to the long dead prophetess and I felt that there was a disobedience that had been pushed to one side. There was much more than just the message that Cailleach had imparted to me in that brief moment of contact. My friends that I had 'called' from the void had no memory of what they had done in their altered state of being. Their memories finished at their deaths and ran on from the moment that I had resurrected them. There are things in this life that we are not meant to know. I could only wonder if some other higher real of existence had intervened?

"High King!" Vita-fjarri spoke in the stunned silence, "Have you the information that you need? Take my daughter you will, to see things that no living troll has ever glimpsed. I cannot look too far into her future, as decisions there may be, that you will need to make that could be misinterpreted, by your knowing too much, too soon! Enough! You have brought 'yfir-grunnr-matr' as an offering of harmony between our peoples. Baked for us long, long ago, the castle gnomes did, before ravished these lands, did the curse of the Dokka'lfar. Come again here they must not!"

There were so many secrets here that I would have given much to ask. We had not reached out to these people, but they were known well by the gnomes that lived in the lower reaches of this castle. Gnomes and their foggy minds! There would be questions that I would ask when I once again spoke to Razzmutt when I had the time. For now there would be a ceremony of shared food-stuffs between these amazing people and ourselves.

Eloen was triumphant as she sat in the control chair of the Dream-shifter. She smiled at the raging elf restrained by the chair. This had gone so well! It was such a satisfactory feeling to know that the High King's mother would hang on the iron spikes until her son arrived. Several days at least! As for the humans that she left behind to delay the action as long as possible, well they were very expendable. She could afford to lose a few men. She had what she wanted most and that was Peterkin's son.

"Dream-shifter, I need to talk with Abaddon. I need a history lesson from very long ago!"

Abaddon's voice slipped into mind, praising her victory over his destroyer.

"What can I do for you precious Lady? What do you want to know about the past?"

Eloen thought for a moment and asked, "How did the High King, Auberon manage to hide the entire remnants of the Ljo'sa'lfar from Molock and yourself on Earth?"

"When Auberon settled the Ljo'sa'lfar on Earth he spent a great deal of time surveying that world before he chose a place to stay. It was the homeland of an earlier type of mankind. This different species of man was later called Neanderthals and they had settled in the north of the planet. They were giving way under the onslaught of a much better adaptable type of man, spreading across the lands. He could see that the new species of man was beginning to dominate. Soon this earlier type of man would vanish and he was concerned about this as the dwarves had always accepted the Light Elves as friends.

This was long before the Dream-shifter had been built, but Auberon knew that it would be only a matter of time before the Dokka'lfar came looking for them. What he did, was to persuade the Neanderthals to enter the territory that was encapsulated by the Spellbinder. He extended the range of the ship to place many hundreds of square miles of good hunting and gathering land under the bubble. Once everyone was settled in, he slowed down time inside. They lived subjectively for thousands of years, with the Neanderthals evolving into what we now call dwarves, while outside, time went on as it does. When humans began using iron in large quantities, things got difficult and sometimes the bubble became breached and isolated humans wandered inside. We got there just after they had left to colonise Haven. We took slaves and whatever else that was of use to us and continued to seek them out. The rest you know!"

Eloen stared into space and asked, "Have you that ability? Can you speed up time instead inside these walls?

"I believe so, my Lady. Somewhere in the memory banks will be the same set of instructions that was built into the Spellbinder. Much of the failings of this vessel were due to my inadequate understanding of all the workings possible. Things are different know. The composite mind that is the new ME is much better equipped to do as you ask. I am no longer insane."

"They are following our track. Alter time inside this vessel now and breach the rifts taking me to another parallel Earth. Once we are off this reality Peterkin will not know where to look and I will have the time to surprise him!

The Dream-shifter slowed time by an hour and the vessel and all of its contents disappeared from Peterkin's reality. Now it searched the rifts for another Earth that would be habitable. Those that had no moon it discarded and continued to seek out a world empty of any intelligence. Finally the composite mind found one and took itself over a landscape very similar to where new London was situated on Alfheimr.

"You have done well my loyal Dream-shifter. This will do admirably! Set us down and extend your presence over a hundred miles in all directions. Then speed up time inside the bubble by a factor of ten. By the time that five years have passed outside we will have been in here for fifty years. That will give me plenty of time to raise a new Dokka'lfar race from the raw materials that I have brought with me!

Within the bubble the sun rose and set just as it always had, but if it were possible to view the outside the days and nights would have been flickering on and off at a fifth of the time inside. Eloen now put the rest of her plan into action and that involved Peterkin's son, Elthred. She entered the cell that the Dream-shifter had provided for his encapsulation.

The Ljo'sa'lfar was tethered by chains at his wrists and ankles that disappeared into four holes in the floor. He was relatively free to walk around his cell as long as he paid out the chains. This finished the moment that Eloen walked into the cell. The Dream-shifter reeled the chains in until he was spread-eagled on the resilient floor with his wings trapped beneath his back. He had been stripped naked by Eloen's attentive dwarves, Hilden and Thorin, soon after capture and washed down.

Elthred writhed from side to side, helpless in his chained condition and stared with hatred at the Halfling. He watched with horror as Eloen disrobed and dropped her clothing to the floor. She walked over to him as a predator would stalk its victim and sat down cross-legged just behind his head, resting the back of his head onto her pubic hair. She put her hands over his forehead and entered his mind. Trapped in the iron collar, he could not stop the intrusion and backed up by the influence of the Staff of Power, Eloen was in complete control of his mind and body. His hatred flared against her and she turned it into lust. The growing fear of what she wanted him to do, she altered into a terrible need. He felt a growing itch that could only be tamed in one way. Eloen pushed deeper into his mind and placed blocks that would ensure that he was incapable of resisting her advances. The pent-up energy of

Molock's Wand gave her a power equal to his, but she used it with a much greater intelligence.

Soon it would be time for him to become tuned to her will and that will, would be unreservedly hers. It had been a long time since Eloen had been sexually active and she was pleasantly overwhelmed by desire. Elthred stared at her with fever-ridden eyes as she wriggled around his chest and sought his erect penis by sliding down his belly. As he entered her she trapped him in there and rode the spike up and down, forward and back until they both oozed sweat and passion juices. Peterkin's son arched his back as he totally lost control and ejaculated deep into the warm wet resting place.

Eloen had released two eggs down her fallopian tubes some time before they began and into her womb to be met by the rush of eager sperm. Her body reacted to the fusion of sperm and eggs immediately and told her that she was pregnant! Leaving her 'partner' still chained securely she had Hilden wipe him down and collect his sperm in a glass jar. She then had Hilden and Thorin impregnate as many of the human women that she had imprisoned in the cell next door, until the supply ran out. This she did by partially wakening them and making them walk into her chamber and assume an easily entered position on a table that the Dream-shifter bade to rise from the floor. Using large hypodermic syringes with the needles removed and the sperm diluted in warm water the dwarves did her bidding.

She knelt by the side of her elfin sperm donor and lifted his balls in her hand and said; "Now my forced love, I will no longer be the last Dokka'lfar. I carry the gene that allows fertilization of a human by an elf. My mother told me that I was not unique, but that my kind were rare to survive from being eaten. So you my love will be the father of Halflings and I shall ensure that the hearts of Dokka'lfar beat in every one of them.

Inside the bubble of the Dream-shifter, we will experience a speeding up of time that will allow the children that you spawn to mature and breed amongst themselves. I shall go forth and add to the sperm bank that I will build up, by collecting Ljo'sa'lfar and bend them to my will. This time the Dokka'lfar will not lose intelligence by interbreeding closely with each other as they did before. Our offspring will be more elf than human and will grow up more powerful than their half-brothers and sisters. A new kind of elf will arise from the ashes of the old. Your father will rue the day he crossed me!"

Part of the way back up to the castle I felt the abrupt loss of my son, stumbled and fell to my knees. The feeling that possessed me was not of his death, but of an absence of him being in any reality and deep down I realised that Eloen had managed to take the Dream-shifter out of time reference.

I heard the voice of Auberon inside my mind say, "She has managed to activate the time manipulation device that I thought only the Spellbinder had. She has managed to rid her sentient ship of the insanity that Abaddon forced it into. Until she relocates into real-time, we cannot face her. We cannot find her."

My people helped me to my feet and I gave them the bad news.

"An alternative path that leads from this moment, brought into being it has by the very situation that you have explained to your friends and I," No'tt-mjool said. "We were not totally certain until this moment, as the future alter can, depending on changes in the present! The ones behind us are other troll-maidens who have been sent to carry out what yet may be. More you will be told at a much later date."

Already the future was unravelling just as Cailleach had prophesied. I would have to trust Night-flower as I was told.

Now matters were out of my hands and I would have to accept that I would be to some respects, a pawn in a greater game. Vita-fjarri had kept quite a lot of her knowledge from me and had waited for me to acknowledge the loss of my son from this reality until she was sure where the direction of future events would go. I looked back along the tunnels leading back towards the troll-underworld and was astonished to see so many troll-maidens making their way towards us. Behind them slightly crouched under the roof of the burrows were a number of taller males. Why would they be coming with us and why so many? A thought entered unbidden into my mind. What if none of them were going to return? What strange future would, or could happen, where the trolls did not come back to their ancestral home? Was this the 'bride-price' that Calleach had insisted that I pay? These trolls were not coming home after this adventure had played out. If anywhere, they would be settled underneath the castle at Haven. If they survived what had to come, they would be colonists. This would account for the sadness that Sees-far had tried to hide at our farewell as she said goodbye to her daughter.

I felt the comforting presence of Ameela in my mind joined with that of my mother.

"Elthred lives, my love. Whatever she is doing, he can endure. There will come a time when we will all return to our homes and then and only then will destiny be finished with us all."

"I will call back Mia to our family. I will need her on Haven if John's research bears the fruit I think it will. I have suddenly realised why there are so many of the Trolls coming with us. No! I will not say yet. There is still too much to be done," I answered and continued to climb the endless steps back into the sunlight.

MOLOCK'S WAND

CHAPTER FIFTEEN

I left the rebuilding of Homecoming Castle to another Ljo'sa'lfar and the survivors of Eloen's attack. I left some of General Price's men as a defence with adequate weapons. Now I had to equip my colonists with rifles and guns. This was something that I had not wanted to do at any price! Price! I had dreamed of a peaceful existence concentrating on filling the empty Earths that were spattered through the multiverse without any need for conflict!

Now due to one Halfling Dokka'lfar, I would have to make sure that all of my people could defend themselves against Eloen's mind-pressed troops! There was no trace of her and no track to follow. No'tt-mjool was my only thread of sanity to cling to. She insisted that all would remain quiet for some considerable time. The trolls had indeed tunnelled deep beneath the castle at Haven and found a cavernous system much like the one on Alfheimr that they soon adapted to their needs. They were still a nocturnal species so I usually saw Night-flower in the evenings to talk and discuss what poor plans that I had. Mostly it was Sam Pitts who sounded her out on her abilities and worked with her to try and work out what advantage her people could give us. I missed my son with a raw ache and feared for his sanity. At least my daughter, Mia had returned to us and Mother had returned to Haven with Spencer.

There at last there came the day that I was hoping for, that tied into the possible future that the influx of trolls had inspired me into wondering about. John Smith and his descendants with the help of the goblins, managed to clone the Spellbinder! From the original vessel they were able to duplicate ten more sentient vessels. Each of them carried the composite mind of the original, but without the genetic key that only allowed the High King or his heirs to mesh minds and control it.

This was the reason why so many trolls had travelled back to Haven with me. The production of the self-replicating Elf-stone became a priority and the process was tricky, requiring the goblins to push their abilities to the limit. The material was a sliding Matrix that could only be influenced by psychic ability. The humans called it a form of Nano-technology that built a neural net into the fabric of the ship. The intelligence that inhabited it could evolve along with the minds that controlled the structure. The fact that we had the uncorrupted copy of the mind of Deedlit, gave us an advantage over Eloen.

This was not to be trusted too much, as she had shown that between her mind and the copy of Abaddon's she had been able to pull out abilities that we thought were singular to the Spellbinder and make the Dream-shifter operate. The voices in my mind were never silent. I had realised that all of them were copies of the people that they once were. Their souls had journeyed on into whatever the afterlife existed, leaving the copies behind, etched into the fabric of the Spellbinder. Copies or not, they seemed very real to me. I was finding out a great deal of information that I had just taken for granted, was not necessarily completely true. Since my exposure to the 'other side' to resurrect my old friends and the meeting with the spirits of Hildegard and Cailleach my mind felt fractured.

The other most difficult item was the construction of the staves of power that brought each ship into operation. It took some time to grow a crystal and join it to the staves. Unlike my wand, these could be operated by any elf, or as we found out, also my resurrected people. We had at last, a real advantage over Eloen should she appear. Each cloned ship carried a powerful laser designed by the goblins, capable of temporary blinding Eloen and disrupting the Dream-shifter. They called them sun-burst lasers and they spat X-rays and Gamma particles.

No'tt-mjool and all of the other Troll-maidens constantly cast their minds into the future without any result. Vita-fjarri's 'children' kept a constant watch and continually matched predictions looking for any possible discrepancies. Sam Pitts and Night Flower began to take out one of the cloned ships and try to pick up a trace of the Dream-shifter, but to no avail. The other ships were pressed into use by the rest of my companions and utilised by transporting weapons to outlying colony sites all over Alfheimr along with trade goods. We were building up strengths dotted all over the two worlds in my domain. Earth was inspected more carefully to find isolated societies that had kept the trappings of civilization and survived the nuclear holocaust. Gradually, knowledge of the Elven kingdom spread over the ravaged globe and the threat of Eloen taken seriously. Many places were far too dangerous for elven influence to be inserted and the knowledge that a simple iron collar would defeat any mental influence soon spread throughout the communities.

My simple, benign dictatorship was not always agreeable to the humans who were by nature fiercely independent. Slowly and steadily my dreams of peaceful co-existence were being shattered. I was beginning to realise that the Earth was not a realm that I could control and as violence broke out over and over again in the pockets of survivors, I considered the withdrawal of those who had voluntarily followed me to Alfheimr for a fresh start. The great problem in all this was Eloen. I had little idea of what she planned and the Earth was an easy place to pick up soldiers and weapons. That I could not allow at any price, or the blight of warfare would march over the lands and innocent or fighter, many would die!

The only real advantage against all these problems was the edge of elven science that went far beyond the mechanical science of humanity. We had combined psychic power with a form of nanotechnology that had produced the Spellbinder and the Dream-shifter. As our mental abilities could not be duplicated without elven assistance, there could be no duplication of the reality crossing ships crossing the Rifts. I decreed that a Spellbinder ship be always stationed on Earth to keep a watch for a sudden appearance of Eloen and her ship.

Once the problem of Eloen was solved, then the isolation of the other parallel worlds would be a simple thing to achieve. My head ached with the effort of coping with all these potential problems and uppermost was the loss of our son Elthred. Amelia had cried herself dry over the uncertainty of not knowing where he was and what was happening to him. I must admit there were times in private that I too had lost control, thinking about him. I had touched Eloen's mind, but briefly and had felt as if my mind had been scraped and dipped in acid.

The worst part of this tableau was that I had to wait until Eloen resurfaced, before I could bring into action any of my plans to defeat her. The frustration built up until I felt that I could explode! Months dragged on into years and still there was no trace of her and her captives. Life carried on as it must and my influence increased across the two worlds of Haven and Alfheimr. We continued to trade with the community at and around the area of Los Angeles, cultivating good relationships with the descendants of the marines stationed at twenty-nine palms. Located as it is in the Mojave Desert of Southern California, the city experienced some high and low temperatures in the past. Since the nuclear episode engineered by terrorists and the destruction of the east coast, plus the knock-on effect of retaliation, much had changed in the weather patterns. The El Niño effect and the melted icecaps had altered the coastline along with the weather. Winters, during the El Niño effect, are warmer and drier than average in the Northwest, northern Midwest, and northern Mideast United States, so those regions experience reduced snowfalls. Meanwhile, significantly wetter winters are present in northwest Mexico and the southwest United States, including central and southern California, while both cooler and wetter than average winters in northeast Mexico and the southeast United States. A new wave of vegetation began to spread into what had been dry lands.

Humanity's home had changed out of all recognition and was not a safe place to be! There were vast areas uninhabitable through radioactive poisoning and whole cities that had exploded into anarchy without electrical power. These were run by feuding warlords and feral gangs. As supplies ran out, starvation took over and diseases did the rest to wipe out all traces of mankind all over the Earth in many areas in the last two centuries. I had done all that I could to save what was possible and had resettled Alfheimr and Haven with a fresh start. Saving the Earth was beyond my powers. The community that had survived the destruction of Los Angeles was self-contained and was building on the ruins of past ages. These people would eventually spread out over the American continent over time and as the scars healed they would proper.

My people were soon accepted by the humans on Earth

and our help appreciated in rebuilding their civilization into a different mould. With the cloning of the Spellbinder a steady traffic built up between the three worlds using these extra vessels. New life was added to the plains of Earth by transporting the more useful dinosaurs into the changing ecology and using them for meat and transport. Soon the cries of the Quetzalcoatlus could be heard in the skies of two planets that had not heard them for seventy million years as humans learnt to ride them and fly on a beast instead of a machine.

Every so often I would grip the Staff of Power and using its augmented influence, send my mind into those empty places between the Rifts searching for our son. I could feel the warmth of sentient thought all around the three settled worlds, but not a tiny inkling of anyone else. Wherever she was, locked down underneath the umbrella of the Dream-shifter and in a different time frame, she was invisible and untouchable.

Once she left the settlement behind and came out, still running on a different time-frame. She was undetectable to my Trolls and made a quick fishing trip. She materialised on Alfheimr at the settlement that Mia had joined and had quickly imprisoned a number of male elves. The whole operation had taken but an hour at the most, as she flicked in and out of the time-stream and once again disappeared. Those I questioned could only tell me that a bright light had appeared in the sky and a choking gas that made it impossible to see through tears spread over the town they had built. Humans wearing goggles and masks had quickly selected only male elves in the fog and female humans. With them was the figure of Eloen who picked out a selection from the captives and discarded those who did not suit her purpose. I could only wonder why she had risked so much to come out of hiding.

CHAPTER FIFTEEN

All at once it hit me! She was collecting breeding stock. It was the incestuous nature of the Dokka'lfar that had produced billions of mind-crippled, defective offspring. The first generation had been born fully capable, but succeeding generations had bred with each other, brother, sister, cousins over and over again. Eloen was a Halfling and was determined to generate a different type of Dokka'lfar that would not be inbred. Under the boundaries of the Dream-shifter she would have the time to do this. My son and the male elves she had 'acquired' would give her diversity to breed into the gene pool of the humans that she had taken from twenty-nine Palms and elsewhere. If she came out again in real-time the Trolls would know and hopefully give me enough warning to be there waiting for her. It all depended how far away she was, when she shed the boundaries of time and space to return to our timeline. To my frustration she did this time and again, each time gathering human females and male elves.

Underneath the umbrella of the Dream-shifter with time speeded up, Eloen bore her pregnancy and became overwhelmed with the sensations of impending motherhood. She was protected by the two dwarves that she had originally mentally pressed to her cause. Hilden and Thorin Hammer-fist could now not remember any other kind of existence than that of serving Eloen's needs.

Using her father's Staff of Power, she had easily overpowered Elthred's mind and now he loved her with a passion that she had come to enjoy. The fact that she used him as a stud beast to impregnate the human females did not bother her at all and he cheerfully did her bidding. She still kept the iron collar safely around his neck to prevent his father being able to even know that he was still alive. He lived in telepathic silence until she touched him and blended minds. In this state his personality began to change.

Now she had other male elves totally 'pressed' into her service and she compelled them to impregnate the human women. With some mind-control on both sides the situation was soon treated as a natural process. As 'time' went by, bellies began to swell and Eloen was satisfied that her plan was becoming fruitful. Soon it would be time for the births and she would be the first. She could feel the independent life-signs from each of the twin boys that she carried. They would be three-quarters elf and one quarter human. She felt that there would be a good chance that they would be winged like their father, but until they were born it was impossible to know. Besides it took some while during puberty for elves to develop wings. There would be the tell-tale buds behind the shoulders where the wings would develop much later.

Hilden kept a fine-tuned eye on her mistress, as she had delivered countless babies for her people in her capacity as mid-wife. The bump that had slowly dominated the once trim waist of the Halfling had begun to slip steadily down, as the birthing time approached. The fact that Eloen would be completely in her mercy just did not occur to her. She now lived for one purpose and that was to serve Eloen in any capacity that she could. Her mate, Thorin was never far from her side. This was the first time that Eloen had allowed herself to become pregnant and some days it seemed that she had never known any other existence! Carrying and developing the twins, was beginning to take a toll on her strength and she realised that her need for a life-force was beginning to be apparent when she noticed the aging of her hands and the wrinkles in her face.

She had more than enough Gnomes to fog the mental signature of the colony so she had the Dream-shifter ready a cell for what she needed to do. Eloen gave Thorin an order to bring her two young male gnomes while she sat and waited on a bench that the sentient ship provided her. She was also aware that the ship needed some extra energy to continue to provide the colony with space-time cover. Soaking energy from the sun was inefficient when time was out of synchronization with reality and the Dream-shifter had not been engineered to do this. Molock had been in a hurry to find and destroy the Ljo'sa'lfar so he had not bothered to try and duplicate all that the Spellbinder could do. Also he did not have the mind of Deedlit encapsulated into the consciousness of the Dream-shifter. With the copy of the mind of Abaddon lodged inside the structure, Eloen had achieved a great deal more than her half-brother and had taken the time to understand a lot more about the Elf-ship and how it worked.

She gripped the Staff of Power and sent her mind out to see what was keeping Thorin from bringing the gnomes to her presence. He was meeting some resistance from the female mates of the two males selected. So he had enlisted the aid of the humans with Curtis Jones, to help drag the gnomes into the Dream-shifter. She felt the anticipation of feeding her now apparent hunger and prepared herself to receive them. Eloen slipped out of her gown and stood naked with her favourite obsidian blade in her hand, waiting.

The two females were left weeping outside the cell door as the dwarf and the human held the gnomes tightly. Now the terror pierced the fog of their minds and Eloen could feed on the emotions that poured out of the small folk as they caught sight of her knife.

"Hold that one still Curtis Jones while Thorin brings this one to me," she ordered and motioned the powerful dwarf to hold the gnome still, against the bench.

The gnome began to scream as she showed him the blade as Thorin held him still. There was no fog to his mind now! The Halfling wallowed in the fear, as she slit his throat and bathed in the blood that soaked her extended body, drinking as much as she could. She felt the years slip away and the wrinkles smooth out as she took his life energy into herself. The blood was hot and so satisfying to fill her stomach with something so alive and fresh. Thorin held the gnome tight until he sagged and dropped him to the floor. There he sank into the substance of the Dream-shifter taking all the spilt blood with him.

"Thorin and Jones bring the other one over to me, so that I can feed him to the ship," said the Halfling waiting with the knife.

"Yes my lady," replied the thing that once was Lieutenant colonel Curtis Jones.

Thorin turned, held the other gnome under his chin with head up, so that Eloen could cut his throat while Jones held his hands behind his back. This she quickly did and silenced the screams abruptly and they dropped him to the floor, where he also sank out of sight. She felt the unborn children kick as they shared the life energy that the gnome had given up with her and the Dream-shifter.

"Soon my darlings, soon," she said and stood while the Dream-shifter washed her down by showering her.

Eloen slipped on her gown, walked out of the cell with Thorin and Curtis into her living quarters, while the Dream-shifter absorbed the cell and all within it. As always after she had 'fed' she felt brim full of energy and young again. The dwarf and the human stood waiting to see if there was anything else she needed.

She did!

"Thorin, find Hilden and bring her here. I think my babies are coming. I felt a squeezing pain that must be a contraction," she ordered and sat heavily down on a bench provided by the ship.

Within moments Hilden appeared and took charge of the

situation. She held her hand on Eloen's belly as another contraction came and nodded to Thorin.

"Soon, I think," she said and gave a grunt of satisfaction as the Halfling's waters broke. "Dream-shifter, provide twin cots for these children and a bowel of hot water and towels. Link to my mind from your mistress and provide what I need when I think of it."

Hours passed as Eloen fought that battle of contraction and rest. She was glad of the energy that she had taken from the gnome as she needed every bit of it. The babies were not small and soon Hilden was working her hands around the first head to enable it to emerge when with another contraction, the first child was free. She did what was necessary and handed him over to Thorin who towelled him dry and laid him screaming in his cot. The next child soon emerged, none the worst for being second and was also dealt with. Once the placenta was got rid of, Hilden placed both babies on Eloen's chest where they soon found the nipples of her milk filling breasts.

Eloen stared at her babies in amazement and realised that the emotion that was thundering through her mind was unconditional love. Now and only now she could appreciate the misery that Peterkin and Ameela were feeling at the loss of their child. Ethelred kneeled by her side so that he could touch his children and she could feel the reality of his love. This was not something that she had placed in his mind, but an honest reaction to seeing his children. He was totally hers now without any of her mental coercion. Soon the other human women would start giving birth to a new type of Dokka'lfar far more intelligent and gifted than the offspring of incest that had followed Molock's rape of the Elven women and the coupling of his children. She had the means and the ability to pursue her purpose of revenge. All she needed was time and because of her domination of the Dream-shifter, she had as much as she needed.

Hilden would soon be very busy helping to deliver all the other children and once they were well into the world there would be ample time to produce more. Her stud farm of male elves, were all satisfyingly compliant and obedient to her wishes. Genetic diversity was the key to the success of the rise of the Dokka'lfar and this was something that Molock never understood. He was just a hedonist intent on satisfying all of his perverted desires with an intense hatred of the Ljo'sa'lfar who loathed what he had become. Eloen carried his legacy in that she thirsted for revenge against Peterkin and all his family. She did not carry his craving for the flesh of the light elves, but if opportunity presented itself she could indulge quite happily. The necessity however did not have the same urgency in this world of plenty, as the amount of food was virtually inexhaustible.

Eloen's twins, Cethafin and Firovel grew well and were healthy and strong. Once they were weaned and could be placed in the crèche, Eloen began to contemplate another pregnancy to increase the size of her family and decided to wait a year until she carried again. Meanwhile the human women began to come to full term and soon there were over thirty children in the crèche and Eloen made sure that they became almost immediately pregnant again. Each and every Dokka'lfar was inspected by Eloen and she found to her delight that all but a few were healthy and strong. Those that were bodily weaker she did not put to death immediately, as all of them would fulfil a purpose and sometimes a lack of strength could be compensated by a mental edge and stronger psychic abilities.

Eloen watched the passage of time with some disquiet as the Dream-shifter began to struggle to maintain the rift in space-time for speeding up time inside its boundaries. She had sacrificed as many of the male humans and gnomes to prop up the energy gap as she dared. She needed the gnomes to continue to spread that foggy blanket and hide them all from inquisitive elfin minds. She would soon have to collapse the umbrella and take the Dream-shifter into direct sunlight for a considerable number of days to fill up the energy banks. Abaddon had driven the Dream-shifter insane by sacrificing hundreds of thousands of almost mindless Dokka'lfar to keep the arch open, when the sentient ship began to fail. The minds that had been surrendered to the Dream-shifter had been whole and had been assimilated into the structure of the ship.

Her first born sons were fast approaching adolescence and to her delight were beginning to grow wings from the stubs on their shoulders. They also had six fingered hands and antennae sprouting from their foreheads. Everything about them was elfin in structure except for their tempers and their indifference to the treatment of the humans and gnomes. In mind-set, they were as Dokka'lfar as their mother. Eloen had made sure of that by nudging their minds onto the same frame of mind as their mother's. She had fed them on resentment of their grandfather and his destruction of her kind. The only history they knew was the one that Eloen had planted in their minds. Her twin daughters, Brianna and Kellynn knew their duty to their mother's vengeance on the Ljo'sa'lfar High King and simmered with hatred for Peterkin. They too were showing signs that they would develop wings just as their father had and would be able to soar into the sky once fully grown.

One thing filled Eloen's heart with joy, was that their minds were developing the same extra psychic power, as herself. They could send their minds into the molecular structure of solid objects and influence them by telekinesis. After the plague had subsided from her frame in those early days, the dormant power had begun to flower in her mind. She had always been able to influence objects, but that ability had grown stronger, as she used it more and more. She realised that it was part of her human heritage and had merged with the elfin ability to practise telepathy. Now she had added the Dream-shifter's enhancement along with the Staff of Power that was once Molock's and found that the more she used it the stronger it got! She could now lift small objects and propel them through the air with ease. Her children all had the gift and now could lift, throw and catch around a circle of the five of them an object as dangerous and heavy as her obsidian blade. They could draw a bow and loose an arrow thinking it into a target with ease. This was something that no elf had ever done or even thought of doing.

Eloen smiled and reached out to her children and Ethelred with her mind and found them all hers.

"Soon High King you will have a problem to solve that will drive you into insanity," she thought and stretched her arms out to her mate.

Ethelred held her head in his hands and kissed her upturned lips and replied, "My father will not know what will hit him when we emerge. All we need is a few more years to grow while his life ebbs away at normal speed. You changed my life when you took me from the ancestral home of my people and have taught me so much! I would lay down my life for you, my love."

"I know," Eloen thought to herself. "I really do know! I will keep that thought safe until I need it."

MOLOCK'S WAND

CHAPTER SIXTEEN

Time crawled by for me and my family as we waited for Eloen's emergence. My resurrected friends were not idle however. The indomitable Sam Pitts and No'tt-mjool organised a rotating watch, using the cloned spellbinders to travel the rifts searching for any trace of Eloen's base that might leak out and give us the edge we needed. Spencer and my mother cruised through the rifts with a pair of bonded Trolls. She used her powerful mind opened to the utmost for a trace of any sentient creature, while the female troll searched the future for any emergence.

I was disturbed by my mother's thirst for vengeance. Do we all carry a Dokka'lfar alter ego in our subconscious mind, I wondered? I reflected, how easily I had 'turned' my people to take up arms and fight back against the Dark elves once I took control. My human mercenaries had shown them the way to fight with the weapons that they had distributed and my elfin people had gone against thousands and thousands of years of pacifism. This ability to take violent decisions was once only the prerogative of the High Kings and it was keyed into their genes. Now it would seem that due to my efforts, any one of my 'Light Elves' were now capable of violence if pushed. Self-control was now something that had to be mastered instead of it being second nature to my people. In a telepathic society there is little ability to lie and anti-social thoughts cannot be masked, so we are all, 'our brother's keeper'!

When we first met, until I altered the humans by contacting them mentally, telepathy was looked upon as a freak of nature or a trick. By using my mental powers to impart information they needed to know directly into their minds, I had given them all a nudge towards that ability. As time went by their abilities increased and they had been able to communicate by telepathy and shut out the constant 'chatter' of Elven speech.

Since I had resurrected my friends and blended Elven genes into their bodies via my own blood, their mental abilities had evolved very close to mine. I could now 'speak' with them quite easily across the strange distances of the rifts, as they searched for any sign of Eloen. Not all of them roamed the multi-universe however. John Smith and his descendants were working with the goblins that almost lived in the research laboratories beneath the castle on Haven. The missile that I had brought back from the military base at Twenty-nine Palms had been stripped down, studied and modified by the inquisitive goblins with the help of the human contingent. They called it a sun-burst device and it had been replaced in the secret compartment that the Spellbinder had constructed to house it. I hoped that I would not need to use it, but deep in my heart I knew that if the time came, I would deploy it.

To my surprise Ameela had no doubts about its use. The long years surviving at the top of the Tower of Ashkelon had left its mark upon her soul. There was a streak of ruthlessness deep inside her mind that was echoed in Mia's as well. My son Elthred lacked that steeliness of purpose in his make-up as he had never been in that situation until now. Time and again the thoughts tormented me by day and night, about what Eloen had done and was doing to him.

Ameela had decided to bear him at what we both understood to be the start of a new age. He had been the symbol of a great and peaceful re-start to our lives. Many of my people had followed our example and brought forth new elves into the empty worlds. For the first time in eons, elves, goblins and gnomes had increased their populations and that rare thing in such long-lived species of people; children had filled the air with happy laughter. The humans and the dwarves had always bred in large numbers as their spans were so brief. Elfish medical and genetically based knowledge had altered this for the dwarves long ago. These techniques had successfully been implicated into our new human allies so that they too could expect a much longer span. Once the numbers filled the empty lands, they too would operate a lower birth-rate and bear in mind how the voracious hoards of the Dokka'lfar had filled a complete world with endless famine.

All races understood this dictate and on that point of view we were united. Unknown to me there was now a new race of sentient beings loose amongst the rifts with an elfin heritage. It was during the construction of the Spellbinder clones, that a greater understanding of the 'staves of power' began to be had. Not only did they activate the Spellbinder that was tuned to each crystal, they augmented the mental powers of the wielder and could create a gestalt mind grouped from the individuals that pooled their strength. It was my scientifically minded friend, John Smith, who stumbled onto this capacity after I had told him of how Waldwick had tapped into the energy fields of Haven. It was during a test of a crystal and its ironwood staff that he had linked minds to the goblins working with him in the laboratory and also his great grandchildren. They had created a gestalt mind controlled by him and using the strengths of the other minds.

The next step was to incorporate No'tt-mjool into the blend

of minds and use the augmented power to 'see ahead' at a far greater range. Once this had been achieved then I would incorporate all of the other troll maidens into the gestalt and take control myself. This was a new ability to be learnt and apply with elfin mind-power. What worried me was the amount of resistance to the siren call of the group mind that I would have to apply. The lure of almost unlimited power was a terrible thing to fight against and if I succumbed, all participants could die leaving mindless bodies to decay. This was something that no other High King had attempted to do. I was on my own in this endeavour.

A sharp mind broke into my thoughts and rang my telepathic 'ears' mercilessly with a scolding that only my mother could impart.

"My son! While Ameela and I have breath, you will not go into that mental maelstrom alone! We will be your anchor! Just as Ameela was when you went fishing for souls into the reaches of the after-life so we will be firmly fixed to this reality here on Haven."

I was then aware of another voice that was just as resolute.

It was my daughter, Mia who had joined what had been a one sided conversation, with the comment, "Father, do you really think that mother and I would let you go without being your compass to get back?"

Whilst I was still unbalanced, Ameela broke in with a statement, "With apologies my dear mother, remember in ancient lore, the maiden, the mother and the crone makes the seal of three. We are all of the blood except for me and I have carried your seed to fruition. That seals the oath! We will be the thread that binds you to this reality and we will remain strong enough to haul you back away from that siren voice! There will be no argument! We have spoken with the same voice. We will be ready whenever you are to seek out the

Dokka'lfar Halfling and if we can, we will have my son back with us. If this is not to be, I have long ago prepared a mourning place in my soul to accept this. Do whatever you have to do to bring this evil creature down without counting the costs to us."

I stood quite still, with tears running down my cheeks, as their love for me surrounded my soul as tight a shield that I could only wish for. The confidence of a king flushed through my veins again as the strength of my three powerful 'queens' added themselves to me.

Under the shield of the Dream-shifter Eloen's Dokka'lfar prospered and multiplied. As soon as the Halfling girls were capable of childbearing, the male elves in her thrall made them pregnant. Their children were born with less human traits and a higher elfin genetic signature. All of them were fed on Eloen's hatred and lies. The original humans bore the brunt of the passing years and by the time that the second birth rate exploded were beginning to show signs of age. Lieutenant colonel Curtis Jones had aged in the twenty or more subjective years that he had lived under the shield. He was now approaching sixty and he was showing the effects of having been under Eloen's mental control for so long. He had a tendency to dribble and dragged one foot due to a stroke some years ago. Sometimes he would be racked with hatred for his mistress when his mind cleared and his hands would twitch towards his knife. A bitter cold grip would descend upon his mind as Eloen 'punished' him and rearranged his thoughts and priorities. Each conditioning would leave him in a weakened state and he would need feeding and cleaning for a few days until he got control of his body again.

The gnomes had been given a harsh incentive to breed and bring more of their hardy race into being. Eloen would have their leader crucified for several days and released to heal, with the promise that if more gnomic children were not born, she would nail him up for an extra day and make it three days instead. As Lorick was loved by all his people they reluctantly did as they were told. She could not easily control their minds because of their foggy thoughts and that was why she needed them. If their numbers fell too far there would not be enough of them to provide the mental blanket to keep the Dream-shifter mentally invisible. It was an insurance that coupled with the time differential, produced by her ship, kept them hidden. There was another problem however, the Dream-shifter was running out of energy and if Eloen sacrificed too many of the gnomes the fog would lift and she had no idea where Peterkin might be. She was sure that he would be patrolling the rifts just on the one chance that she would become visible.

As time passed she was contacted by the mind of Abaddon.

"My lady, unless you sacrifice a great deal of gnomes and what is left of the humans, I will not be able to maintain the shield for much longer. There is a limit to how much life energy I can use in this situation. There is an energy leakage through the time differential shield inwards, but not enough to enable me to maintain the speeding up of time for much longer. I need direct sunlight in massive amounts, so I must lift up beyond the atmosphere in real time to replenish the banks. The time has come to take a risk."

"Very well", she replied. "I will ensure that the gnomes are distributed evenly around the complex we have built here over the years. My people will keep them under control while we replenish your energy levels."

Over the next few days the Dokka'lfar moved the gnomes to be evenly distributed about the complex and extra iron collars were forged so that every human and elf hybrid would be shielded from any telepathic probe. The settlement had been made from logs hewn from the surrounding woods and where the ground had been cleared to grow crops. They had learned how to be self-sufficient in all matters of agriculture including the taming of livestock including horses. Once the land had been cleared, ploughed, harvested and managed, the Halflings turned their talents to weapon making, dominating the landscape under the Dream-shifter's umbrella. As the Halflings matured, the human males were treated as slaves and were easily mentally controlled by them. The women were conditioned to breed only with the elves and a simmering hatred began grow in the hearts of the pressed humans. Eloen and her children kept a tight control on their minds whenever they became aware of any slackening of purpose. The knowledge of the use and maintenance of the human weapons brought through the rifts were taken from the humans and their memories stored into the Dokka'lfar minds so that when the time came they would be quite capable of using them.

Curtis Jones had managed to recover from the last 'pressing' that Eloen had enforced upon his mind a little quicker than he usually did. After all these pain-wracked years he had developed a small growing resistance to her reinforcements. He managed to acquire one of the iron bands that had been recently forged and sprang the torque around his neck. The chance of being noticed as telepathically shielded, before the Dream-shifter shut down the time slowing field was a risk that could be pushed in his favour if he could only persuade one of the gnomes to accompany him to the edge of the barrier. He had in the past many dealings with Lorick and the two of them shared the hatred for Eloen and all her 'children' that dominated their lives.

He made his way behind the log cabins, leading a horse and pony to where the gnomes had their own segregated area and edged close to the back door of Lorick's cabin. The

Dokka'lfar had left him in his cabin along with his family and had moved the other families into hurriedly constructed shelters spaced in a wide circle around the settlement.

He tied the horse and pony to a hitching post and rapped a stick against the door to get Lorick's attention and the gnome's leader opened the door.

"What do you want, Curtis Jones. Has she sent you to do more harm," he bitterly said as he looked up at the lieutenant colonel.

"Listen to me, Lorick," he said. "I may not have much time to try this. Forget what I have been forced to do in the past. This is a chance to get outside of the Dream-shifter's time-dilation field. I need a gnome to travel with me, to make my disappearance less possible to be observed. I must get outside of the shield's boundaries before those hell-spawn return and hope that my thoughts may be picked up by Peterkin and show where we are. Do you understand?"

Lorick stared at the instrument of suffering to his people that the human had so often been and almost recoiled at the idea. He had so many fearful memories of his people dying at the hands of this man as he aided Eloen in her sacrifices to the Dream-shifter that he found it so hard to believe him. Incredible as it seemed, he had to believe him. The man he knew and feared would not act in this manner unless he was free of Eloen's mental thrall.

He came to a decision and beckoned the human into his house. Curtis bent his back so as not to knock his head on the low ceiling and supporting beams. He found it easier to go down on his knees and rest against the table.

"Before we go any further, tell me more," Lorick said bluntly.

"Eloen must take the Dream-shifter above the atmosphere with her children, so that the energy banks can be replenished by direct sunlight. The ship cannot maintain the time-distortion field for very much longer without sacrificing more gnomes and what humans are left. For a brief period the shield will be shut down and that is when I will make a break for it," Curtis said.

Lorick's son Olaf moved out of the door's shadow and put his knife away.

"I will go with him father. Throw some food into a sack and we will ready a horse and pony." Olaf asked, "When will she shut down the field and lift off? What time do we have?"

"I have a horse and pony tied to the hitching rail outside. I have provisions, but extra will be useful. She will lift off in the dawn to catch the morning sunrise so we need to make our way this evening to where the edge of the time-dilation field operates. Once that barrier goes down we will need to get well away from that point. What state the countryside will be in, I cannot guess, as it will be quite wild. Inside the barrier we have cleared the ground and farmed, raising live-stock. Outside it will be as if we had never been here. We will need the weapons that I have stolen to make sure that we survive. There will be wolves, bears, wild pigs and even perhaps lions that we may have to face. Staying alive will not be easy and there will be no coming back here," Cutis insisted.

Lorick turned to his son and threw his arms around him and said, "Go now before your mother comes back. I will explain to her where you have gone and why. If there is any chance that we can help stop that hell-spawn, we must try. We both know what this human has done to us in the past. Forget it! Eloen was in his mind and he has been her puppet all the time that we have been forced to live here."

Lorick opened the store-cupboard and swept the contents into a sack, handing it to his son.

"I will father. I do understand. Come then Curtis Jones let us be on our way as the evening sun begins to drop as we talk," Olaf said and lifted the sack over his shoulder.

Lorick opened the back-door and looked carefully into the gardens behind the house. Apart from a few gnomes harvesting vegetables and fruit there were none of the Dokka'lfar to be seen. He beckoned them out and held the horse and pony by their reins, as they settled into the saddles.

"Go well my son. We may not meet again. Do whatever you must to bring this tyrant down. I will deny all knowledge of where you are for as long as I can, so make haste. I will not see you go because if I do not see what direction you travel, she cannot have that information from me," Lorick declared and went inside.

"Which way?" asked Olaf.

"We will not make straight for the barrier as there is another vital thing we need before we ride hard towards it. I did not dare to tell your father, but we need a Dokka'lfar to be our mental beacon. My mind is not strong enough to be picked up by elves. But a Halfling will do fine. So we need to capture one, bind, gag and collar it with iron and get it outside before she comes back. I think that as soon as the energy banks are full she will return and put up the time-dilation umbrella. By the time she realises that we are missing we should have been on the other side of the barrier for a considerable time. A few days inside will be speeded up by a factor of ten while we will be in real time outside."

Olaf stared at Curtis and asked, "How do you know that she does not have that knowledge and has set a trap for you?"

"I have been her puppet for so long that she does not regard me as a threat. Every so often she reinforces her rule over me and makes me obedient, but a long association with that control builds resistance. When I am near her I sing old songs in my head and it amuses her to listen. The rest of the time I wear the iron torque around my neck under my shirt collar. Her children treat humans with contempt and the

Halflings laugh at us as we hurry to do their bidding," Curtis bitterly lamented. "So it will not enter their heads that we might just do something rebellious!"

The last rays of the sun were dipping behind the hills when the two of them stopped short before a well-lit log cabin tying the horse and pony to a rail. Curtis had told Olaf of his plan and crept to the hinged side of the door and waited with his club ready. Olaf waited until Curtis was prepared and stood some way in front of the door holding out his sack of provisions.

"Master," he loudly cried out, "I have your food ready as you ordered. My wife has baked you a pie and there is fresh fruit to go with it!"

The door swung open and a Halfling stared at the gnome with surprise, "What are you on about gnome! I asked for no food to be delivered, but I will gladly relieve you of that sack. I quite like gnome-baked pies," he said, stretching his hand out to the sack that Olaf dragged away from his grasp.

"You can't have this then, it must belong to someone else," Olaf replied and the Halfling walked out of the door's protection to grab the sack.

Curtis brought the club down on the back of the Halfling's head and he dropped like a stone. It was then that he saw the girl stood wide-eyed in the light of the candles inside the cabin. He quickly jumped inside and delivered a punch to her stomach that emptied her of wind and fixed an iron torque around her neck as she lay upon the ground. He dragged her outside and dumped her by the side of the male.

The human quickly bound and gagged them, dragging them both to his horse. He quickly hauled them over the saddle and bags, tying the both of them securely in place. Curtis fitted an iron torque in place around his neck. He heard a wicker from the stable at the side of the house and rapidly saddled up the horse that was tethered there. He led him outside and gathered the reins of the packhorse, riding steadily into the dying sunset. There was a reasonable road running along the side of the fields heading towards the edge of the barrier. Olaf and Curtis made use of it and kept going until it got too pitch dark to see. They then climbed off the pony and horse and walked them as far as they could and finding a stream, decided to stop there till morning. They opened the sack and shared the pie that they had tempted the Halfling with. The Halfling male began to come to and began to moan around the gag. His hands were tethered to his front and a link ran down to his feet and ankles. Some blood trickled down his forehead and matted in his hair. The female had got over the punch to the stomach for some time, but could do nothing tied to the back of the horse. Hatred shone from her eyes as she tested her bonds. Curtis released the bindings to the horse and the two Dokka'lfar fell to the ground.

Olaf had made a quick inspection of the cabin and had relieved the food cupboards of anything useful. He had also helped himself to an assortment of knives, arrows and a bow. He had then shut up the doors and put out the candles, popping those into his pockets as well.

Cutis spoke to his two captives and said, "You have a choice. I can remove the gags as we are far from the settlement as no-one can hear you and I will allow you to drink. Or if you will not obey me, I shall leave them on. If you do give me trouble I will remind you of several things. One you are in my power. Two, for what I need you for, I do not need you to see. My gnome friend here would love to put out your eyes with the point of his knife. So what is it to be?"

Curtis had hit the right spot as Olaf had caught the threat and had produced a mean looking knife that reflected the moonlight with a steely silver gleam. He grinned at the two captives and pointed the blade at them.

"Believe my human friend, Halflings; nothing would give me greater pleasure than to inflict on you, what your people have done to us."

Olaf stood and slowly approached the two terrified Dokka'lfar, keeping the knife visible all the time. Both of them nodded vigorously as Olaf knelt beside them. He took his time cutting through the bindings savouring the moment as he stripped away the gags.

He gave them both a drink, well laced with a sleeping powder that Curtis had brought with him.

"What are you going to do with us?" the male asked. "You can't hide from her for too long out here in the woods. What do you think you will gain? She will punish you in ways that you cannot imagine!"

Curtis ignored the tirade and waited until the sleeping draught soon took effect. Both of the Dokka'lfar slipped into a heavy sleep and the human and gnome relaxed.

"Come the dawn my friend and we will cross the barrier as she lifts it. As I have no idea how wide the time-displacement umbrella is, we must put as much distance away from it as possible," Curtis urged and stretched out on the ground, wrapped in his cloak. "You get first watch Olaf." He took off his wrist watch and gave it to the gnome and said, "Make sure that you wake me at two o'clock and I will wait for the dawn while you sleep."

Olaf sat quietly wrapped in his own cloak and watched the hours go by as he held the human's watch. The moon had long since set and the darkness amongst the trees was oppressive. He had no regrets with throwing his destiny alongside the human. He could only wonder what terrible pressures had been put into Curtis Jones's mind to force him to bend to Eloen's will. Gnomes were telepathically shielded from the minds of the elves and could only be read when in physical contact. The humans had no such defences and could be easily pressed into service and made to do what Eloen wanted.

When the watch showed the time to be near two o'clock, Olaf woke Curtis and said, "Your time to lie awake my friend. Dawn will be in about four hours. I just hope that you are right in what you say about her relaxing that field after dawn. If you are wrong she will come after us and our deaths will be an example to all the others."

MOLOCK'S WAND

CHAPTER SEVENTEEN

Curtis watched the Dokka'lfar as they still slept soundly in their drug induced torpor, as the early morning mists began to settle on all of them. This was a desperate measure he had taken, with no definite way of knowing if they would succeed at all. The only way he would know his bold scheme had born fruit would be if they were contacted by Peterkin. Outside of the barrier they would exist in real-time and it would be their only chance. He had no idea just how many years had passed 'outside' but he was sure that the High King of the Elves would never give up searching for Eloen and his son. He checked the ropes binding the Dokka'lfar to make sure that they had not worked loose during the night and that the iron torques were secure around their necks. He was pleased that they had managed to capture two of the Halflings as that would double the mental output from his captives. It made their detention more difficult and hazardous, but it might just be enough to get them noticed. The sky began to lighten and the birds began to sing in the branches above his head.

"Olaf! It is time for you to awaken, my friend. We have things to do," he said. "Our guests are still flat out from that sleeping draught we gave them, so it should be easier to load them onto the horse."

The gnome gave a grunt, stretched his arms out and wriggled out of his cloak to stand by his human companion.

He looked up at the sky and said, "Well it will be soon be time to see if you are right. Let us tie this scum onto the pack-horse so we can be on our way. We have no idea just how long she will take the Dream-shifter to the edge of space and return. We can eat breakfast as we travel."

Curtis nodded and dragged the male Halfling to the tethered horse and with Olaf's help managed to drag him over the saddle and tie his hands under the beast to his feet. The female was lighter and was not quite so difficult to heave over the saddle-bags. She too had her hands and feet tied together under the belly of the horse. They were smaller than the human but larger than the gnome. The horse had no problem taking the double load. The two of them mounted the horse and pony and continued to make their way through the forest, towards the edge of the barrier. The ground was flat and it was not too difficult to forge a pathway through the shrubs as the sun came up.

They became aware that there was an odd fuzziness in front of them stretching left and right as far as they could see. The vegetation rippled as if it was being shaken. Colours came and went in bands that rose and fell into the ground and up into the sky.

Curtis pulled the horses to a stop and declared to Olaf, "This must be it. We must wait and see if it changes. When and if it does, we must get through that area as quickly as we can."

As the sun rose the barrier changed before their eyes, first becoming a mirror and then the forest the other side of where the barrier transformed. The trees this side were older and well established, while the other side was as overgrown, but younger growth. Olaf rode a little closer and threw a stick through where the barrier had been. Nothing happened!

"Ride through Olaf and pick a path that I can follow with the two horses. Make haste! I don't want to be in there when the umbrella goes back up," Curtis worriedly asked the gnome!

Olaf pushed the pony to force his way through the easier parts of the underbrush leaving a track that Curtis could easily follow. The Dokka'lfar were beginning to wake up, as moans and whimpers sounded from the pack-horse. Curtis ignored the sounds of misery and urged the horses to keep up with the gnome's progress. They reached an area where the trees thinned out and they could make good progress. The ground began to climb upwards and they continued to urge the horses on, sometimes at a steady trot. This increased the moans of pain from the captives, but neither the human, nor the gnome paid any heed to pleadings to stop. They were now climbing steadily into summer sunshine and had reached a height far enough up the hill to look back onto the cultivated lands that had been hidden from view by the Dream-shifter's time-dilation field. Curtis got out his binoculars and searched the area around where they had captured the two Halflings. There was no movement and as all the Dokka'lfar were wearing iron torques to mask their thoughts, as well as every human, then there would be no telepathic searching. There would be a mental silence throughout the settlement and that would work in their favour. The colony of gnomes would also 'fog' any telepathic signal.

By now the moaning and pleading was getting on the nerves of both jailers and Olaf could stand no more. He rode his pony back and slapped the faces of their bound captives.

He pressed the point of his knife just under the eyelid of the male and said, "Your eye for quiet. A good trade I think!"

Curtis turned and said, "Leave him his eye Olaf; we don't want infection getting into the hole. He is no use to us dead! Let us keep moving up the hill and over the top before we stop and make camp. I have no idea how far the outside the edge of the bubble extends when it is working. We will keep moving just to make sure that we are well outside of the field when it goes back up."

Olaf took the point of the knife away from the Halfling's eye, but cut his cheek instead, as an incentive to keep quiet. He re-mounted his pony and took the pack-horse reins and followed Curtis as the human pressed on up the hill. The bushes thinned out until they could make a far better travelling rate as the sun climbed higher in the sky. Once they got to the top of the hill, Curtis could see where a spring had broken through lower down up on the other side of the hill and had filled a pool.

As Olaf caught up, Curtis pointed to the sight of the pool below them and said, "That's ideal, my friend. We can stop there and make some kind of a camp. This is where we will stay and see if my plan will work?"

"If! What do you mean, if? I thought that you were sure of what you were doing," Olaf exploded.

"Think about it, Olaf. Why do you think she has lived under that time distortion barrier all this time with everyone wearing an iron collar most of the time? It's because she is terrified of Peterkin hearing a telepathic signal from anyone! These two Dokka'lfar will sing well without those collars around their necks. Once the barrier goes up again, the collars come off and we wait. Olaf my friend it was the only chance we would have. She would stay under that barrier breeding more Dokka'lfar until she has an army, while my people die of old age serving her as her puppets!"

At that very moment there was a thunderclap that echoed round the hills and shook the trees on the lower slopes, making the horses rear and plunge as Curtis desperately hung onto the reins. The Dokka'lfar screamed in terror as the pack-horse kicked her heels and bucked, shaking her load till their teeth rattled. Olaf pulled his cloak over the horse's head to quiet her and slowly her terror diminished. As soon as the horse stood still, he cut the ropes under her belly and the two Dokka'lfar dropped onto the hard earth. Curtis dragged the two of them away from the possibility of kicking hooves and tied them to a nearby tree. He turned a deaf ear to their pleas to have the bonds loosened.

"Keep an eye on these two and do not take an eye out while I am gone! I would think that clap of thunder was the Dream-shifter returning. She is early! I thought that we would have several days until she returned. I will ride up to the top of the hill and see if she has switched on the time-displacement field. If she has we will take off the iron torques from around these Halflings' necks and start them broadcasting," he said and mounted his horse.

Olaf took his knife out and began to sharpen it again on a hard stone he had picked up, anxiously watched by the two Dokka'lfar.

"Don't be too long, or I might get bored," he replied and winked at Curtis.

The human rode quickly to the top of the hill and took out his binoculars. He stared down at what seemed to be a large bubble that stretched over the cultivated lands that he had helped to build. The bubble flickered in and out of existence and when he focused on the effect he could see that inside everything was speeded up. The field was definitely back in place. As time was speeded up inside, Curtis realised that it would not take long for Eloen to realise that some of her people were missing. He turned the horse downwards and rode fast to where the captives were tied to the tree.

"Take the iron neck-bands off Olaf and don't be too worried about being rough!"

The gnome removed both torques and sang a gnomish dirge to fog up his mind even more so the Dokka'lfar could not reach into his mind and control him. He also moved well away so that his mind did not interfere with the broadcasting effect of the two telepaths. He hung one of the iron bands around his neck as insurance and handed the other to Curtis, who added it to his.

"I'm glad to see that you have started a fire, Olaf. Get some more dry wood and we will build it up a little while I remove their shoes," Curtis grimly asked. !"I am going to roast the Halflings' feet. That should incite them to increase their telepathic shout!"

As he began to cut through the leather straps the two Halflings screamed and begged to be set free. The human ignored their desperate pleas for mercy and raked the fire steadily towards the bare feet, taking his time. The Dokka'lfar suddenly stiffened and went unconscious.

I sat in the control chair of the Spellbinder and began preparing my mind for the joining. What I was about to do had never been done before and the risks were enormous. If I failed and lost my mind in probing the future I would take with me all of the minds joined to mine. There would be no leadership of the Elvan kingdom left, except the few individuals that commanded the cloned Spellbinders. All of my people would be lost, leaving everyone at the mercy of Eloen. I systematically went through the calming exercises in my mind and pushed the sheer terror of what I had to do aside.

Sat cross-legged around me in a tri-angular formation were my mother, wife and daughter. Scattered throughout the rifts and placed close to any likely possibility, were the clones of the Spellbinder. Each sentient ship carried a troll maiden accompanied by elves, or one of my resurrected people. All of them began to relax and open their minds to the presence of the High King to allow me to take control. Each ship retained a pilot with three gnomes sat in a triangle around him to prevent me from absorbing his mind by accident, leaving the Spellbinder clone without any control.

I closed my eyes and reached out to the waiting minds of my friends that I had called back from death. Sam Pitts was the first, followed by Mellitus, John, Hoatzin, Spencer, David and his twin Steven. I was aware of my three anchors sat around me and my mind rose out of my body, seeking to make a solid base of elfish minds. Through the patterns of the Rifts I searched for them and found them inside the Spellbinder clones.

At the same location were the minds of the trolls and I added them into the gestalt, layer by layer, led by No'tt-mjool, who sat cross-legged behind the control chair. I built a launching platform around the fan shaped search pattern that the Troll minds set up and hurled through future time using their abilities. Night Flower had sought me out the night before and spoke seriously to me.

"Tomorrow High King, will test the powers of my sisters to the very utmost. There are many different paths to take into the future and some will end in death. I dare not say more, except to say that I do not yet, immediately see my tomb or yours. Much of what will happen will rest on the day and whether an outside force is applied. I cannot say more!"

My questing mind was swept along with the Troll maidens, as day by day, they scanned the future carrying my seeking mind. A week went by in subjective time, followed by a month and then several months rushed by. I increased my control by invoking the Spellbinder's Staff of Power and added the minds of the long dead Kings that I carried with me. Now I became a godlike entity with countless eyes and ears searching through rift after rift, many months in the future.

A wisp of thought, of fear and pain, caught my attention. The mind signature was different to an elf's and it was more comparable to one of my resurrected people. There was a faint aura of humanity about it. The pattern of the Rift became set in my mind and the time in the future that the mind was broadcasting from, became known to me. The minds I touched were Halfling! I had what I needed and a feeling of triumph surged through my mind.

Yet I was all-powerful. What was the point of what I was trying to do? This was how I should be! A siren temptation beckoned to my being. The layers of minds within my mind were mine to use. I could be supreme! I could be a god! There was nothing that could be denied me in this state, but for that annoying thread that pulled at my soul. What was that? Did I need to cut loose from its influence?

Feelings of love and need flooded my being, channelled by that very thread I sought to cut. It was then I remembered why I was there and individual minds that were not mine to take began to be recognised.

A babble of voices all clambering to be heard filled my mind, but loudest were the minds of the dead kings ringing in my head, all of them shouting, "Go back while you still can!"

I was spinning in the void, not sure which way to go, when something empathetic touched my mind. It was someone who I had known and trusted, long ago it seemed. It was an anchor that brought me to a stop.

"You are, Peterkin, the Long Shadow," Hildegard reminded him. "You do not belong here! This is not your place to be!"

"Hildegard! Am I dead?" I asked in astonishment.

"You will soon be in that state, if you do not follow the thread back to your body, along with all the others with you.

Concentrate on the 'seal of three' that is the trinity of your mother, daughter and wife. It is their love for you that will pull you back."

I was fast becoming much more aware of the individual minds that had been part of my gestalt and began to gently release them back to their parent bodies. I began to feel a sense of direction and a steady pull. Finally I became aware of myself and the ragged breaths that my mortal frame was struggling to take in. A terrible weakness flooded my nervous system along with a burning thirst that clawed at my throat. I opened my eyes to see my beloved family stretched out on the floor, collapsed with fatigue, attended by our ever devoted gnomes.

"Drink this sire," said Razzmutt, my faithful confidante and friend. "It's honey and water. The ladies will be attended to. You may find that all of you are in need of a good bath, my King. You have been in this state for over two days. We have tried to keep you as clean as we could, but we dare not wake you from the work that you were doing. Were you successful, Sire?"

"Yes, I was, Razzmutt," I replied.

It was then that I realised that I was bleeding from the palm of my hand that held the crystal at the top of the Staff of Power. My other hand was locked around the staff and I was having trouble opening my fingers. Razzmutt leaned over me and undid my fingers one by one and rubbed them to bring back the circulation into my hands. The bleeding soon stopped as the ability of regeneration that my species have, 'kicked in' and the skin began to knit together. It still hurt and burned however. I began to move my arms and legs to overpower the vicious cramps that knotted up my muscles.

My family were all suffering the same symptoms and were struggling to get to their feet, helped by our gnomes. There was nothing that I could do for them as I could scarcely move myself, except to tell them all the news.

I took another swallow of the honeyed water and opened my mind to make contact again with the ones who had offered me their very minds to use, live or die.

"We found them! I know where they are and when they will surface briefly," I told them. "I have time to plan and organise. Come home to Haven and sit at my table again. We have much to consider."

I walked away from the control chair on unsteady legs and hugged my family to me. We were all in desperate need of a bath or shower, but we did not mind. We were alive and none of the gestalt had suffered mind damage. I shuddered as I thought what could have been had it not been the long dead spirit of Hildegard thrusting me away from what was calling to me. This must have been the intervention that Night Flower had hinted at. The outside force had been the very soul of Hildegard that had crossed over from her realm to mine and helped me to get back. Had it not been for her, I am sure that I would have lost my way and we would all have sunk into death. She had said not one word about her daughter, locked into madness and a servant of Eloen. Her only concern was for me, or could it have been that she knew the alternative future that could have collapsed onto us all?

According to what I had experienced I now knew what spatial rift Eloen had gone to hide in and when she came out to replenish the Dream-shifter's energy banks. No'tt-mjool warned me of the possible paradoxes. We must wait until after she has returned to the alternative Earth before we did anything. If we were too early, the Halfling minds would not be heard because Curtis could not make the journey outside of the time-distortion field, if we did anything to alter that timeline. I seethed with impatience. Yet I could understand Night Flower's logic about alternative futures. The good thing about it was that it gave us plenty of time to plan and the element of surprise.

Now I also had to wrestle with the moral issues. The brief mind-touch I had with the Halfling gave me some information that gave me pause for thought. Eloen had brought these new Dokka'lfar into existence and apart from the cruelty they had shown to the gnomes and humans, they did not warrant extermination. Eloen had made them the way that they were and had 'pressed' their minds into obedience from babyhood. The other problem was the fact that the gnomes had been captured, forced to breed to provide a mental screen and were blameless. Somehow we needed to rescue them from the Dokka'lfar along with any humans that were left. This was going to take some planning!

It took a few days before all of my people journeyed back through the Rifts and made it back to Haven. I had fully recovered by then, as far as anyone could with all those voices in my mind clamouring for attention. They all had good advice to give, but it was me that had to carry it out. I drew much comfort from my father, who although he had never ruled, had sound guidance to give in matters relating to people. It was he who had put forward an idea about dealing with the Dokka'lfar, if we were to attempt the rescue of the gnomes.

The morning sun was shining through the balcony and over the round table that I always had our meetings around. My resurrected friends, the Troll maidens, and the dwarves sat around along with an assortment of goblins and gnomes.

Thorinson had received my news badly about his parents. I had extracted enough information from that brief mind touch with the Halflings to understand that there was little chance that his parents were still sane. Who they once were had been buried under many years of domination by Eloen. She had made these two stalwart dwarves her own creatures, willing to die in the defence of her. From what I had seen, they were instrumental in carrying out her deranged commands. It was these two that had nailed, Lorick, the leader of the gnomes to the wooden frame, to compel his people to do what was required. She had left him there for two days before she instructed Thorin and Hilden to remove the nails. Under that sort of duress, the gnomes did as they were told with no rebellion, knowing that Lorick would be the sufferer for any of their indiscretions.

I opened my mind and showed the council what I had discovered and the location and time of Eloen's brief emergence. I threw the option open for ideas and discussion.

John Smith opened the debate by handing over the 'floor' to Mallindar, who was one of the goblins that had taken apart the atomic weapon that I had taken from the marine base of Twenty-nine Palms. He had studied it and had modified its function to directly disrupt the nannite structure of the Dream-shifter, without destroying the life housed inside the sentient ship.

"There is one problem," Mallindar pointed out; "when the weapon is deployed it will also take apart the vessel carrying it. The host ship will have to hover over the top of the time-displacement bubble and spread itself over it, to be a mirror, so that the intense light will be reflected into the Dream-shifter. This will take it apart as well!

We all stared at the light green, roundish face of the goblin and thought about what that meant. His large, dark eyes sought each one of us in turn and his long eyelashes opened wide in concern. His spindly fingers interlocked and came apart into fists showing the amount of agitation and stress that he was under.

He pulled at the long tufts of hair growing from his double pointed ears nervously and added, "This grim choice is the only certain way to totally destroy the Dream-shifter. The adapted neutron bomb would now deliver an Electromagnetic pulse, not the lethal radiation that was intended by the originators of the device. Done this way there would be no margin of error. If this was done by a winged elf, then using darkened goggles should be sufficient to stave off blindness by the activator. The elf responsible could then soar upwards while the cloned Spellbinder is destroying both vessels at the same time. The shape of the ship would need to be open at the top so that whoever sits controlling the vessel can fly away. The host ship will rain down elf-stone onto those who are inside the Dream-shifter as it comes apart burying anybody there. Also we have no real idea of what the Dream-shifter will do as it dissolves into inert nanotechnology."

John Smith stood up and added, "A pulse of that intensity could do all manner of things to a telepathic being. We can only guess what the effect might be, but be assured it may well do permanent damage to all of the people under the main theatre of operations."

Eduardo stood up and stated, "I volunteer for that post, High King. I could see that you were about to take on that responsibility for yourself. The answer to that idea is a big no! I can and will be the one to carry out that part of the mission."

Sam Pitts then took the floor and ran with the innovative idea and added, "All the other cloned spellbinders have been fitted with the sunburst lasers that will send out a cone of intense light, temporarily blinding all of the people under Eloen's control. During that induced blindness we will need very fast snatch squads to collect the gnomes and the humans if possible and stow them onto the cloned spellbinders. I know just the people to do this. The raptors helped us before when we destroyed the Dokka'lfar. I'm confident that they would help us again. We need to be no more than five minutes after the 'nova' bomb goes off to maximise confusion."

I spoke earnestly to my friends, "There is no certainty that my son is still alive and if he is he may well be so well mind pressed by Eloen that he will be completely untrustworthy. The same could be said for the new Dokka'lfar that Eloen had bred. What I picked up from the two Halflings minds in the brief contact was that they have all been conditioned to hate us and me in particular."

Mellitus stood up and addressed the meeting raising a question that Thorinson dared not ask, "Thorin and Hilden are dwarves! They are my kin and though they are insane to our standards, surely they can be salvaged? May Thorin, Aradun and I try to capture them so that perhaps their bodies and minds may be salvaged?"

"If it proves possible, you have my blessing Mellitus old friend," I replied and added, "I must go across the plains of Scion and find the descendants of Prime's people. I shall take you with me Mellitus, along with the two gnomes who first brought new of Eloen's appearance on Haven. Rassel and Lorena have met with the raptors before and will be recognised. It will give the 'Folk' a chance to recognise the scent of gnomes as well as their smaller stature."

MOLOCK'S WAND

CHAPTER EIGHTEEN

I still had plenty of time and could easily spend it searching out the Velociraptors on the plains of Scion. I had the company of the two gnomes who had been rescued by the 'raptors' and brought to the outskirts of the elven lands. Both Rassel and Lorena were excited to be meeting these intelligent dinosaurs again. I also took Mellitus, Arundel and Thorinson with me, to be able to explain the loss of the dwarves from the Stormgalt, now that Mellitus could converse using telepathy.

I left a great deal of activity at the laboratories at the castle at Haven. Sam Pitts had taken a Spellbinder clone back to Alfheimr with Night Flower as company, to inform Vita-fjarri of what the Trolls had helped me discover. I had asked her on no account to look into the future in case some small thing altered what I had decided to do. I had to have faith in my own abilities that the decisions that I had set in motion would be carried out. I had the hope that the spirit of Hildegard could also travel through the rifts of time and had she felt the outlook bleak, would have told me in some way to make me alter things. She had remained silent and had not followed me back in time for me to reclaim my body.

"This is the area that I recognise, my Lord," Rassel said and grasped my arm, bringing me out of my inwards musings.

"Look! I see smoke, High King and where there is smoke the raptors will be somewhere at hand."

I stared through the transparent panel of the Spellbinder and sent my thoughts into the jungle below. I had made the shape of the Spellbinder into a great silver cylinder and extended four legs with flattened feet. I used my augmented senses to 'see' where the village huts were situated and brought the Spellbinder down onto a mass of ferns that were out of the way of the dwellings. Once the vessel had settled I opened the front and stepped out into the humid air.

I was met by a throng of raptors, all of them quite aware of whom I was and who the two gnomes were who followed me outside. I had quite forgotten how much taller than elves and dwarves the raptors were. They would strike terror into anyone who was not acquainted with them. The sight of the teeth alone would do the trick, along with the sabre looking talons spreading from both hands and feet. Add into the mix, that the vision of anyone near the Dream-shifter when it was destroyed would be very blurred and then the sight of these giant predators would paralyse anyone with fear. The new Dokka'lfar had never seen them, but some of the gnomes had and had passed on the stories of how they had helped to destroy Molock's offspring. They would quickly understand when hell broke loose and the raptors gathered them up and ferried them back to the waiting Spellbinder clones.

I opened my mind to the velociraptor's mental band and was instantly aware of the lead raptor.

"You are High King. You have need of us. Speak in my head and tell me how my people can help. I am Prime of the 'Folk' descendant of the Prime that led the way against the common foe. It was I who rescued the small people from the Great Plains and took them to you."

I was amazed at the clarity of the thoughts that I picked up from her. In the generations that had been hatched since I had last been here, a rigorous form of selection had been carried out. I scanned her history and was taken aback over such ruthlessness. Any raptor that failed to measure up to the standards set by the leaders was driven out of the community to fend for themselves. Only the most intelligent were permitted to breed and once the hatchlings forced their way into the world, they were watched and judged. My use of telepathy to communicate with the first 'Prime' had triggered off a cascade. What had happened since then had sharpened their minds so that they could communicate amongst themselves. Those that retained that ability were encouraged to mate with the best of the best.

They had increased in size since I had last seen them. The feathers were still a variation of browns that were barred with darker stripes. They were easily as tall as a human and some of them were taller. The three fingered hands were more dexterous and quite able to fashion tools. They all had the big feathery ruff around their necks and what were almost flight feathers on their arms that they kept slanted back, out of the way. The long ridged tail had also increased in the number of flight feathers, so that it could aid them in changing direction when they ran. This was not quite right however as I was conscious of a shadow over us and looked up. A raptor had launched itself from the top of a tall fern and was gliding towards the village with arms or wings outstretched and the tail fanned out behind it. This was a new talent that I instantly file away for future use.

"There have been great changes in the long years that have gone by since I visited you last," I projected into her mind. "You are right, descendant of Prime. The elves would use your abilities if you are amenable to help us rescue many of the small people, kin to those who stand before you. There is once again an evil in the lands of the elves and the 'Folk'. It is contained at the moment and I will deal with it and try to keep the bloodshed to the minimum. We have Dokka'lfar amongst our people, but far from the many mindless ones we fought before. These are not to be eaten for they are as sentient as you. They have made captive, many of these small people and I wish them to be freed."

"I am Mellitus," interrupted my friend using his new found power of his elfish mind. "I see that you carry the glass that I gave to your ancestor, many years ago in that carrying bag around your neck.

"You are the one who was given the egg and gave us the means of creating fire. You also gave us the secret of the bow! Ask of us and we will repay you," the raptor promised.

"This man's parents are captive to the Dokka'lfar. They will be difficult to capture as the Halfling has turned their minds and they would gladly die defending her. I want them taken captive without damage. Can you do this?"

The new Prime circled Thorinson and logged his scent into her memory. She studied him carefully, staring long and hard at Rassel and Lorena, noting the differences, taking their odour.

"You will need many more than the people from this village. How many days can you stay here before your carrier takes you away?"

"We can stay here for no more than thirty sunrises before I must leave." I asked, "How far can you reach out to the 'Folk' to bring those who can be spared from their duties here?"

"As far as a signal fire can be seen! We will light a big one tonight that will be seen all across the Great Plains. My people will come from far and wide. Once the fire is seen then minds will be attuned to one purpose. Then you will be able to contact them along with me. We will join together and reach out to all of the leaders of the clans."

I was in awe of the changes that had taken place amongst these enterprising people. They had evolved so far and all due to their involvement with me. Ripples in a pond, I thought. What had been started would have no end. Now above all else I was determined that the raptors would become part of the lives of all the many sentient beings that lived on the two elf worlds.

That night the raptors lit the bonfire and within an hour, tiny lights shone out in the darkness all across the Plains of Scion. My people sat on logs and stones enjoying the feast that Prime's people had collected and roasted on the bonfires flames. Ameela, Mia and I sat a little apart from the others and we dwelled on Elthred's fate. He had been the symbol of the peace that we had achieved and had been the first elf new born in the Kingdom. The need to fill up the empty worlds had enthusiastically driven elves, gnomes, goblins and dwarves to increase their numbers.

I had never forgotten that when we had destroyed Molock and his mother had handed over her rape-child to me to see fit whether she could live. I had looked into that child's timeline and I had seen Molock's shadow fall across the tiny defenceless creature. I had told Olivia that the time of the Dokka'lfar would end with this infant. I had sworn an oath that I would care for my people and now once again a hard choice would fall to me. I remembered so well the night that Elthred had been born. My heart had danced with joy. It was I that had cut the umbilical cord and separated him from his mother. I had been so confident that here was the future leader of the many species that would live together under elfin rule. I had thought that the evil that lay untapped in every heart would remain hidden. I had watched my son grow up with so much joy and had taken a great part in his rise from childhood. I had never watched Mia's childhood unfold, as much of it had been spent in Waldwick's dungeon. As the centuries had passed, Elthred had grown into a fine elf and had taken up the task of refurbishing the ancestral castle we called Homecoming. We had been so proud of him and all of his accomplishments on the home-world of Alfheimr. I had been so sure that when that day came, he would take up the reins of High King and discharge that duty well.

Now the curse of the Dokka'lfar had risen again and Molock's offspring had been brought into this multi-verse by one Halfling consumed with hate for me and my family. I could only surmise what she had produced under that time-distorting bubble! My contact with the Dokka'lfar had been brief, but I had picked up enough information to give me a good clue. I at least knew that lieutenant colonel Curtis Jones was still alive and was the instigator of bringing the Halflings out from the time–distortion barrier so that I could pick up their mind signatures. I realised what a brave man he was, to do what he had accomplished. He would be the first that I picked up, as his knowledge would be invaluable, but this was in the future and was yet to come.

I also realised that as time was speeded up inside the Dream-shifter's influence then I would not have very much time to assimilate his information before Eloen realised that something had changed and two of her Dokka'lfar were missing along with her one-time puppet, Curtis Jones! The one thing I had learnt to my cost was that she was an incredibly intelligent elf. She had outwitted me time and time again, but not this time. Now I knew where she was and when I could strike without creating a paradox. I would have to time things very carefully or things could unravel. I needed the knowledge inside Curtis Jones's mind to direct the theatre of action. If I took too long understanding it, then Eloen might realise what had taken place and disappear through the Rifts taking the Dream-shifter and her people with her.

It was then an idea surfaced in my mind and I sent for Night Flower. It was not long before the troll appeared with Sam Pitts very close to her side. The light danced off her black curly hair from the bonfire as she stood in front of me.

"No'tt-mjool," I asked, "there is something that I need know about your abilities."

"Ask, High King," Night Flower replied.

I walked towards the two of them, reached forwards and held her hand in mine and asked, "What we did collectively as a group mind, can we two do as a couple, travel forwards in time to that time and place now that I know the co-ordinates? There would be a possibility of gathering more information, if I could just spend a few minutes at that location and time. I can then return here with that information and plan accordingly."

"Possible it may be, High king, but dangerous it could be for the two of us. Anchors we would need again to make sure of a return," the Troll deliberated. "Choose do I, the Halfling Sam Pitts, as his love for me will draw into returning. Your daughter, Mia would be of your blood and that will call you back! Sit and link hands and we will enter the future together."

Ameela went pale as did my mother at the prospect of me once again plunging into the rifts of the future. The fact that they would be left out, made them all the more anxious. I gave both of them a kiss and a hug and sat down linking hands into the circle. Sparks shot into the air from the bonfire as we prepared to join our minds together in a lighter capacity. Thoughts had been passed from mind to mind that I was willing to risk our combined lives on yet another quest. There was a stir in the crowd that had gathered as the new Prime pushed her way through and squatted down beside me. Her three fingered hand tightened on my left wrist and she held onto Sam Pitts' right wrist.

The velociraptor opened her mind to me and said, "Show me what you would do. I would learn this power of the mind. I will be part of this union. My strength will be yours to draw upon. What you know, I will know and when you need my people they will understand far better what is required of them if I do too!"

This was something that I had not planned for, but I could not think of any way I could refuse her. I was reminded of something that I had been told by No'tt-mjool and that she had not 'seen' my tomb or hers. It could well be that the addition of the velociraptor's mind would tip the balance in my favour?

I came to a decision and gathered in all the minds in the circle and thrust forwards in time to a point two minutes after I had first made contact and to the place that Curtis Jones was torturing the Dokka'lfar. The co-ordinates rushed towards the gestalt and as we approached that point in time and space I slowed the speed right down until I just passed that point of time when I had departed and slipped through the rift. I reached out to the mind of the male Dokka'lfar and took control of his body.

Curtis Jones and Olaf had seen the Halflings stiffen and stop trying to keep their feet from the heat of the fire. As quick as that moment faded and the Dokka'lfar began to wriggle away from the fire obviously back in control of their minds and bodies something else took place.

The male turned and spoke to Curtis Jones with a completely different voice.

"Put the iron bands back onto the Dokka'lfar and take yours off. I am Peterkin and we do not have very much time. I need the information in your mind, now! I do not have the time to explain; just do it!"

Curtis slipped the iron torques around the Dokka'lfar's necks and added his as well.

Instantly he was aware of the High King's mind in his, storing his memories and he added, "Take cover and to be safe, kill the two Halflings. Do not look over the top of the hill until I say so. I am from the past and at this moment I cannot tell you with certainty what my plans are to deal with this situation. I need to examine your memories and make decisions in my own timeframe. All I can say is that it will happen in the next few minutes. Replace the iron collar."

Curtis grabbed the male by his hair, dragged his head up and cut his throat immediately, replaced his collar and directed Olaf, "Kill the other one. What is about to happen will happen soon. Peterkin knows where and when we are so take cover."

The gnome smiled and slashed his knife through her carotid artery and allowed the gush to put out the fire.

"I can't tell you how good that made me feel, Human," he said and wiped his knife clean on her hair. "It worked then Curtis! You made contact with the High King. What happens now?"

"We stay as flat to the ground as we can and stay there until he sends for us," replied the human and buried his head under his crossed arms, making sure that all the fire was out before he did so.

Because I knew where and when we were I was able to keep the bond steady and return to the bonfire along with all the members of the gestalt without any problems. Indeed the clarity and strength of Prime's mind had wrapped around the group. She had been the push that got the entwined mind of No'tt-mjool and myself, wrenched away from the here and now. I knew where we needed to be and when we needed to be there, but it was the clean logical mind of the velociraptor that had propelled us there fuelling the abilities of the Troll maiden. The two anchors that were comprised of my daughter and my old friend Sam Pitts had been just the right emotional bond to drag us back. I found myself dragged away from the bonfire by Ameela who seized me by my pointed ears and kissed me over and over again, tears streaming down her cheeks.

"Stop doing that Peterkin. You scare me too much! I could only stand and watch as your mind disappeared from your body and something else swept away! If you had not returned then I would have sang the dirge of un-being and joined you in the afterlife."

"You know that I do what I do out of love for you and all who call me High King. I cannot turn my back on my people! You know that! I never asked for this and remember it all started with the rescue of you! I am the Long Shadow and I cannot change that prophesy," I reminded her and held her tightly. "Besides I got what I came for. I have Lieutenant Curtis Jones's memories of what has transpired under that time distorting umbrella. I need to make sense of what I have learned and impart that knowledge to the others."

We all needed to sleep, so we removed ourselves to the comforts of the Spellbinder where I soon found out sleeping was something that would not come for me. I sat in the command chair and ran the human's memories forwards from the time he had been 'pressed' until the present day. By the time the dawn had risen my grudging admiration for Molock's Daughter had grown another notch. It was her cruelty that I found an abomination. Her ruthlessness was without parallel as she rolled over anything in her way. Curtis had been kept close to Eloen's side and had been mentally dominated for over thirty years. He had been 'pressed' to do some terrible things to both his own kind and to the gnomes. The fact that he had still managed to formulate a plan and keep it secret from her amazed me.

I wept as I realised that my son was lost to me. The use of

the wand and her augmented mental powers had altered his personality to the point that he now worshipped her. As for the four grandchildren I now had, they had been brought up on a constant diet of hatred for me and my family. There were two sets of twins and were one part human to three parts elf. The two males-Cethafin and Firovel and the females;– Brianna & Kellynn, were far more elf than anything else, but pure Dokka'lfar in their hearts. Also they were born with the wing nubs that all elves develop into fully fledged wings upon puberty. By now they were adult, fully winged and old enough to give and carry children of their own. There were many of these 'new elves' produced by the mating of the male elves to Halflings all with a one quarter human heritage. They were a new race of beings created on purpose by Eloen. The taint of Molock was present in each and every one of them, but not the colouration of the original Dokka'lfar species. Amongst the off-shoot of this elfin race, were none of the bright red or coal-black types brought about by the incestuous coupling of his children. Eloen had masterminded a new intelligent species that would obey her every whim, as their minds had been twisted by her from birth. Svartálfar was the closest that our old language could get to what they were. We had no real name for them as they were less than pure elf and had human genes in their makeup. The fact that we all evolved on parallel Earths might be the reason that we were genetically compatible. The darkness was evident in their minds, rather than their bodies and that had been planted there by Eloen's vengeful efforts.

A hand lightly squeezed my shoulder and Ameela said, "Peterkin you have sat here all night. You must sleep or you will be too tired to give direction and leadership. Go to bed my dearest love. You will rest, because I will make it so! I have forbidden anyone for any reason to interrupt us in the bedchamber. Come with me."

I rose from the moulded chair and made my way into our bedroom, noticing that Razzmutt and Mellitus had sat against the wall preventing any disruptions. My head was spinning and my limbs cried out for rest as I lay upon the bed. Ameela removed my clothes and hers and massaged my aching body eventually finding my flaccid penis. She worked her magic on my manhood and popped it into her mouth until it rose proud and steady. Ameela straddled me and drew me into that warm, wet place of pleasure. She squeezed me hard and tormented me with her presence until I could stand no more and ejaculated deep into her receptive womb where two eggs awaited my eager seeds.

She rolled onto her side and held my head in her arms and said, "There will be two sons awaiting the outcome of this confrontation. If we have lost our firstborn son to Eloen, then there will be two that will take his place in times to come. Now sleep my King and I will watch over you until you wake."

I felt her mind slip gently into mine humming a lullaby that my mother had sang to me when I was a child. Sexually gratified and at peace with what I had sorted from Curtis Jones's memories I at last sank gently into slumber.

That morning and every day the clans moved across the plains of Scion to the summons that the descendant of Prime had set in motion. As each clan forced their way through the ferns and wild jungle, they were made welcome at her 'village.' The logistics of feeding so many began to tell on the raptors hosting the gathering. Many of the newcomers had brought beasts of their own to slaughter and did so without dissent. The bonfire needed to be replenished and carcasses were hung over the smoke and flames. Each clan were determined to pledge their best and fittest males and females for the expedition in hand. Prime had used her mental gifts to impart to each clan just what it was that we were about to do. By taking her with us into the possible future and sharing the information we had gained, it had been so much more straightforward in passing on what we needed her people to do. From the information that I had downloaded from the mind of Curtis Jones I knew where practically all of the gnomes had been placed so that they gave maximum coverage of their unique blanking effect. Eloen had positioned them around the perimeter of the time-distorting field. They would be the furthest from the EMF pulse when the cloned Spellbinder dropped on top of the Dream-shifter and activated the weapon.

I had spent a long time planning this day; all I could hope for was that it would at last rid me of this hate-filled Dokka'lfar creature. At what cost, I could only speculate. I feared that it would cost me my son and that would be the 'bride-price' that Cailleach had warned me of through using Vita-fjarri and her people's abilities. I swallowed my anguish and clamped down on that pain; coming to terms with the awful decisions that I and only I had to make.

MOLOCK'S WAND

CHAPTER NINETEEN

Eloen sat in her command chair and fretted about the time spent re-charging the energy banks. The Dream-shifter had expanded every possible light-sensitive panels and turned them to the sun. Long-starved of energy except for the life energy syphoned off the gnomes and humans, the sentient ship greedily sucked in the starlight and banked it.

"Abaddon! How much longer must we soak up energy? I feel exposed," Eloen asked the sentient ship!

"Lady Eloen can you detect the ones beneath at the settlement? All on board are wearing the iron and cannot be detected," the Dream-shifter replied.

The Halfling cast her mind beneath and could not detect any telepathic 'chatter' as the gnomes she had settled around the inside edge of the time distortion field fogged the complete area. She sighed with relief, but she still felt uneasy and exposed.

Elthred reassured her and said, "My one true love, my father is just an elf! He has no special powers at his disposal. You are equal to him in all your powers and your other gifts that we have mastered, will put him at a disadvantage. I have never seen my father move things with his mind! Our children have talents that he could never dream of!"

"Mother, when can we remove the iron band from around our necks?"

The voice had come from behind Eloen and was one of her sons.

"Be patient, Cethafin and you, Firovel as the Dream-shifter will soon be fully fuelled and we can return to the planet below," Eloen insisted and stood to embrace him. "Once we are yet again under the time distorting field, we can carry on the plan. This will take time my impatient son, but when we emerge back into Peterkin's world we will carry a punch that will overcome your grandfather and bring all that he has done crumbling around his knees. I too wish to bring that day forwards but we need far more of the improved Dokka'lfar than are clustered around the settlement. We will carry out a series of hit-and-run raids that will destroy the order that he thinks that he has built. It will just take time and we have all the time we need, once the Dream-shifter has replenished its energy stores."

Brianna and Kellynn were both pregnant by one of the elves that Eloen had kidnapped and 'pressed' into servitude. They were halfway through the gestation process and had not yet begun to show very much. They had both been taught by their mother how to release multiple eggs for fertilisation and were carrying quads. These children would only carry an eighth of humanity in their genetic makeup.

Eloen would make sure that from birth onwards, these new elves would be Dokka'lfar in their minds and would mature into the same hate-filled attitude to the Ljo'sa'lfar, as did their grandmother! The new race of elves that she had genetically crafted would grow and increase soon to dominate the weaker 'Light Elves' and rule them all. Eventually the elder race would cease to exist and Molock's descendants would dominate all of the parallel worlds. Eloen would be there to make sure of that and with the power of Molock's Wand at her disposal she would dominate all who came before her. As for the humans; their service as weapon makers and slaves would satisfy every desire that she could need. The aversion to iron had been bred out by incorporating human genes into elfin bodies although its negative effect on telepathy was a double benefit. For the first time in elfin history that sense could be turned off by a simple iron collar worn around the neck. The isolation was difficult to suffer for long periods and she would be very pleased to return to the settlement and be free to use that sense. This close to the Dream-shifter it was possible to communicate by loosening the torque around her neck. She opened the collar a little more and cast her mind outwards for a brief moment and was comforted by the feeling that there was no indication that any mind was 'out there' waiting to pounce. Even then Eloen felt uneasy and exposed.

Several rifts away the Spellbinder and ten of its clones, patiently waited for the time to pass until Eloen returned to her base and switched on the time-distortion field. Peterkin knew the precise time to home in to the rift that Eloen had hidden in and the co-ordinates of where the settlement existed. He had relayed the points that the other Spellbinders and would need to touch down, to be as close to the gnomes' areas as could be made possible. After Eduardo had detonated the bomb and the electromagnetic pulse had destroyed the Dream-shifter, he would move in as close to what remained as he could.

I was linked telepathically to each commander of the cloned spellbinders and had spent some time with them before we embarked, training them to resist the urge to join with me. Each mind had to stay individual and not form a gestalt with me, when I briefly dominated them and sent them on their way. I would have to send the co-ordinates to each of them one minute after I had sent Eduardo to his probable death. My brief connection to Lieutenant Curtis Jones had given me the layout of the settlement and all the outlying farmhouses.

Whatever lay slumbering in the hold of Eduardo's Spellbinder had never been tested. The conversion done by the goblins and John Smith had altered the nature of the bomb. General Price had called it a ten kiloton device and quite small measured against some of the weapons from hell that humans had made.

It needed to be detonated high above the Earth's atmosphere so that the Electro-magnetic pulse would be at the maximum, without a fireball removing the entire settlement. The EMP would contain enough energy to destroy anything and everything electronic.

John Smith explained it to me and said, "Think of it like a powerful lightning bolt that will destroy all electrical usage." He shuddered and carried on, "And when I say destroyed, I mean burned out and not repairable. But even if your radio or computer was still somehow working, there would be no electrical power in the grid to run it; - for a long time. All of the transformers would have to be replaced and new wiring installed and, of course, their generators themselves would need to be rebuilt. The entire infrastructure would be gone; - in an instant. We have experimented on the elf-stone that comprises the Spellbinder and the nannite structure falls apart and stays inert. Anything iron based will instantly possess a strong magnetic field.

What the pulse would do to elves that used telepathy to communicate by would remain to be seen. As for the collars that they wear around their necks whilst Eloen is aloft, to shield their telepathy from detection? That too is a matter for conjecture!"

We would be a rift away and separated from that universe. Maybe Eduardo would not! He had insisted that he would program the cloned ship to rise after setting the timer on the bomb, release it and slip back into the same rift that we were stationed in. He would need to be quick as there would only be a space of two or three minutes until the bomb detonated, flooding the area below with the gamma radiation pulse. John Smith and his team had fitted a hovering device that would fire rockets for a short space of time, keeping the device stationary above the Dream-shifter, one hundred and fifty miles below. The amount of fuel was limited and would not last more than five minutes.

If the bomb dropped into the atmosphere it would send a fireball down over the settlement, taking out every living creature over a hundred square miles. There were hundreds of gnomes settled, just inside the time-distortion barrier. I could not exchange the lives of so many to redress the balance and destroy Eloen and her 'children.' John had built several prototypes around the weight of the bomb and was quite confident that the bomb would hover in place, giving Eduardo time to translate across the rifts before it exploded; - theoretically!

I could feel that the time that I had contacted Curtis Jones was coming closer and closer. It felt strange to know that my mind was reaching out to the human while the present 'me' was waiting for that moment to pass! Neither of us could have knowledge of the other. My mind and those of my attacking force were separated from that universe by the Rift so we did not occupy the same space, but we were in the same time! It made me shudder.

I felt an incredibly strong pull on my mind as my former identity was hauled back to his present time and space. The sweat poured off my body as I resisted that insatiable urge to leave this place and go 'home' with him. Suddenly, as quickly as that feeling came, I was once more alone with my thoughts. It was then that the haze retreated and I realised that now was the time.

"Eduardo, go now and do what has to be done," I instructed my loyal friend. We will follow in five minutes.

"Goodbye High King," he replied, "and do not grieve for me if I am delayed."

It was then I realised that he would ride the bomb far up and out of the planet's atmosphere until it was positioned above the Dream-shifter. Eduardo would make absolutely sure that the bomb was primed and hovering in position before he tried to leave. He would stay there if he was unsure and go with the bomb into oblivion.

I knew that he was there already.

Eduardo sat in the command chair and ordered Spellbinder 6 to cross the rift and watched reality change and a new planet form underneath him. Beneath him was an iridescent bubble that stretched for hundreds of square miles across the countryside.

"Spellbinder, rise above the target and set the height to 150 miles. When we are at that height, activate the device," Eduardo ordered.

"All systems are 'go,' Eduardo," answered the ship and the elf sat back in the command chair and waited. The bomb fell away and the rockets fired keeping it in station, Eduardo lingered for several moments to be sure that the bomb was where it was meant to be and took the cloned ship out of this reality and as far north as the vessel could fly and away from this area to take up his designated position as a 'spare' gnome haven.

Eloen's patience had stretched thin by the time that the Dream-shifter informed her that all energy banks were full and she commanded, "Abaddon, take us down and activate that time-distortion field as soon as we touch dirt!"

"Yes my Lady. We are fully charged and returning to the settlement," the sentient ship replied. The moment we are set down I will do as you say and activate the field."

The moment that the Dream-shifter switched on the shield Eloen took off the iron torque and sent her mind out into the settlement to check that all was as it was left to be. She immediately felt a loss in the mental spectrum and realised who was missing!

She concentrated her augmented powers with the Wand and gave a mental shout, "Curtis Jones! Take off that iron collar now! Where are you hiding?"

There was nothing! She immediately knew that he was outside of the barrier. What had he done? Another loss registered in her mind. Two Halflings were missing!

High above the settlement the device almost ran out of fuel and activated.

Eloen's mind felt a roasting hot pain instantly screw her mind and the crystal shattered in her father's staff. All around her the Dream-shifter began to dissolve, along with it all the minds held captive to give it a personality. She was aware that her children were screaming and flat on the ground, that was rapidly appearing through the retreating substance of her ship. Everything around her was coming apart. The energy banks released all the captured starlight in a blinding flash of light. Now she was temporarily blind, as well as mentally deaf. Every Halfling and elf hybrid struggled to cast off the heated torques around their necks, as they writhed upon the ground in blinded agony, all across the settlement.

The pulse knocked the gnomes unconscious and they fell where they laboured. They were far enough away from the dream-shifter so that they were not blinded by the release of the energy banks. There was however a second sun high above them for a few minutes that would make it hard to see for a while.

Curtis Jones and Olaf hugged the ground as a bright light expanded over the lands of the settlement and a series of thunderclaps heralded the arrival of Peterkin and his compatriots. Even at this distance from the epicentre there was a flash inside the eyelids.

Curtis looked across at Olaf and said, "I think they're here! It worked my small friend! I believe that we should re-mount the horses and make our way back."

"I should not be in too much of a hurry my human friend. What's going on over that hill will be best left to the High King to sort out. Bring that fire back to life and I think we should leave the dead Halflings to the scavengers and take our time. Plenty of time tomorrow to make our way back. Besides I could do with a rest. So let things settle down for a while. The 'Long Shadow' will send for you if he needs you," the gnome wryly remarked and encouraged the fire back into life. "Fancy a brew?"

The Spellbinder clones dropped as close to the gnomes' scattered settlements as they could and the velociraptors sped out in long loping strides. They gathered up every gnome that they could find, very often with one under each arm. Fortunately the tales of their involvement during the destruction of the Dokka'lfar had passed into legend and there was no panic amongst them. Once they were inside the Spellbinder's safe haven they were soon attended to and reassured that Eloen's reign of terror was ended. Meanwhile I materialised the Spellbinder as close to the remains of the

Dream-shifter as I could. I sent the velociraptors out in the field to find as many Dokka'lfar as they could find. These allies were swathed in iron plates and collars so there was no chance of mental subjection or a knife thrust into a vulnerable place. They soon rounded up the dazed and disorientated of Eloen's genetically bred people. Some of the rifles had shattered due to the metal getting too hot and the cartridges exploding. Those that were winged were bound in such a way that they could not use them, but remained undamaged.

The mind-controlled elves were rendered unconscious and detained in Eduardo's Spellbinder under the care of some of my mind specialists. I was relieved to see him back and I told him so!

Eloen's Dokka'lfar were all locked into iron rings around their necks, so that they remained mentally shuttered and unable to use their powers. In amongst all of this I at last saw the new 'royal family' that had planned on taking over the parallel worlds.

My son sat on the muddy ground with his face turned towards me, distorted with hatred and madness. His features twisted with the overwhelming urge to kill me! Ameela stood by my side with tears falling down her cheeks and clutching Mia's hand. He never noticed them, as all his attention was directed at me.

My bound grandchildren also stared at me with a baleful animosity that showed that Eloen had done her work well. They were beautiful to look at and would have passed as a full blooded elf with little of their human heritage showing. The two boys had grown into handsome male elves and the girls were lovely and beginning to show signs of pregnancy. It would seem that I would soon have great-grandchildren. They would forever be lost to me.

Eloen had aged. She was wrinkled and creased, her beauty

gone without the life that she had stolen from others to sustain her, removed by the nuclear pulse. I could only guess how long she had held onto her youth by stealing it from others! In her hands she held the remains of Molock's Wand. Her clothes hung on her thin and twisted body with her mind irreparably damaged. The raven hair had fallen out and her bald skull lay naked, showing sores breaking out in the paper thin skin.

Still a malevolent hatred shone from her face that made me all too conscious of Molock himself. I have never forgotten the baby I held in my arms and stopped that tiny heart to prevent all of this happening. I had missed this Halfling and she had almost brought my 'kingdom' down. Her cruelty and disregard for any other sentient creature right to live was genetically set in her very DNA. She was Dokka'lfar through and through. Her efforts had brought into this world, a race of elven-human hybrids that were instilled with a hatred for me and all the many races that I 'ruled' and the need to dominate them. This I could not allow.

"Eloen! Listen to me," I insisted. "You are an abomination, as I can plainly see. You keep young, by stealing life from others. This, amongst everything that elfdom values; cannot be tolerated. You have taken from the gnomes, goblins, dwarves and the humans who are forced to serve you whenever you have felt the pangs of age. This will now stop and you will die!"

To my horror I saw my son, Elthred loose his bindings and gather the wrinkled creature in his arms and feely give her every last piece of life energy to make her young again. Before my eyes I saw my son wither and die so that this evil thing would live!

As she rose from the near death, she called out, "Kill him!"

From behind them, unseen and rising from the ground,

two dwarves brandishing steel knives bounded towards me, their faces twisted with hate. It was Hilden and Thorin bent on defending their mistress. Thorinson and Mellitus became a wall that they could not pass. A mailed fist took Thorin in the side of his jaw, as his son delivered a paralysing blow. While my old friend Mellitus snatched hold of Hilden's wrist and snapped it, making her drop the knife. His elfin speed and surety was his shield. To him she was moving in slow motion. Thorinson quickly bound his father's hands behind his back while he lay unconscious on the muddy ground. My two faithful dwarves carried the two mind pressed victims away from further harm. Thorinson wept over his mother as he took her from the arms of Mellitus and I used my mind to put her and his father into a deep sleep.

I stared into the now beautiful face of the Halfling and came to realise what the 'bride price' meant that Cailleach said that I would have to pay. My once handsome son lay withered, grey and very dead. He looked as if he were thousands of years old and human. Eloen had discarded him the moment she had leached out all of his life force.

There was a scream of, "No!" and Ameela swept by me in fury. She reached out to the Halfling's throat with her obsidian knife that she had kept by her side ever since she was incarcerated on the Tower of Absolom. The scalpel-sharp blade sliced through Eloen's carotid artery and into her windpipe. The spray of blood drenched her children sat before her as she fell. I watched as her eyes grew dim and the last of my son's life ebbed away from this evil Dokka'lfar.

I smiled sadly at my blood-spattered queen and wondered, "Are we all Dokka'lfar underneath?"

As the day wore on we collected together all of the human beings that were left in the settlement and had assessed the damage done to their minds by Eloen. Many of them had not had dealings with her, except the females who had become breeding creatures to produce more Halflings. The men had just been used as slave labour. To my satisfaction none of them were as mentally damaged as I had believed to be. They could be re-settled on the elf home world or the Earth that they had come from.

At last two figures came into sight, one on a horse and one on a pony. It was Curtis Jones and Olaf returning to the settlement. I met them by the side of my ship. The human swung his legs off the saddle of his horse while the gnome stayed mounted.

"It's good to see you, High King," said Curtis. "I was never that sure that you would hear that mental shout from the Dokka'lfar."

"I heard them alright! Toasting their feet certainly did the trick. It's a shame that they had to die. It was too risky for you to leave them alive. Had they shed their metal collars they would have made you stop your hearts. As you can see, we are here and yes, Eloen is dead. Her children remain however and so do all of her genetically produced offspring."

"High King," Olaf asked, "Do you need me? If not, I would like to see my parents and assure them that I am alright. I have had enough of killing!"

"Olaf, you and this human, Curtis Jones, did a perilous thing. If it had not gone as we planned you would be at Eloen's whim and that would have been a bad place to be. Go home my friend with the High King's blessing."

Curtis Jones watched the gnome ride his pony out of sight before he said, "He was very brave to do what he did with me. It was a crazy idea and I had no surety that it would work. After the things that Eloen had made me do to them, it took some persuasion for the gnomes to help me. I count him as a friend, High King. Now what is the next step?"

"You will find that little has changed outside of the time distortion field. For us a matter of about five years have passed, but for you many more, living here. If you want to go back to Earth then I am sure that General Price will be pleased to see you back again."

"I would like to see my old friends back at Twenty-nine palms," he replied. "I've had enough of this kind of life. No disrespect but I would like to be where there is little likelihood of someone poking around in my mind!"

"Whenever you are ready, you can go," I said. "There are many Spellbinders operating now, so transport is not a problem.

After a week had gone by, all of the gnomes had been settled in the Spellbinders and been translated back to Alfheimr. I now had to deal with Eloen's 'children' and had thought long and hard about the problem. All of them had been fitted with an iron collar that could not be undone without a bolt-cutter. They had been under constant surveillance twenty four hours of the day and had been placed inside a compound 'grown' from one of the Spellbinders.

This world was now empty of humans and gnomes. The only people here were elves and the new Dokka'lfar. Now my problem was what to do with them?

I called for the four of my grandchildren to come with me, into my Spellbinder. They came by armed escort, as trusting them was out of the question. I could still sense the unreasoning hatred for me even with the collars in place. Trying to undo the 'pressing' that Eloen had immersed their minds in since birth, would do more damage than good. So I would talk to them. The Spellbinder had built a set of benches with restraints and each one of them was handcuffed by the left wrist. I waited until all of them were seated and safely manacled.

"I have been advised that the easiest solution to this problem that your mother has left me is to have you all put to death. That way I have eliminated all threats in the future, but I am not Dokka'lfar! I am Ljo'sa'lfar; a Light Elf who has not been bred to kill, although I can. I am looking for a peaceful solution to the continued existence of your kind."

My grandson, Firovel shook his manacles and answered, "Is this your solution grandfather? Are we to be in chains for the rest of our lives? For if you do not keep us imprisoned, we will seek you out and kill you!"

"I can only hope that with the passing of the years some kind of mental balance will prevail and this unreasoning hatred of me and what I stand for will go. You are reasoning beings! You are more elf than human so think like an elf!"

"What are you offering?" asked Cethafin, "Eternal servitude? Is that what we can look forward to?"

"Listen to me my grandchildren and think about this for the rest of your days! At any time I could drop another bomb here where you live and explode it in the atmosphere. This would expand into a fireball hundreds of miles across destroying everything here. That is the power that I have at my disposal. That is what I have been advised to do! But, I will give you one chance and only one chance for you to listen to me. What I will do is to release you and all of your people to rule this world as you wish. All advanced weapons have been taken back to Earth where you cannot reach them. I have removed all trace of the Dream-shifter so there will be no resurrection of that evil machine.

The settlement is all yours to develop. I will keep an eye on you from time to time and I hope that eventually you will ease back into sanity. When that day comes you will be welcomed back into the society that I shall build. That is the promise that I give you. Let the children that Brianna and

Kellynn carry, grow up in a world of light, not the darkness that your mother planned for you."

I stood and beckoned to an old friend.

"Eduardo cut the collars from their necks and give the bolt cutters to Firovel to remove all the others. Escort them off the Spellbinder and we can go. Goodbye my grandchildren and good luck. You may see me in a hundred years or so. I will be there, you can count on that!

MOLOCK'S WAND

EPILOGUE

It took over five hundred years before all of Eloen's poison filtered out of their minds and I kept my promises. There are many elf-human hybrids in my kingdom and I still have my friends with me that I 'called' back from the dead. We grow old together at a more sedate pace. We have linked the Spellbinders to a program of discovery and prowl through the rifts of this parallel set of universes. One day we may meet evil again and will need each other. I still have the velociraptors as my unyielding allies. They now take Spellbinder ships out, searching for another dinosaur planet and others of their kind. Who knows what they might find?

ND - #0468 - 270225 - C0 - 229/152/22 - PB - 9781861510037 - Matt Lamination